W9-BJZ-160

PAST LIFE

"THOR..."

Also by David Mark

Novels

THE ZEALOT'S BONES *(as D.M. Mark)*
THE MAUSOLEUM *
A RUSH OF BLOOD *
BORROWED TIME *
SUSPICIOUS MINDS *
CAGES *

The DS Aector McAvoy series

DARK WINTER
ORIGINAL SKIN
SORROW BOUND
TAKING PITY
A BAD DEATH *(eBook only)*
DEAD PRETTY
CRUEL MERCY
SCORCHED EARTH
COLD BONES

* *available from Severn House*

WITHDRAWN
CHARLESTON COUNTY LIBRARY

PAST LIFE

David Mark

SEVERN
HOUSE

First world edition published in Great Britain and the USA in 2021
by Severn House, an imprint of Canongate Books Ltd,
14 High Street, Edinburgh EH1 1TE.

Trade paperback edition first published in Great Britain and the USA in 2022
by Severn House, an imprint of Canongate Books Ltd.

severnhouse.com

Copyright © David Mark, 2021

All rights reserved including the right of
reproduction in whole or in part in any form.
The right of David Mark to be identified
as the author of this work has been asserted
in accordance with the Copyright,
Designs & Patents Act 1988.

British Library Cataloguing-in-Publication Data
A CIP catalogue record for this title is available from the British Library.

ISBN-13: 978-0-7278-9092-4 (cased)
ISBN-13: 978-1-4483-0592-6 (trade paper)
ISBN-13: 978-1-4483-0591-9 (e-book)

This is a work of fiction. Names, characters, places and incidents
are either the product of the author's imagination or are used fictitiously.
Except where actual historical events and characters are being described
for the storyline of this novel, all situations in this publication are
fictitious and any resemblance to actual persons, living or dead,
business establishments, events or locales is purely coincidental.

All Severn House titles are printed on acid-free paper.

Typeset by Palimpsest Book Production Ltd.,
Falkirk, Stirlingshire, Scotland.
Printed and bound in Great Britain by
TJ Books, Padstow, Cornwall.

'Death must be so beautiful. To lie in the soft brown earth, with the grasses waving above one's head, and listen to silence. To have no yesterday, and no tomorrow. To forget time, to forgive life, to be at peace.'

Oscar Wilde

'The deeper that sorrow carves into your being, the more joy you can contain.'

Khalil Gibran, *The Prophet*

PART ONE

PART ONE

PROLOGUE

A pig of a day.

Afternoon bleeds blackly into evening: big dark shillings of rain tumbling down from slow-moving, pot-bellied clouds.

The land, featureless, beaten down. Flat, in every direction; a green-brown cloth draped across the earth and stamped until the wrinkles are smooth. A visitor here could be forgiven for believing the planet to be a disc.

A long, straight road, heading for the coast.

A copse of trees.

And *here*, the last house before the water: the final man-made structure before the soil becomes the sand; becomes the sea.

A plume of smoke, emerging from a red-brick chimney like an illustration in a nursery rhyme.

Inside, now. The door isn't locked.

Here.

A murky little room.

An overhead light throws a yellow glare upon a horseshoe of coloured picture-cards. The cards are encircled by a small henge of different crystals: their glittering stones reflecting fire; a jagged coral reef of serrated edges – each tiny spike sharp as a tooth.

A plump woman, long hair, clever eyes, half lost in a swirl of incense.

This is Dymphna Lowell. She talks to the dead. Sometimes, she gets a reply.

Opposite, a man in a sodden overcoat, dark trousers, boots leaving muddy prints upon the carpet: a triangle of ankle peeking out from between the unlaced tongues and the sodden hems. Upon the skin at his heelbone, an ugly ridge of scar tissue, as if burned by hot iron. In his dark coat, he's a bundle of kindling: a corn dolly, burned black.

Dymphna is thinking of the money. Telling herself that the

smell of him, and the sight of him, and the muddy prints on the floor, are worth enduring for the inch of crisp notes he had placed in her hand. She's never been the sort to turn somebody away. Would never deny her gifts to those in need. And money's money. She's been inconvenienced. Had to deal with a knock on the door on a wet afternoon. Here, at the end of the road, where a person could be forgiven for expecting peace and quiet. Only right she gets what she deserves.

'It is important not to take these things at face value,' she says, with an encouraging smile. 'The widower card, well, it doesn't mean you've necessarily lost somebody, or are about to. It's about loss. About a sense of bereavement, yes, but that doesn't mean a life. The other cards inform it, you see.'

A quick glance at his left hand, starfished flat on the wooden table. A gold ring, on the third of his big, pink fingers. It's a little loose. There's clear space between gold and the flesh. She hadn't noticed it at first, having been focused instead on his fingertips. He has no nails. The nails have been bitten down so far that there is virtually no cuticle: each tiny strip of nail a letterbox in a pinkly wrinkled door.

He used to be bigger, she tells herself. *Suffered, this one. You can see it in his neck, too. That loose skin. The collar of his shirt's a little frayed, as if it used to rub against stubble. Been through something. There's so much pain in him it's like he's full. Like he's been a sponge and now he's saturated. Like pain is spilling out a tear at a time . . .*

'The *militaria*,' she muses, examining the pretty, colourful card. 'One of my favourites. Very encouraging. Not a soldier, by any means, but somebody with purpose. A mission. Perhaps a belligerence, a devotion to a duty. Am I getting warm? Stop me if I'm getting ahead of myself . . .'

She glances up at his face. He's barely spoken since he arrived. Hasn't responded to much of her chatter. She finds it a little rude, if she's honest. She hasn't got much enthusiasm for idle prattle, but most of her clients expect it, the same way they expect a little gossip at the hairdresser's or some borderline racist invective during a cab ride. She counts it as part of the service. With this one, she may as well have said nothing at all. Just lit the candle, wafted the incense, and got right down to business. Not much of a one for foreplay, she decides. Probably hasn't played the field. Married young, and for life.

She makes a theatrical display of examining the cards. She doesn't need them. Can read this man just from the way he looks; the way he smells; the catch in his voice as he said he was desperate, that he would pay twice her normal rate. The money had been enough of an incentive to overlook her own protocols. She doesn't like walk-ins. Likes to be suitably prepared. Some of the cynics suggest she only accepts advanced bookings so she's got a chance to Google the shit out of each new client, acquainting herself with every aspect of their character. She doesn't rise to such suggestions. She knows she's the real deal. Always has. Can read a person like a pop-up book. The cards just give her something to look at while she's letting an innate empathy draw a picture of whoever is sitting in the chair. The crystal ball; the palm, the tea leaves, they're all mostly props. She could tell this man's future just by looking at him, and none of it rings with promise.

'Now that's interesting,' she says, peering at a colourful picture card, soft yellows and gleaming red. 'This is a feeling card: a state of being, you might say. *Amore*, that's love. And love means love. It doesn't take much explaining. You feel it, or you've known it, or will again. That's where this *esperanza* card comes in – a sense of hope. And I can see the power there, how you long for something. There's a sadness in you, something beyond gloom. If I were to describe a kind of wistful, delicious melancholy, a nostalgia for something fondly remembered, would that mean something to you?'

He doesn't reply. Blinks, once or twice. She watches the little pearl of saltwater build. Take shape. Bulge, reflecting tiny prisms of iridescence. She has to force herself not to pull a face as the tear finally spills over the lip of his drooping eye. He's wept, one-sided, since he sat down, though there has been no accompanying sound. His eye, tugged down as if with an invisible finger, glistens pinkly. A steady drool of tears oozes from the lip of the lid, charting a course down yellowy, unhealthy-looking skin. He spends most of his time indoors, she thinks. Hasn't known much sunlight. And that smell. Like something on the turn . . .

'Ah, so this is one of my favourites,' she says, cheerfully.

Considers the cards. She's pleased to be considering the images again: studying the Oracle with the same warm feeling as others might consider an old photo album. She is among friends, here. Knows each image like her own reflection.

'Hmmm, that one facing towards me . . . that's unusual . . .'

Glances up. She's grateful for the smoke from the incense burner. It blurs his edges. Conceals the worst of the fungal, earthy aroma that seems to seep out of his skin. She feels an urge to stick her nose above the scalding surface of her herbal tea. There's something about this man that makes her think of spores: of something rotten. Can imagine him coming apart into a million tiny points of flesh, billowing away like seed heads to be distributed by the breeze.

'Who is that?' he asks, his voice low, the words hard to discern. She wonders whether English is his first language. He's staring at the card as if it were written in his blood.

'Ah, well, that's next, but if you're eager, well . . .'

'Who!'

She gathers herself. She's no stranger to raised voices, heightened emotions. Telling the future, disentangling the present, providing guidance from the spirits: she can forgive outbursts of emotion.

'An interesting card,' she says, quietly. 'You've chosen an unusual spread, as it happens. But, well . . . *L'Amica* is the Female Friend, but she can also represent friendship in a general sense – similar to the Dog in the Lenormand deck, though we're getting fairly advanced territory there. L'Amica brings valuable aid, especially when she appears upside-down. She can be a safe harbour in a dark storm. She won't make all of your problems disappear, but . . .'

'I don't know her,' he says, and the sound is harsh, grating: a hiss through locked teeth.

'Well, obviously, it's not saying this is a specific friend, it's implying somebody with that kind of relationship, that closeness . . .'

'What do you mean "obviously"?'

She smiles, to show she hadn't meant anything offensive. Does her best to look the way her clients want her to. Friendly, plump, a little Bohemian: an ethereal being emerging through the fog of incense carrying opaque messages from beyond the veil.

'Perhaps there is somebody from your past – somebody who may be returning, to listen, to offer counsel . . .'

'No.'

She glances at the item he had placed upon the table. It's pretty. Well-made. Antique, if she's any judge. She likes all of the charms, but it's the horsehead that makes her smile. She can imagine herself wearing such a piece, though she would hang it on a chain.

'The person who wore this . . . she's in pain, yes? She needs help.'

Another tear spills over his ruined eyelid. He blinks, slowly. The damaged eye does not close all the way. She is left staring into the milky grey of his lower eyeball: a Cheshire cat smile beneath the puckered lid.

'If you could select a card from this pile, please, perhaps we can get . . .'

He shakes his head. Opens his eyes. 'You're a liar,' he says, candidly. 'I thought for a moment you understood. But no. A charlatan.'

She bristles. 'Hey, back off there, mate, not everybody likes what they hear but I've been doing this for twenty-odd years and—'

'How much money have you made in that time?' he asks, staring a hole into her. He's not looking her in the eye – seems to focus his burning gaze on the very centre of her forehead.

'I provide a service, mate. You don't like it, I can sympathize, but you came to me, don't forget. You're in my kitchen, my house. You've known pain, I see that, but we've barely begun and you're calling me a liar, and that's one thing I'm not. My daddy taught me to always tell the truth . . .'

'Another liar,' he says, sadly, shaking his head.

She rises, furious, knocking the table. A curl of ash falls from the incense stick: cards slide across one another, the pattern and meaning lost. 'How dare you! Don't you ever think you can—'

He picks up a crystal from the circle surrounding the stones. It's heavy and sharp: sparkling and brittle.

'Liar,' he says, again, and hits her in the side of the head with such force that the jagged edges of the twinkling rock embed themselves in bone. There is a grotesque slurping sound as he pulls the gory crystal from the wound. She slumps forward. He hits her again. Harder, right at the back of the neck. Takes a fistful of her rosaries, and pulls.

The chain snaps.

Beads fall like hail.

He lets go before she dies. Pushes her onto her back. She's heavy, and there's a thud as she topples back onto the floor. One of the cats, nosing near her feet, gives a hiss before it darts away.

He crouches over her. Opens her eyes and peers in.

There's life in there, he tells himself. A consciousness. Something that can still feel.

'Charlatan,' he says, leaning down so his lips are by her ear. 'Deceiver.'

He considers the pupils in her dulling eyes. Changes his angle until he sees his own barely-there reflection in the glassy surface of the eyeball. Peers in as if searching for something. For someone.

Smiles, as he finds it.

'My love,' he whispers, and puts one hand to his heart.

He pulls the blade from his pocket.

Reaches into her mouth and seizes her wet, dead tongue.

Begins to carve.

ONE

Not much of a moon tonight.

Typical, thinks Mr Dash. *They can't even do that right.*

He squints through the binoculars. Rubs at the lenses. Thumbs at the focus wheel as if tuning a radio.

'Not a bloody dicky bird,' he mutters, pressing his skin again the eyepieces. 'Not a sausage.'

He isn't surprised. Whole bloody world's going to the dogs. It's the same with the weather. Used to be proper weather. Winters used to look like Christmas cards. And puddings. Used to get proper puddings, once upon a time. Children had proper names. Shoes lasted. Hotels gave you a proper key . . .

Mr Dash is not a sunny individual. He is well-suited to the bleak panorama into which he gazes. Remote, joyless, unremarkable: he and the landscape could be twins.

It's cold, now. Cold and bitter and still. If he were to strain his ears the same way he forces his eyes, he would be able to hear the Humber estuary, sucking and pulling and chewing at the land. Instead he can hear little save the shushing of the trees, and the low, mournful wail of next door's cats.

'Last chance,' he mutters, raising the eyeglasses and training the blurry circles on a distant spot of darkness. There's a waning crescent, out there, apparently: somewhere over the shimmering blackness of the water. According to the website, some eleven per cent of the lunar surface should be visible. Gazes into nothingness. It does nothingness well, this part of Holderness, out on the very eastern edge of Yorkshire.

He pushes out a wispy grey cloud of air. There is a brief whiff of denture-paste and Ovaltine, before it is gathered up by the chill wind and carried inland. He considers emitting a true *hurrumph* of dissatisfaction. Decides to keep it in reserve: a weapon in his arsenal in case the electricity goes off or the French invade.

'Ah, there's the blighter . . .'

He finally sights the moon, just out there, just above the tree-line, peeking out of the lower reaches of a great wall of cloud: a silvery arc – a curved blade puncturing a gut. Thinks of a shark's eye, almost closed. Thinks of sickles and slash hooks.

He holds the glasses steady, enjoying their heft. Wartime glasses, still complete with the original leather case. He likes how he feels when he's holding them. Can make-believe he is on the deck of a battleship, scanning the horizon for any sign of the *Bismarck*. Can feel quite the hero, out here, on the front lawn: a vision in slippers and raincoat.

He gives a nod, satisfied. He'd feared the worst. Very little surprises him anymore. A missing moon? Very much par for the course, these days. Too many softies, that's the problem. Too many bleeding-heart liberals and not enough speed cameras. Mr Dash is in no doubt that the world is 'going to the dogs'. That civilization is 'off to Hell in a handcart'. He feels that he is living through the end of days. Young people have no respect, no drive, no bloody backbone. He's all for the short, sharp shock, is Mr Dash. Would like to see the return of National Service, the birch, and public executions for benefits claimants and vegans.

He looks up again. Not many stars, neither. He can see a distant smattering, out where the sky is at its darkest, at the place where the sky meets the sea. Swings the glasses back to the moon. The clouds have moved on. It sits there, a clipped thumbnail, discarded on the dirty black sheets of the night sky.

Waning Crescent, he muses. Sounds like a nice place to live. Can visualize a row of well-tended trees and high, terraced properties shielded by wrought-iron, black-lacquered spikes. Can imagine a child, sitting in a distant skylight, staring through a telescope and jotting down constellations in a neat lined notebook. He'd like to live on Waning Crescent. Would like to live anywhere other than here, truth be told. Four years they've been marooned on Sunk Island and each day has been more disappointing than the last. The wife had promised him magical sunrises and vast skies; a private wilderness teeming with rare birds and serving up nightly celestial spectacles. Fat chance of that. It's cold and bleak and miserable, and while he believes that all suffering breeds character, he considers himself, at sixty-eight, to have developed sufficient character to be excused having to build any more.

He *hurrumphs*, unbidden, lost in crossness. Feels better at once.

A light flicks on, not far above his head. He doesn't change his position. Just keeps his vigil, standing here by the gatepost in front of the sturdy Victorian farm cottage, gazing into the air above the Humber estuary as if willing a trawlerman home safe from a storm. The light from the house serves as a timepiece. He knows it to be 10.05 p.m. His wife, Dinah, will have finished her programme, made herself a herbal tea, and made her way upstairs. For the next ten minutes she will busy herself with whatever it is that women do behind closed doors, and then she will head to bed to read the next three chapters of whatever silly romance novel has been bringing a blush to her cheeks this week. Mr Dash will join her in an hour. He prefers her to be asleep while he completes his ablutions. There is a creakiness, an uncertainty, in his movements of late and he does not wish his wife to see him becoming enfeebled. She is ten years younger than him. There's still a lot of life in Dinah. Life and light and lustre. There was life in Mr Dash once. But the buggers forced early retirement on him, and his youngest daughter died of the cancer, and they lost a fortune selling off the family home at just the wrong time. And now he's here. Sunk Island. Somewhere between Hull and the arse-end of bloody nowhere. Half a dozen houses spread out around a church and a crossroads; making do in one of the smattering of old homes that hunker down, hidden behind bow-backed trees, sheltering from the merciless gale that howls in from the sea. His hobbies are what keeps him going. Birdwatching. Astronomy. And Dymphna, next door.

In the darkness, Mr Dash purses his lips. Raises his eyeglasses. Twitches them sideways. Plays with the focus until he sights the bedroom window in the left-hand corner of the last house before the water. The light's on. The light's always on. The curtains are always open too. And one blessed evening, several months back, Dymphna had stepped out of the shower, squeaked a porthole into the condensation on the bedroom window, and managed to give Mr Dash far more than he had expected to see when he stepped out into the spring air and attempted to spot the rare Montagu's harrier he had been given to believe was inhabiting the little wooded area near the water's edge.

The image remains imprinted on Mr Dash's mind: a memory so perfectly clear that he wonders whether he has had to forego other memories in order to make it. He can't fully recall the faces of his nieces and nephews, or his best friend's birthday, but he can see every glorious particle of that magical evening. Can visualize her perfect pink roundness; the damp glistening on scorched skin; the tattoo winding up her ankle to her fleshy buttock; the two metal bolts pinned through her big pink nipples. He had not thought her more or less attractive than Dinah. She had simply been different. And by God, how he longs for different.

He stares through the glasses. Stares, and hopes beyond hope that she will waddle, wetly, buxomly, onto the big yellow screen of the bedroom window. He has only sighted her on a handful of occasions, and never in anything more evocative than her swishy pale blue kimono. On the other occasions she was fully clothed, bustling about, laughing and chatting into a mobile phone, or carrying a laptop around in front of her, the screen filled with an unfamiliar face, as if bearing a head on a tray.

He's had little to do with Dymphna in the flesh, much as the thought warms him on cold nights. She was already living in the little house when he and the wife upped sticks and set out for the very edge of civilization. They'd lived in a little market town twenty miles inland before Dinah got it into her head that sea air and bracing winds were what they needed to make their retirement go with a bang. Dymphna had popped by as soon as the removals men had driven away. Brought them a little basket of gifts. Dinah had dealt with her. Chatted for an age while he was on his hands and knees trying to work out which cable went where in the back of the TV. She'd brought odd gifts: multi-coloured candles; greasy soaps filled with real flowers; little voile bags packed with crystals and tied with red silk. She hadn't turned his head, of course. Not then. Not at five foot nothing, with a big fleshy middle and a backside that wobbled like half set trifle. Mr Dash hadn't known what to say, so he hadn't said very much at all. Forgot her name and was too embarrassed to ask her to repeat it. Left it to the wife. Got chapter and verse once she'd gone, of course. Quite taken with her new pal, was Dinah. Fortune teller, or so she claimed. Medium and clair-voyant. Palmist. A whiz with the old Tarot cards and no stranger to journeying into the great beyond to ask lost souls if they had any messages for those left behind. Mr Dash had no time for any of that nonsense. Put a stop to that friendship before Dinah could be tempted to cross anybody's palm with silver or ask for guidance about what lay in store.

Still, thinks Mr Dash, as he stares, wide-eyed, at the rectangle of yellow light, and yearns afresh for a glimpse of his round-hipped neighbour. Sees her in his mind's eye. Chats with himself, as if with a trusted friend. Something about the gypsy look, isn't there? Something beguiling. Blue eyes, bare feet; that touch of the dirtiness in the way they sway their hips. That certain something that speaks to a part of a gentleman in a way that nobody else ever seems to. He read mucky books about filthy gypsies when he was a young man. Books about seductresses in headscarves and long skirts.

He hadn't had her pegged as Romany at first. Hid it well. The hair was short and mostly grey and she favoured silly little plastic earrings over big gold hoops. The eyes gave her away though. The eyes, and that mucky, sand-blown tan.

For a moment, Mr Dash suffers a brief flaring of discomfort. He feels at once embarrassed and ashamed, the way he had when Dinah came downstairs for a couple of painkillers and caught him watching some saucy French movie on one of the subscription channels. He sees himself, in this moment, for what he is. Unpleasant words fill his head. *Peeping Tom. Voyeur. Perv.* He doesn't like it. He fancies he's probably just about old enough to be thought of as a dirty old man. Sees himself, as if looking back through the binoculars. His paisley, flannel pyjamas, his fleecy, blue dressing gown and tartan slippers, his big waterproof coat; binoculars on a strap around his neck, half obscuring his round, porcine face. He feels dirty. Mucky. Pervy.

The light flicks off behind him. He should turn away, go back inside. Should lock up, put the keys on the hook, and make one last cup of malted drink to help him get off to sleep. Doesn't get more than a few hours these days, and those are broken up by the ceaseless trips to the bathroom.

He can't help himself. Needs one last peep.

Mr Dash swings the binoculars back to his neighbour's window. Plays with the dial, seeking a clearer picture. Blurs become shapes; shapes delineate into figures. He glimpses movement. Sees the two furry outlines up on the windowsill, smearing themselves exotically against the glass. Two cats. Two fat, white cats. Two fat, white cats with grubby, red faces, scratching at the glass with rust-smeared paws.

Fear, now. Mr Dash feels the hairs rise upon his skin. Feels gooseflesh spreading across his arms, his shoulders, his thighs. He blinks, rapidly, behind the glass. He realizes he has ceased to breathe. Forces himself to gulp down some air. Focuses again. It's clearer this time. Clearer, now he knows he is watching two cats scrabbling at the glass: a collage of bloodied paw-prints staining the glass. He squints. There is redness upon the faces of the cats. Each time they open their mouths to mew, it is as if they have been lapping at red wine. Teeth, tongue, little pink nose, all caked in dirty, crusted red.

Mr Dash lowers his glasses. He feels very cold. Feels sick. Feels like he would very much like to turn his back on the gypsy woman's house.

He can't help himself. Raises the binoculars again.

A third cat leaps up onto the windowsill. This one is a tortoise-shell, its fur a little patchy: skinny at the ribs and a little arthritic in the hip. It can only mew from one side of its mouth. There is a scar down its face, on the same side where its jaw hangs, slack. It has a drugged look. It moves floppily, awkwardly, as if dragging something heavy. The other two cats back away.

'Here, kitty . . .' mutters Mr Dash, in the silence, and feels like laughing at the absurdity of it all.

The cat turns as if it's heard him. Through the glass, it fixes him with a baleful yellow eye. It drops the thing it has been carrying in its jaws. Noses it, playfully, like a plastic ball. Arches its back, its features locked in a rictus hiss, as the nearest of the two white cats take a step towards the find.

Mr Dash feels a grim, warm wetness spread out from his groin.

Around the binoculars, his hands turn white.

He can't seem to tear his eyes away.

Can't stop looking at the eyeball, complete with a rat-tail of ragged tendons, that the malformed cat pats at with its paw.

Can't look away, even as it sinks its teeth into the glistening white orb.

He is a moment too late in closing his own eyes.

Sees the cat close its jaws, and the squirt of putrid, jellyish liquid.

Blue, he thinks, through the static in his thoughts. It was blue. Then . . . *Dymphna.*

And then there is just the sound of running feet, and the distant slurping of the water against earth.

TWO

Victoria Avenue, Hull

She wakes with a yell, jerking upright and swinging madly at the air. Thrusts up a knee, taking her invisible attacker in the balls.

'Dontyoufuckingdare . . .!'

The dream fades. Turns to pixels. To vapour. To spores.

She raises her clammy hand to her neck and seizes damp cotton. The bedsheets have formed a loose noose while she slept. The crocheted blanket has managed to bind her legs.

She coughs. Tastes red wine and microwave moussaka. Tastes ash.

Feels something wedged between tongue and cheek. Spits it into her palm. It's a cigarette butt, half chewed and soggy. She fell asleep smoking again. Must have swallowed the ember. Fancies the day will bring a little heartburn.

The new flat, she tells herself, as consciousness creeps in. *Don't fret. The girls are all sorted. Sophia's got the new place. The others are with Mum. Anders is dead. You've moved to Hull, remember . . .*

'Oh fuck,' she slurs. 'Hull.'

She hauls herself into what she hopes is a sitting position. Realizes that it's not. She's malfunctioned somehow. Her hair is touching carpet, dangling blackly off the edge of the bed. She fumbles for the light. Makes sense of herself. She's at the far end of the bed. The door is on the wrong wall. Nobody's stolen the curtains, they're over there.

To herself, aloud: 'Fuck, Trish . . . when Alzheimer's comes along, you won't bloody notice . . .'

The trill and buzz of a mobile phone, somewhere nearby. She dangles a hand down to the carpet, nausea rising up her throat. Closes her hand around the blessed coolness of an empty wine bottle and presses it to the sweat on her forehead. Rolls somewhere that feels like it might be to her left, and lands on the rag rug with a clatter.

'Oh, you bastard,' she mutters, hauling herself upright. She stumbles to the bedside table and manages to switch on the little light. Illuminates a square room with a high ceiling. Clothes in various states of their usefulness are scattered over ripped cardboard boxes, their contents spilling out in great archipelagos of paperwork and books and photo albums, their edges forming a rough pathway from the doorway to the bed. There's a dried-up pot plant by the door: a housewarming gift from her girls. A mirror, at the foot of the bed, streaked with make-up and handprints.

Looks up, sharply. The damn phone again.

She grabs her cigarettes from the bedside table. Lights up. Takes a breath and gives a coughing fit that makes her ribs hard. Watches a photo album fall from a tower of hardbacks. Looks at the picture for a moment. Blows a kiss and tells herself to fuck off when she feels the tears prick at her eyes.

Spots the phone, skittering around by the door to the hallway. Grabs for it and puts on her best phone voice, even as her inner South Yorkshire lass is telling the caller that 2.10 a.m. is a bitch of a time to call somebody.

'Detective Superintendent Trish Pharaoh,' she says, in the accent she uses to talk to the chief constable and her daughters' schoolteachers.

She looks at herself in the mirror as the duty sergeant pours violence into her ear. Looks away, appalled with herself. Focuses on the report of a suspicious body, called in by a neighbour, out at Sunk Island, on the arse-cheek of East Yorkshire. Signs of violence. Uniforms at the scene. Becomes more of herself as the words drop into her mind: coins into a jar.

Blood.
Brutal.
Mutilated.

Trish Pharaoh comes together as if the words are triggers: blinks away her hangover and the wisps of lingering nightmare as surely as if she were responding to a hypnotic suggestion.

'We'll take it,' she says.

THREE

He stares into her. *Aches.*

It is a thudding thing, this love. It is a feeling with teeth and claws. It is built of need and hunger; of healing caresses and the warmth of skin on skin.

He carries her essence inside himself: makes a safe space for her within the wide, half made boat of his ribcage, feels the nearness of her warm, hot heart pushed up tight against his own. Sometimes he feels he is looking out through her eyes, and she through his.

She stands at the bedroom window, staring out. The sodium glow of the streetlight caresses the hollows and curves of her thin, sylphlike frame. She makes such tableaus into art. She's slender. Dark. There are silvery scars on her legs from a bad injury a few years ago and the telltale shimmer of stretch marks across her taut belly, but she remains extravagantly beautiful. Her dark hair hangs loose, the tips forming inky hieroglyphs and scripture amid the colourful tattoos that pattern her shoulders and back.

She leans forward, elongating her neck, her face in profile. Looks out towards the world beyond the glass with a yearning that all but breaks him. He knows she is seeing something other than the greys and browns and shimmering silvers of the old, familiar view. She is not seeing the little patch of grass, nor the shingle-and-shale beach that lies between their own white-painted cottage and the brown waters of the Humber estuary. She is not seeing the majestic span of the bridge overhead, nor the black bulk of the woodland that hugs the coastline. She stares at something intangible; something that stirs her blood and chills his own. She is staring at the horizon. Yearning for something he cannot give.

He watches, his heart seeming to double in size. Around him, the air is so full of feeling that he could take it in his fist and squeeze tears from it.

'Roisin . . .'

His voice soft, breathy, gentle.

She turns to him. There are tears on her cheeks. She sniffs and rubs a hand across her face. She tries to smile. It closes in on itself: petals at night-time.

'Did I wake you?'

'I always wake when you do.'

'I'm sorry. Go back to sleep.'

'Come back to bed.'

'I will. I'm OK.'

'Are you? I can hold you . . .'

'No. Soon.'

Aector McAvoy gazes upon his wife down the length of his own naked body. Tries not to dwell upon his own ridiculousness and to focus instead upon his wife. His flesh is a map of scars and tortured flesh. He's a big man. Huge. There's the look of a sated Viking about him, in this light: his red hair and beard muted by the dark of the room. There is certainly no mistaking the strength in him. His arms, clasped at his sides, are barrel-thick, and his shoulders so broad that when his children sketch him, he rarely stays within the frame of the paper. He reaches out and strokes her side of the bed. Feels damp sheets. She's had the dream again. Woken, drenched in sweat, and slithered her way to the window and the chill night air. Soon she will return. She will climb in beside him and rest her head upon his chest. He will wrap her in himself and allow her to seep into him. He will give her his warmth. And she will sleep. He, unsettled, will lie still. He will stare at the ceiling. He will fret, and worry, and try to fill his head with pleasing thoughts so they may silently transmute themselves into her essence and allow her to sleep sweetly. And he will tell himself that when she wakes, they will talk. That today will be the right time.

That come the morning, he will be brave enough to ask her what she is hiding from him.

In the darkness, he swallows, drily. Shifts himself around with practised soundlessness. Their two children are asleep in the nearby rooms. Both are sound sleepers, but McAvoy is a considerate man. He has a big man's fear of disgracing himself: of clumsily smashing precariously placed ornaments or crunching down on discarded toys with his size twelve feet. He tries again, desperate now.

'Can I get you anything? Do you want to talk?'

'It was just a dream.'

'Same dream?'

'I don't really remember. It's just a dream.'

'There's nothing to be scared of, I swear.'

'Don't, Aector. Don't make promises you can't keep.'

'I'm sorry . . .'

She shrugs; so much sadness in one simple act. Self-consciously, she worries at her mouth, tugging at her lower lip, chewing the skin on her thumb. He watches her flick her tongue against her teeth. She says the dream is always the same: a shadow, a patch of jagged darkness, following her relentlessly through an unfamiliar house; the sensation of nearness, the certainty of pain; dirty, bloody fingers in her mouth; teeth coming loose and falling like spilled jewels, tumbling into her lap, glaring gorily up at her in two perfect concentric rings . . .

And then she wakes. Wakes, and slithers from their bed, and seeks the comfort of the great open spaces beyond the glass, over the claustrophobia of their bed.

McAvoy has always known they would reach this point. His wife is an Irish Traveller; a *Pavee* to her very bones. The road is calling her. And he, a police officer all the way through, knows that soon, he will have to make a choice.

He can't stand this. Can't stand her fear, her pain, her yearning for something he knows he cannot give. Do it, he tells himself. Say something. Demand to know what she's hiding. Why the phone calls; the texts, the second phone. Ask her who he is.

The darkness hides the blush that blooms in his cheeks. He is disgusted with himself. Would whip himself bloody for his disloyal thoughts if his suffering did not cause his wife so much pain.

She slips into bed beside him. He pulls her close. Presses his mouth into the crown of her head. She twists her fingers in his chest hair. He feels her tears against his skin.

Just try, he tells himself. This isn't how it's meant to be.

He steels himself. Whatever she is hiding, he needs to know. So do the children. They deserve better than this. Deserve the mum they know: effervescent, ferocious, funny, raw. They deserve Roisin McAvoy – not this listless, distracted wraith who drifts in and out of their lives and who wakes in terror that only seems to be soothed by the vastnesses beyond the glass.

'Roisin, whatever it is, I swear, whatever you need, or whatever you think you might have done . . .'

Her whole body stiffens in his grasp; her fingers clutching at his skin as if afraid of falling.

Then the buzz. The damnable vibration of the work phone on the nightstand. The sudden blue light, illuminating a name, and a picture of a formidable looking woman with dark hair and blue eyes.

'I'm sorry,' he begins, but Roisin is already rolling out of bed; already shrugging on her leopard print dressing gown and giving him that smile of hers; the smile that breaks his heart.

He gathers himself. Answers as quietly as he can.

'Trish?'

Detective Superintendent Patricia Pharaoh, a little drunk and a lot more than half asleep.

'Hector,' she grumbles. 'Are you decent?'

He looks down at himself. Draws the quilt over his nakedness and feels the blush return. Pharaoh is his boss, his best friend, and something between a mother figure and a lost love. She is also the new head of Humberside Police CID.

'Suspicious death, out at Sunk Island,' she says, briskly. 'Get your arse up. You can pick me up in forty-five minutes.'

'Sunk Island,' he says, head spinning. 'Holderness . . . how suspicious?'

'Very,' says Pharaoh. 'There's a big spike of blue stone sticking out of her chest cavity and half her face is gone. I'm not getting ahead of myself, but I don't think she did it to herself.'

McAvoy screws up his eyes. Combs his beard with his fingers. 'Name?'

'I'll brief you en route. All I know is she was a clairvoyant.'

McAvoy's head fills with static. He can hear nothing but the sudden roar of blood inside his skull. For a moment, the years fall away. He is back in uniform. He's friendless; afraid of his own shadow, all blushes and good intentions. And he's on his back, as a man with red-rimmed eyes pushes a curved blade into his face and forces him into the sodden, blood-soaked earth. He is fading. He is fighting for his life, and losing.

He strokes the scar; the white line half hidden by his greying beard. Chews his cheek, and tastes blood.

'I'll get it out of my system now,' says Pharaoh, her voice muffled for a moment as she pulls a garment over her head. She curses, having briefly set fire to her top with the tip of her cigarette. 'Should I? Just get it out of my system . . .'

'Get what?' he asks, his voice faraway, his thoughts skittish.

'The clairvoyant . . . she never saw it coming.'

Neither of them laugh. They both feel a responsibility to treat the dead with respect. Both know that the day will bring pain and suffering to those who have done nothing to deserve it.

'She's a clairvoyant?' asks McAvoy, cautiously.

Please no, he thinks. *Not after all these years . . .*

'She reads cards. Palms. Crystal balls. I bet your Roisin would love her.'

And the whisper in his head becomes a scream.

Out there. Out *here*.

Now.

Moonlight on brown water, the shimmering ripples flecked with foam.

Beneath the bridge. Just where the pea-green channel marker bobs above the sandbank, and the shadow of the bridge cuts the estuary down the middle.

A shadow. A silhouette in perfect shimmering black.

He watches. Stares at the figure in the window, and drinks her down like ale. He feels a little giddy. Feels energized. He cannot quite believe that this is happening; that the fantasies he dreamed up in the dark are about to be made flesh.

Pretty house, he tells himself. *Prettiest in the row. Done well. Done better than she deserves.*

Then: *She's going to fall so fucking far.*

Clings to the rusted metal, teeth chattering like hooves on cobbles. Holds himself tight, refusing to let the cold reach his bones. He's endured worse than this. Far worse.

Feels himself rise and fall, his body eddying, up and down, down and up, as if dancing with the water.

Stares through the infra-red scope at the soul he has come to take.

The window frame makes her a portrait: a slender Venus: domed breasts; elegant neck; gently splayed fingers resting on the loveliness of her soft, warm stomach. He is not a man of carnal desires but he identifies the slow, hungry warmth that spreads through his lower reaches as something akin to arousal. He wonders whether it is relevant. He's heard that she has certain gifts; a talent with herbs; a way with wild animals; an ability to soothe.

Perhaps, he thinks. *Perhaps this is an enchantment. Perhaps you are bewitched. Her people – her clan. Touched by the angels, blessed with the sight . . .*

She retreats from the window. Is replaced by the big man. Broad shoulders, red hair, sad eyes. He's formidable, in the way that a cow can sometimes become a bull when its calves are threatened. He would rather not have to face him, if it can be helped. To do so would be to spoil the marvellous things he has planned.

He leans back, both hands clutching the green metal channel marker, the sea canoe tied to his foot by a length of cord. Looks up and around him. Raises the scope to his eye again and stares at the moon as if trying to read an inscription on it.

Above, the dark air above the Humber estuary becomes a kaleidoscope of shifting, shimmering shades. The clouds take upon the allusion of playful horses: all dapple-grey rumps and coiled tails, their muscular flesh scored with palette knife scratches. The darkness behind insinuates infinite colour: dried specks of sugary white picking out unfathomable constellations amid the spilled diesel and glistening coal of the night sky.

He rolls onto his stomach. Stares again at the little row of fishermen's cottages; twee and saccharine in their picture-postcard sameness. Listens to the sound of a car engine coughing into life. Hears the swish of a lorry rumbling on the bridge overhead. Feels the slap of icy black water against his skin.

He takes a breath. Pushes it out and takes another. Rapid, shallow breaths now, followed by a deep, final gulp.

Slips into the water like a seal from an ice-flow. Surfaces twenty metres away. Makes for the shore in long, smooth, powerful strokes, dragging the cumbersome little craft behind him. He'd like to climb aboard and paddle to shore but to do so would risk drawing attention. Half submerged beneath the waves, he could easily be dismissed as an errant log or some scrap of discarded cargo. And so he swims. Kicks against the suck and pull of the currents. Tastes the salt and oil and brackish foulness of the shallows as his feet strike muddy earth.

Drags himself forward, mud up to his neck, hands and knees and feet scrabbling for rock.

Slithers onto the muddy, moss-slimed shore; caked in earth, slime upon his shoulders, mud and yesterday's blood upon his hands.

Makes his way towards the house: a sea serpent made flesh.

FOUR

B lack, wet September air, hanging thick as cloth. The scents of decay, of rotting wood; of life becoming death; earth becoming sea.

An arrow-straight road, framed here and there by crooked trees, pointing inland with the wind at their back.

A sensible saloon car, heading east. The clock on the dashboard reads 4.02 a.m.

At the wheel, Detective Sergeant Aector McAvoy. Grey suit, blue shirt, old-school tie. He wears his glasses when he drives, and they give him a teacherly appearance, though the piratical scars upon his face could just as easily imply a gangland enforcer with a court appearance.

In the passenger seat, Detective Superintendent Trish Pharaoh. She's fifty-two now, but has managed to find a way to confuse the issue by accessorizing herself with leather jacket, biker boots, and a pair of sunglasses that sit on her forehead and hold back her long, black hair. When McAvoy casts her his habitual sidelong glances, he tries not to dwell on the smudges of dark beneath her piercing blue eyes. She's tired. Run ragged. Wrung out. He feels instantly disloyal for letting his gaze linger on the new wrinkles, the laughter lines and crow's feet that peek out from beneath the haphazardly-applied make-up. Looks away before he feels compelled to remark upon the red wine stains that colour her lips. She has always been this way. Has always drunk, and smoked, and eaten what she fancies and done what she's pleased. She raised four daughters and a stepson like this, all while caring for a bedbound husband and rising to the upper echelons of CID. It's just starting to extort a heavy price.

'According to the satnav, we're in the sea.'

'Close,' he replies, gesturing out of the window at the vast blackness. 'Over there, I think.'

'And you'll have been here, of course. Read the guidebook. Got chatting with a lovely chap who runs a little museum . . .'

'Not here, no. But there's a gentleman in Patrington. Has some very interesting exhibits.'

'And the guidebook?'

'I might have had a wee flick.'

'Hector, you are three geeks stuffed into a skin-suit.'

'Thanks.'

Silence, as she plays with her phone. The sizzle of burning paper as she takes a drag, and fills McAvoy's family car with the flavour of Auntie Trish. She holds her long black cigarette between her mid and index fingers, the glowing tip punctuating her speech and flaring each time she sucks down another half an inch. McAvoy looks across at her. Experiences a flash of vivid memory – that cold, blue day in November when Trish Pharaoh cremated her husband. She had worn a dress of fuchsia and gold and insisted that the mourners wear bright colours. The songs had been happy, the sermon short; the coffin disappearing behind the purple curtain while 'If You Don't Know Me By Now' boomed from the speakers and the vicar tried not to laugh. There were so few mourners that McAvoy had found himself in the front row, six paces from where the shrivelled body of Pharaoh's husband, Anders, lay awaiting the rush of the flame. None of the dead man's children cried. Sophia, the eldest, barely looked up from her phone.

Pharaoh had hidden her eyes behind dark glasses. Her fingers were bare of jewellery, the nails a gaudy red. There were no flowers on the casket lid but she'd placed a bottle of Jamaican rum into the coffin before they nailed him in. The funeral directors had been wrong in thinking it was a tender gesture. She told McAvoy she would have rather used lighter fluid. Said that if she could have afforded a proper burial she'd have filled his coffin with sex toys, just so that archaeologists of the future would know he was a wanker too.

Should have done it years ago, she'd said, as the coffin disappeared behind the drapes. *Seems wrong that we had to wait until he died.*

McAvoy had struggled to know what to feel. Anders had been a bastard. Charming, gregarious – but still a bully. He'd hurt Pharaoh. Hurt their kids. Run up huge debts and lost the family home. Got into business with some very bad people, then succumbed to the blissful insensibility of a brain aneurysm just when she needed him the most. Pharaoh stuck with him. Nursed him. Fed him, bathed him, clothed him. Climbed the ranks and got enough money together for a little place in Grimsby. Moved him into the garage. Paid for his care and for the equipment that enabled him to make some attempts at communication. She gave him her best years. Anders never got better. He started suffering seizures a few months back. Couldn't be left alone. Pharaoh couldn't afford round-the-clock nursing and had refused all talk of a hospice. The girls took it in turns to sit with him, monitor him, read to him. He died in October, aged fifty-one. There would be no headstone, and his ashes were scattered in the car park. Pharaoh drove over them on the way out. Dropped her girls off with her mum and went to drink to the bastard's memory. Nine hours later she called McAvoy from Cleethorpes beach, drunk out of her mind. He'd never heard her cry before. Never heard her feel sorry for herself. Never heard her so unsure what to do next. He'd stayed on the phone throughout her long walk home. Listened as she unburdened herself. Told him what Anders had done to her. What he was capable of. How frightened she had been of him and how that fear remained even after he was incapacitated. It had been like talking to a stranger. He hadn't known whether to offer sympathy or vindication; to tell her she had done the right thing. In the end he had simply listened. It was easier than talking. He could never disguise the sound of tears in his own voice.

'About a mile, I think,' she says, squinting at her phone and tutting at the sporadic network coverage this far east of civiliza- tion. 'Wish I'd have known we were going to be underwater. I'd have insisted you wear trunks. Still, that's a problem easily solved. I should imagine a spot of skinny dipping would be rather bracing. You first.'

McAvoy smiles. Says nothing. Their conversations rarely require much from him. He just has to agree, and blush, and try not to set her off.

'So it's an island, yes . . .?'

'It's called Sunk Island,' explains McAvoy, again. 'Hasn't actually been what you would think of as an island for nearly two hundred years. And it didn't sink. It rose.'

'Sorry? Are we off to Atlantis?'

'I don't think it would quite claim that. But it did emerge from the water. It was just a big sandbank at first. You've seen how the cliffs erode on the coast here. They washed up here. Became this little stretch of land. It's quite interesting . . .'

'No it's not,' says Pharaoh, with authority. 'You tell me things like this all the time, and you always say it's quite interesting. This has never been proven true.'

McAvoy hangs his head. Looks up in time to see the spire of the little church. A piece of trivia bubbles up from the muddy sea in his mind. Pops, and informs him that this, at four metres tall, is the highest point for miles around. He decides to keep it to himself.

A light, bright behind him. He glances in the mirror. Makes out the shape of a low, sleek car. He slows down and watches it drop back, turning away down a side road he hadn't even noticed.

'Excitement?' asks Pharaoh, noting his preoccupation with the mirror.

'Ford Cougar,' he says, embarrassed. 'My first ever car. You don't see many.'

'Cougar?' asks Pharaoh. 'Can't see that, myself. I presumed you'd have been clattering about in a Land Rover. Maybe a battered old Rover 75 – the one that looks like it might be worth a packet but isn't . . .'

'I had one for a while,' says McAvoy, licking his lips. 'It had a cup-holder I was very proud of. Slid out from a walnut dash – very elegant.'

'You're so pretty,' says Pharaoh, shaking her head.

They drive in silence for a time. Pharaoh lights another cigarette from the tip of her last one. Pulls faces while she massages her temples, then admits defeat and puts on her sunglasses. Sits in the passenger seat like a rock star on a come down.

Ting

'Oh here we go,' says Pharaoh, triumphantly, brandishing her phone. 'Right, right . . .'

McAvoy knows little about what is waiting for them. Pharaoh will tell him in her own good time. She was still wet from the shower when he picked her up an hour ago. She's finally moved over from the South bank and has got herself an apartment in the Avenues – Hull's leafy Victorian suburb. She's been there four months and has yet to annoy any of her neighbours, which is remarkable in an area where the battle for parking spaces can be ferocious, and the off-licenses run a home-delivery service. She had towelled her wet hair and spritzed herself with perfume while sitting in the passenger seat. She may as well have been an animal rubbing her scent on him: an olfactory cattle-brand, the message 'mine', seared large. McAvoy knows that she does such things for no other reason than to annoy his wife, with whom her relationship is more than a little fraught. They both use him as a sounding board for their opinions about the other. It turns social occasions into a complex affair. Pharaoh spends a lot of time with the McAvoys. Her daughters are all getting older. Her eldest, Sophia, is one of Roisin's closest friends. Fin and Lilah think of Auntie Trish as real family. McAvoy sits in the middle of it all and watches the false smiles and the barbed compliments and wonders whether the whole set-up is a punishment for a crime he cannot remember committing.

'Anything on your missing anarchist?' asks McAvoy, to fill the silence.

'Waiting for the tide to answer that one,' says Pharaoh, quietly. 'His dad's losing his mind. Daft sods on Cleethorpes beach threatened him with a caution if he didn't stop bothering the lifeboat crew. I mean, a bit of compassion wouldn't go amiss.'

McAvoy gives a grunt. Pharaoh's case load is immense, but the missing person case being dealt with by Grimsby CID is weighing heavily on her. The 'anarchist' in question is twenty-three-year-old Christopher Timothy Stoker, though he's known to his followers as Topher-T. He lives with his father on the outskirts of a little village in North Lincolnshire, and left school at seventeen to pursue his dreams of becoming a political activist. He's been arrested several times for his involvement in various protest marches and stunts, using his skills as a climber and outdoorsman to maximum effect. He managed to scale Grimsby Dock Tower in 2018, hanging a huge great banner urging the locals to Eat the Rich. He's as much a performance artist as a rebel, and Pharaoh thinks he'd do more good for society if he put down the spray paint and had a wash. Pharaoh can't make sense of which movements he's against and which he's in favour of. He's a lithe, straggly-haired young man with facial piercings and purple dreadlocks, seemingly incapable of talking in full sentences and steadfast in his belief that the police are fascists. Pharaoh reckons he's probably been born in the wrong decade. She's watched some of his YouTube videos and rather likes him. He's earnest in a way that stops just short of real conviction. She was present when his father picked him up from the station following his last arrest, and saw a pleasant-looking old hippy who couldn't seem to decide whether his only son was doing the family proud, or making a prick of himself. Topher went missing nine days ago. He'd promised his few hundred social media followers that he had 'something special' planned. His dad believes he may have been the target of agents of the state, determined to silence him for disrupting the establishment.

'He thinks he's gone in the water?' asks McAvoy.

'Flippers are missing from the garage,' explains Pharaoh, tapping at her computer. 'I'll have to head over at some point. His laptop's gone for analysis, which means we should hear back in about a year . . .'

'I can come, if you like,' says McAvoy, quietly.

She looks across at him, a little smile on her face. 'Day trip? A walk on the beach? Maybe an ice cream . . .'

'If you like,' he says, again, and the darkness in the vehicle does nothing to hide his blush.

'Ah, it's alive,' says Pharaoh, as the screen fills with images. 'So . . . right . . . call came in at 10.46 p.m. Neighbour, Edwin Dash. Bloody daft name, innit? . . . reported seeing the body of his neighbour . . . concerned for her welfare – well you would be, wouldn't you? – uniforms dispatched, back door open, discovered the occupant deceased . . . contacted CID, wheels in motion, call went to senior officer on call, DI Grover, who doubtless remembered the fact that he's a fucking moron and made the wise decision to head out and get a look at the situation before alerting me . . .'

McAvoy has had few dealings with Grover. He pictures an ebullient, fitness-obsessed chap. Short, but wiry. Shaved head, and long ears: a sporty goblin. Late thirties, perhaps – younger than McAvoy and already a rung higher up the ladder. He drinks protein shakes and cycles to work. Draws elaborate mandalas in his notebook to help himself centre his thoughts. They haven't had much of an opportunity to work together, and even less to chat. Their one attempt at conversation – conducted at the temperamental vending machine at Priory Road police station – had seen Grover enthusiastically extolling the virtues of vitamin D supplements and the ingestion of powdered ants, while McAvoy gave well-meaning nods and stared longingly through the glass at his captive Galaxy Ripple.

'He's there now?'

'Yep, with two uniforms. Science officers are on alert but haven't set off – same with the dog unit. We'll have a look see. The accountants wouldn't thank me for popping my cork this early.'

'And the victim?'

'Dymphna Lowell,' she says, pulling out the ashtray and crushing out the stub of her cigarette. There's a trace of red wine on the filter tip – a gift for Roisin. 'Only name on the electoral register, lives alone. No formal ID, of course, but you and I both know it's going to be her. Would be nice to think it's an accident. Maybe an aneurysm. Painless. Just drops, and whatever comes next, that's just meat . . .'

'Lowell?' asks McAvoy. The name is vaguely familiar. 'You said something about a clairvoyant.'

'Aye. And anybody who says that she never saw it coming has to put a tenner in a charity jar, yeah?'

'You said that, Trish . . .'

'I'm allowed to. I'm funny. I tell bad jokes well. The shrink says it's a defence mechanism.'

'But the clairvoyance,' presses McAvoy, trying to keep her on track.

'Oh, right, Grover said that when he woke me up. I'm trying to find something on her now but this bloody phone . . .' Her tone changes, as she makes connections. 'Oh, of course! That's your Roisin's world, isn't it? Tea leaves and reading palms, or reading palm leaves and leaving tea, or however it all works.'

McAvoy is grateful for the darkness. Feels his cheeks colour. Feels her eyes on him. 'She's a herbalist. And she's helped a lot of people.'

'I know,' says Pharaoh, brightly. 'All of her lotions and potions – bloody godsend. That elderberry stuff shifted Sophia's bronchitis overnight and she sorted Fin's earache with an onion. That's not a talent to be sniffed at. No, honestly, I know she's good at all that. It's just a shame she was born in the wrong century. They used to burn witches at the stake.'

'Trish . . .'

'Oh shut up, man, I'm just playing.'

She lights another cigarette. Glares through her own reflection into the blackness beyond. In her hand, the phone gives a weak vibration. She opens the message, and barks a little laugh.

'All good?' asks McAvoy.

'Message from Thor,' she says, a different timbre to her voice. 'Inside joke. You wouldn't get it.'

McAvoy clamps his teeth together. The hinge of his jaw bulges like a flexed muscle. Pharaoh has developed a close friendship with a large, bearded police officer in rural Iceland. She keeps telling McAvoy all of the funny, charming and interesting things that he says to her. McAvoy doesn't like the sound of him at all. Thinks, in his private moments, that Thor needn't have applied for the position of favoured confidante. The role is being adequately filled.

'Ah, right. Found her. Dymphna Lowell. There's a picture here. Christ, they're some mad eyebrows. Looks fiftyish, maybe more.

She's wearing one of those scarves around her head. Purple. She looks a friendly sort, though I doubt she'd have a Facebook profile where she's holding a cleaver . . . let me see . . . national and international clairvoyant, Tarot readings, clairvoyance, medium, healing, reiki, crystal healing, animal healing – what's that, does she tell your gerbil's future or something? Fucking hell, she keeps herself busy . . . and she's a cosmic mythologist, which must come in handy . . . from a long line of people touched by "the gift", so she claims . . . oh and this is good to know – her great great grandfather was soothsayer to a Hungarian emperor. You don't get better references than that . . . uses Tzagine Oracle cards, whatever the—'

McAvoy shoots her a look. 'Tzagine?'

'Thought that was a Moroccan casserole . . .' She stops messing around as she meets his eyes. Becomes a different person entirely. 'Familiar?' she asks, quietly. 'You've gone white. Hector?' She raises a hand, about to grip McAvoy's in her own. Makes a fist, then drops it again. 'Sorry. If I went too far . . .'

He shakes his head. Turns back to the road. There are lights up ahead. The darkness reassembles into police cars and a white, sturdy-looking house. He feels tension in his arms and realizes he is gripping the wheel. Pictures start to flash in his mind: a strobing flicker-pad of memories long buried. He bites down on his cheek, regaining control.

No, he tells himself. *No, it's not familiar. No, it's not like before* . . .

'You OK, Hector?' She asks it with genuine concern. For all her bluster, she feels people's pain every bit as keenly as McAvoy. She's just better at hiding it.

'I'm good,' he mutters. 'A case, that's all. An investigation. When I was starting out.'

She doesn't reply. Lets him pull in to the side of the dark road. Waits until he has turned off the engine and they are sitting, silently, in the smoke-filled dark. He looks at her through the haze, his soft, sad eyes filled with memories.

'Hector?'

There is a knocking on the glass. It's Detective Inspector Rick Grover. McAvoy buzzes down the window. Looks up into a face he doesn't know well, but which isn't supposed to look like this.

He's pale as milk, and the spray of burst capillaries across his usually tanned cheeks betray the fact he has thrown up everything he's eaten, and more. There's no smile in his greeting. He can barely manage to get his words out.

'Guv,' he says, ignoring McAvoy and peering across to Pharaoh. He shakes his head. Swallows, and it seems to pain him. 'Horror show, guv. Fucking horror show . . .'

Pharaoh is out of the car in an instant. Becomes the force of nature that at once terrifies and inspires her team. Within moments she is at Grover's side, a warm hand on his back, rubbing his shoulders like a drunken teenager as he rests his weight on the bonnet of the car. She tells him that it's OK – that he's had a shock, to get himself together and do his best . . .

McAvoy hears him through the open window. Hears the sheer bloody ugliness of what the poor sod has witnessed. Feels the hairs rise on his arms as memories rise.

No, he tells himself, again. *He's gone. He's dead. They put him in the ground . . .*

On his cheek, the scar begins to ache.

FIVE

Twelve years ago
Kingsway Flats, Scunthorpe

Eva-Jayne Puck, sparkle-eyed and jolly, bumping off the doorframe as she bumbles, moth-like, into the poky little living room.

'That was your daddy,' she says, grinning madly, as she rubs her forearm with plump, gaudily ornamented hands.

'What was?'

'On the phone, I mean. Bad line, but he's sorting it. Sorting it out.'

The girl on the sofa picks up the TV remote control and mimes blowing her brains out. Manages a decent sound effect too: the spatter of blood hitting woodchip; brains sliding down voile.

'Oh. That's all right, then,' she says, wiping her mouth. 'Send him a fruit basket, shall we?'

Eva-Jayne sticks her finger in her ear. Wiggles it; bracelets clanking, rings catching the light. 'Sorry, Ro? You got my bad ear. Anyway, he sends his love.'

'Did he? Big of him. Send it back.'

She plonks herself down. The sofa squeaks in protest. Ro, inadequate as a counterweight, bounces up and into a sitting position. *'Doinggg,'* she mutters, flicking her hair behind her ears.

'Don't be like that, Roisin,' says Eva-Jayne, placing bare, chubby little feet in the girl's lap and making a little whining sound that suggests her aching trotters may benefit from affection. 'He didn't start this fight. What did you want him to do – just roll over and take it?'

Roisin picks up her aunt's foot, big toe pinched between forefinger and thumb. Deposits it back on the sofa as if dropping a dead pigeon into a pedal-bin. Gives Eva-Jayne her full attention. 'It would have been better than this, wouldn't it? Hiding out, scattered to the four fecking winds, stuck waiting to be told that everything's OK again – that Daddy and the boys have sorted it all out, like it's the nineteenth fecking century and I'm some helpless fecking female, the *bollocks* . . .'

'Roisin, you shouldn't talk about him like that. You're his princess. You're his wee darling.'

'I'm not anybody's princess. I'm nobody's wee darling. I'm nearly eighteen, for God's sake. None of this is anything to do with me!'

'It's just how it goes.'

'Well it's bloody stupid.'

Roisin Teague sits on the sofa, legs drawn up, hugging a cushion. She's scowling into the cold, smoke-wreathed air that fills the ugly little flat where she has been staying with her Auntie Eva-Jayne for three excruciatingly dull weeks. She's sick of it. Sick of keeping her head down, of having nobody to talk to, of worrying constantly about her mammy, her sisters – even Daddy, in the moments when she's not consumed with fiery temper. She feels trapped. Feels like a prisoner. It's as if the air around her is thick and stale: as if she could scoop handfuls of it like gone-off batter mixture. Even in the moments when she stares out of the window across the grey expanse of road, she can see nothing that gives off any kind of spark.

She broods. Chews on her thoughts as if they are all fat and gristle. Jingles the charms on her bracelet.

'Rings on her fingers and bells on her toes,' says Eva-Jayne with a smile. 'That's a beautiful thing, so it is. A present from your daddy?'

Roisin shrugs, grumbling into her lap. She folds her arms so she isn't tempted to play with the pretty silver charm bracelet that Daddy gave her two Christmases ago. Antique, or so he said. French-made. Six charms already, just to get her started: a teddy bear, a bowtop wagon, a teapot, a cauldron, an open book and a star. She's added two horseshoes and the head of a pony since then. It makes a lovely noise when she shakes it, like the sound of a nearby Christmas sleigh.

'You'll give that to your daughter one day, I shouldn't wonder,' says her aunt. 'Nothing's clear when it comes to you, my girl, but there's a shape in your future – a lovely wee lassie with dark hair and fierce eyes and a love for her mammy that could start fires.'

Roisin wrinkles her nose, hiding the smile. Forces herself to stay cross. Thinks upon the Heldens, and curses every last one of them. Hating the Heldens is something the Teagues learn at the breast. Childhood in her family is marked by first words, first steps, and first curse against the dirty thieving murdering bastards with whom her men have been at war since long before Daddy's granddaddy was small. She understands that the Heldens and Teagues are cousins, after a fashion. She can't help but seeing them as mirror images of each other. Both are Galway families. Both are clans to be reckoned with; to be respected and feared. Both are led by formidable patriarchs who've served lengthy stretches inside. United, they could be bloody terrifying. But to be a Teague is to hate the Heldens, and to be a Helden is to hate the Teagues. That's the top and bottom of it, apparently, and anybody who asked questions about what any of it actually matters, could expect accusations of rank disloyalty, and of being a little bit sweet on the enemy. Her sisters and brothers understand this. They have no doubt that when their best men clash in bare-knuckle bouts down damp, dirty country lanes, victory feels like Christmas and defeat brings damnable shame. She's seen them coming home: uncles, cousins, her father. Seen them with faces bashed in, ribs taped up, face the colour of uncooked beef, smoking cigars and swigging whiskey from the bottle, celebrating a slight avenged.

It's gone too far, now. To be a Teague, is to be living on borrowed time. The feud between the families has erupted into something that can't be set right by fisticuffs. It's all shotguns and slash hooks and petrol bombs now. It's not just the combatants who are vulnerable to attack. Anybody with a connection to Papa Teague runs the risk of being put in the ground. All the old rules have been ripped up. The women, the children, the older members of the extended clan – they've all been put on notice. A pregnant cousin was run down and crippled at a halting site in Dundalk; her fiancée hacked bloody with slash hooks and a machete. An uncle, long since disconnected from the main body of the family, was crucified on the roof of his caravan, his dead son's ashes decanted into his throat from a gleaming silver urn. Two associates out at Waterford were blasted with shotguns, the barrels sawn so close to the butt that the nearer of the pair didn't so much die as evaporate.

The slayings are said to be the work of a man that her father won't speak of without blessing himself. The Heldens called in a family associate; a man they quietly call 'Cromwell' due to the amount of Irishmen he has put in the ground. She's heard all the rumours about his origins. Born in the bowels of a mental hospital, or so they say. Smuggled out by authorities afraid of a scandal. Raised in total isolation by a half feral brother and sister who made a living recommissioning weapons and crafting self-assembly handguns and shotguns from items that wouldn't set off alarms. Cromwell started killing people for money before he was sixteen. Thirty years on, he's almost a myth, and the mere suggestion that he had taken the Heldens' money had been enough to persuade Papa Teague, as head of the clan, to send his children into hiding. His sons and daughters have been scattered out among distant relatives like different pieces of a treasured stained-glass window, ready to be reassembled after the war. It is Roisin's misfortune to have been placed with Auntie Eva-Jayne, here on this godforsaken estate in the Soviet-looking steel town in the colon of Lincolnshire.

'It could be worse,' says Eva-Jayne, good naturedly. She's a cheerful sort: plump and dumpy but pleasing to the eye. She's not far off fifty, but years of chain-smoking and fizzy pop have taken their toll and her features are a mess of wrinkles and empty gums. Her long hair is dyed purply-black, like her fingernails, but there is nothing about her that could be called unremarkable, from the big fleshy holes in her earlobes to the constellation of mirrors on her floaty red skirt. She's wearing her unicorn slippers today: two multi-coloured foam horns poking out from beneath her hem. She's wearing a huge fleecy hoodie too: a doe-eyed, baby seal-cub on the front. There are rainbow braids in her hair. Roisin finds herself unable to maintain her temper in the face of this riot of joie de vivre. She has to look away before she feels her temper begin to fade. Grins into the cushion and keeps the temper in her eyes.

'Could be worse? I'm in Scunthorpe. You realize that, yes? The only town in Britain with the word "cunt" in the title.'

'He wouldn't like that language, young lady,' says Eva-Jayne, plonking herself down in the armchair and returning the phone to its cradle on the table at her side. Her presence seems to make the room seem jollier: as if she were a patterned blanket thrown over an old beige sofa. None of the other fixtures or fittings are particularly inspiring. It's a miserable room: woodchip on the walls and haphazard swirls on the ceiling; a mustard-coloured two-seater sofa and easy-chair; a glass cabinet full of Royal Albert knick-knacks and ceramic animals; a bookcase full of DVDs and a gift parcel waiting to be posted. Roisin, who has grown up in a series of halting sites across the UK and Ireland, has seen nothing to suggest that there is anything about the life of the countryfolk, the *Gorjas*, to aspire to. Then again, she's seen nothing about the life of the Pavee that doesn't make her want to run away.

'Not your daddy,' says Eva-Jayne, a naughty smile on her face. 'Your sweetheart. Your knight in white satin. Your policeman.'

'Don't start with all that,' says Roisin, determined to bite back the smile before it can dash across her face. She's unsuccessful. A bright white smile transforms her features. Light seems to dance in her eyes. She looks down at her bare arms and sees the hairs rise like the rigging on a flotilla of yachts. She feels at once shy, self-conscious, and very young indeed.

'Ooh Roisin, you've gone all peculiar,' laughs Eva-Jayne, delighting in the transformation. 'Your auras turned sunset-red. Honestly, it's like you're glowing!'

Roisin looks at herself, peering at her skin as if searching for a hitherto unnoticed freckle. She can't see what Eva-Jayne sees, but then, not many can. She has the *sight*, does her auntie. The gift. She's a second cousin to Roisin's mother, and is originally from a Spanish Gypsy family that settled in Wales not long after the war. Eva-Jayne's mother married an English Traveller, and her cousin ended up falling for a bright-eyed, dark-haired Pavee from Galway. Her blood is pure Roma. It means she sees things. Senses things. She can see the future in the dregs of a cup of tea, can tell whether there is hope for a love affair just by staring into the bubbles on top of her washing up. She reads palms, Oracle cards. Has a crystal ball somewhere, just for the look of the thing. She's been settled in this manky little flat for the last five or six years, but she holds onto her roots with a grip that is fierce. She's made good money from her 'gift', since setting up home here. Two or three days a week, she's Madam Zingara. She tells fortunes. She reads palms. She sells crystals and banishes the bad energy from spaces where the spirits feel ill-at-ease. Half a dozen different women have arrived at the flat while Roisin has been staying here, coughing up cash to contact loved ones across the void; to ask for a prayer of protection for a troubled loved one, or begging for any indication that their life will change; that there is something more exciting ahead than behind. Madam Zingara manages to send them home happy. Roisin isn't sure what she believes, but there is certainly something magical about the bubbly, effervescent woman who sits in the armchair with her feet on a biscuit tin and smokes a cigarette held between forefinger and thumb.

'It's not going to happen, is it?' asks Roisin, softly. She shrugs, already knowing the answer. 'It's . . . I don't know . . . a fantasy. It's a dream, or something. I mean, I've not seen him in years. I don't know anything about him. He's probably married, or at least in love. And it's not right, is it? To think that you deserve something because of the bad stuff that's happened. I mean, we all have bad stuff in our past – it's just mine was, well, horrible, wasn't it? What they did. But then if it hadn't happened I wouldn't know somebody like him exists, which is just the worst way to think, but that doesn't stop me thinking it. And every time I think of being with somebody, of a future with somebody, and I think about what I want – I think of him . . .'

Roisin drops her head. Presses her face into the rough material of the cushion. Smells stale cigarettes and Chinese food. She wonders if she should just stay like this. Wonders whether perhaps she could find a way to meld her features with the fabric. It would be an achievement, of sorts.

'I see what comes over you when you think of him,' says Eva-Jayne, gently. 'It's the real thing, or at least, it feels like it. And I'm not going to sit here and tell you it can't happen, because sometimes miracles crop up, don't they? I know it drives your mother up the wall. Is it true you write to him every week? That you sometimes send yourself replies?'

'Don't,' says Roisin, clamping her jaw shut. She can't stand being picked on. She can hear her younger brother, Valentine, taking the piss in his sing-song voice: snatching her journal from her hand and trying to read out her words in a fake French accent. She's blacked his eye for it plenty of times but the lad doesn't seem to know how to stop.

'Roisin, it's OK. Everybody has their fantasy man.'

'I want to ask you . . .' begins Roisin, fighting with herself. 'Ask you to read for me – just give me something, y'know? Some idea if it's all going to happen . . .'

Eva-Jayne looks conflicted. She makes a face. 'That's for them,' she says, jerking her head at the door to the flat. 'People who need to be told what they want. I'm a bloody clairvoyant and I can't say for sure what the future holds. All I would say is that it's no surprise that you've never forgotten him. I mean, after all that happened, what they did . . .'

Roisin shakes her head, not wanting to hear it. Not wanting the memories to rise. She scrunches up her eyes, willing the pictures in her brain to catch fire. She's not fast enough. For a moment she sees them: the farmer, his boys. Sees herself back in that barn, on the country road not far from the site where the

Teagues had spent a few quiet days. For a moment, she feels the same burning pain. Feels rough skin against the soft flesh of her wrists and the sudden cold air upon her bare skin. Looks up into dead eyes, flared nostrils; animal grunts of exertion; sweat falling upon her face like rain. Sees him. The police officer. The one who talked to her family like they were worth every bit as much as everybody else. The big man, with the kind eyes and the red cheeks, who'd fumbled over his words and dropped his notebook in the mud outside their caravan door. He was suddenly there, above her, grabbing the bad man and smashing a big, ham-hock fist into the side of his head. Through the haze of her tears, she sees. *Remembers*. The way he had taken them apart like scarecrows. And then he had picked her up so gently that for a moment she had felt as if she were flying. It was hazy after that: shouts and screams and the glug of petrol and the crackle of fire; her father's voice, telling him to leave it alone, to go; to put the whole sorry business from his mind. And then his big eyes looking into hers, all sorrow and regret and apology. He'd walked away without looking back. She can see it so clearly that it feels as if she could reach out and wipe the blood and dirt from his ripped shirt. She's loved the memory of him every day since.

'You do pick 'em,' says Eva-Jayne, cheerfully. 'A Pavee and a copper, eh? Hey, stranger things have happened.'

'Have they?' asks Roisin.

Eva-Jayne grins. Gives her a look that twinkles with mischief. Glances at the screen of her mobile phone and sucks her cheek, weighing something up.

'What are you thinking?' asks Roisin.

'About your run of luck. How many years ago was it that it happened? Six? Seven? Maybe we should put our minds to the current problem, eh? The bloody Heldens. God, but these feuds get tiresome. Never used to be like this. The ladies and the babbies were never caught up. It was for the men to deal with. For them to bring in somebody like him. Like bloody Cromwell . . .' She crosses herself as she says his name and spits on the rig at her feet. Pretends to smile – to find something to be positive about. 'Anyway, your father said things would be sorted soon. And we've seen no reason to worry, have we? And with you climbing the walls, mooning over your

flame-haired Thor from years back, and me having a chance
to make a few quid . . .'

Roisin feels her spirits rising. God, she'd give anything for a
change of scenery. A walk – a chance to sit on a swing for
a while and think about nothing, and everything, and *him*.

'Keep your phone on you, and don't talk to any dickheads,
which won't be easy considering the neighbourhood – back for
nine, yeah? I've got a tenner somewhere, get yourself some chips
or whatever. Bring me back some Marlboro Red – I won't be
seeing my guy off the boats for another week. And if you get in
trouble, you tell everybody you sneaked out and it wasn't my
fault, yeah? We can do some more crystal gift bags later, if you
like. You seemed to enjoy that. I know it's been hard, but I've
enjoyed this time together, Ro. You're good company sometimes.
Mind like a bloody rocket and too pretty to be let out alone, but
I know from experience, you can't keep a nightingale in a cage.
Go on, and for Christ's sake take your daddy's blade.'

Roisin leaps up and crosses, half dancing, to her auntie. She
wraps her arms around her, kisses her hair, squeezes her as if
she were a teddy bear, breathes in incense and perfume and smoke.

'Oh go on,' says Eva-Jayne, pushing her away with a smile.

Roisin rushes to the tiny spare room, pulling clothes from her
animal-print suitcase and holding up tops, jeans, cardigans and
hoodies for inspection. She feels like she's getting ready for a
wedding. She fishes out her iPod from the mess of dirty laundry
at the side of the bed, and slips in her little earphones. Feels
genuinely giddy with the excitement of actually leaving the damn
flat. Shuffles through songs that make her move her hips.
Backcombs her hair at the little white dressing table. Spritzes
herself with perfume. Tries on different combinations of
shoes, jeans, skirts, jackets – bounces through Beyoncé, Lady
Gaga, Shakira, Mary J. Blige – grins at herself in the mirror as
she brushes glitter onto her cheeks. Half an hour goes by. An
hour. She's enjoying the getting ready so much that she half
thinks about not even leaving. But eventually, she looks so good
she feels it would be a shame not to show anybody.

At seven forty p.m., she opens her bedroom door and walks
down the hallway to the living room, Girls Aloud hammering in
her ears.

Stops short. The air feels wrong. The scent, the taste, even the way the air flows over her skin.

And then she sees him. A figure, clad in black, on his knees as if in prayer.

Eva-Jayne is laid out on the floor in a spreading pool of sticky red blood. There is so much red around her mouth that for a moment Roisin cannot make sense of what she is seeing. There is something vampiric about her face; something ghoulish in the pure whiteness of her face, the agony in her expression, the crude knife strokes scored into her flesh.

Everything slows down. For a moment, she is perfectly still.

Then the figure shifts his position.

Turns.

Roisin never sees his face. Just the hammer. The long shard of bluish stone. The gaily-coloured card that the killer holds, firmly, upon her auntie's lifeless chest.

Her senses come back in a flood.

A hand, bloodied, reaching up, fastening around her wrist.

She yanks backwards; her bracelet tearing, charms falling: a rain of silver into a pool of blood.

And then Roisin Teague is running for her life.

SIX

3.48 a.m.
Sunk Island

Grover hadn't been exaggerating. Dymphna Lowell's death was brutal. She lies partway between the living room and the kitchen: her lower half cushioned by carpet – her ruined torso stuck to the linoleum with clotted red-black blood. Her top has been pulled down. A shard of crystal, patterned in shades of blue, pokes out from her mangled ribcage. The beaded necklace with which she has been strangled has sunk into the pulpy flesh at her neck. Her face has been partially denuded of flesh. Fingers too. There are little teeth marks around the orbit

of her eye and a great flap of hair and scalp has been yanked
loose; flopping over the excised eye like a pirate's patch.

'Jesus,' says Pharaoh, crouching beside her and angling her
head. She stares into the mess. Doesn't let herself look away.

'Don't know how much of that the cats did,' says Grover, from
the door. 'Three of them. Been having more than a nibble.'

'Bowls are empty, then?' asks Pharaoh, still squatting low.
'Water bowls too?'

'Dry as a bone,' says Grover, quietly, from his position by the
door. 'Bin's been knocked over. Everything edible's been
consumed. Litter tray's empty.'

'Milk?'

'Four-pinter. Half full. An inch or two on top.'

'Fridge?'

'On its side. Counter.'

'Dishes?'

'Breakfast and lunch in the sink, licked clean. Three mugs.
Empty pint glass on the drainer. Nothing else.'

'Through in a jiff.'

McAvoy is standing in the centre of the kitchen, holding
himself together. It feels as though there are birds inside his skin:
a maelstrom of beating wings and needle-sharp beaks. From
where he stands, the bulk of the refrigerator blocks his view of
the corpse. He's grateful. He's already seen enough of Dymphna
Lowell. Has made his promises. He has seen too much death;
the ruination of too much flesh. It does not revolt him – just
makes him monstrously sad. He tells himself that the thing on
the floor is just spoiled meat – that the best part of her, the
essence of her, is in whatever place she believed in. Tells himself
that his duty is to justice – to those left behind – and not to the
dead. But he feels her. Feels the person she was. Can see her
fingerprints in the streaks and dust on the TV screen; can hear
her laughter in the silly saucy postcards stuck to the side of the
microwave with magnetic fruit. He feels an urge to throw open
a window – to let her soul billow away across the low, wide
landscape and into the unknown.

He's trying to make himself useful. Has had as much of a look
around as he feels able without contaminating the scene. He has
squeezed himself into a white suit and blue booties and is making

sure to step lightly. Things will be done properly come the morning light. The science officers are on their way; the dog unit too. He has personally called each member of the Serious and Organized Unit and told them that for the next twenty-four hours at least, nothing else matters. An extra van-load of uniformed officers are already milling around outside, setting up the perimeter of the crime scene and closing the road. The houses here are too spread out to warrant a door-to-door search during the hours of darkness but every resident of this secluded, windswept road will be questioned before breakfast.

'Where are the cats now?' asks Pharaoh, quietly.

'Bolted,' says Grover, on sentry by the front window. 'Soon as the uniforms gained entry. Straight out the back.'

'Lovely job for somebody,' says Pharaoh, arching her back. She looks around her, taking stock of a vacated life. The little living room is a pleasingly haphazard affair: a mish-mash of classics, retro and the gaudily new. The carpet is a gaudy swirl of burgundy and red, offsetting walls covered in cream wood chip. There is a yellow patch on the ceiling above the high-backed armchair, which still carries the imprint of a previous occupant's rump. A glass ashtray sits atop a tower of magazines on the floor. The three-piece suite is wood-framed, with squashy, battered cushions. One is more threadbare than the others, the hem half worn away. A person taller than Dymphna's five feet two inches has spent long enough sitting here to wear it away. Along one wall, imitation brickwork surrounds an imitation fireplace, designed to look like an old-fashioned stove. Each nook and alcove is home to different crystals. The light catches in their edges and shallows; a dazzling display of soft reds, purples and blues; as if sunlight is cascading through stained glass and pitching radiance onto a church floor. There are chunky frames on the wall, showing off a mismatched array of watercolours, photographs, certificates and prints. Pride of place above the fire is a huge print of a grinning bride, barefoot on a white rug, a plump, blue-eyed child returning her smile and throwing a handful of petals and confetti into the air. The little girl from the picture is centre-stage in most of the photographs: wrapped up in a thick red coat on a muddy path, or sitting bareback on a Shetland pony, delighted to be outside – up past her bedtime in grubby pyjamas.

Grover is distractedly examining the little pile of books by the TV. 'Big reader,' he mutters. 'I've had nowt new to read since they stopped printing the Argos catalogue and the missus said I couldn't take my phone with me to the toilet . . .'

'Grover,' says Pharaoh, pointedly. 'The cats. It needs doing.'

'Guv?'

Pharaoh, who has spent ten years enjoying the services of a bagman who does what she wants before she's even ordered it, gives a low growl. 'I just said. Whatever they've eaten, we need back.'

Grover, his face still grey, attempts a laugh. Pharaoh fixes him with a look. Even from behind the face mask, she has a penetrating stare. 'I mean it, detective inspector. One of the vermin is digesting evidence. I don't know her family yet but one of the poor sods is going to have to identify her.'

'Oh,' says Grover, nodding. 'The eye's upstairs. Windowsill.'

Pharaoh nods. Sighs. 'That's a bonus,' she mutters, then eases her way past the body and into the kitchen. McAvoy is staring through the darkened windows at nothing very much, watching as a smudge of pinkness begins to take shape, separating the sky from the sea. He turns, sensing Pharaoh. Feels her give his arm a squeeze. He's grateful for it. Hopes she can't feel the way he is using every ounce of self-control to stop himself from trembling.

'Three days at least,' says Pharaoh.

'Guv?'

'I read somewhere that it takes that long before your skin's loose enough for them to get their teeth in.'

McAvoy shakes his head. 'At least four days – you can see from the milk. But the face thing? The elasticity of the skin? No. Back home there was an old widow who fell and broke her hip. Lived alone in a croft on the road past Slaggan. Drifted in and out of consciousness for twenty-four hours. Came to when her cat started eating the fat of her hand. They'll go for you once they're hungry.'

Behind the mask, Pharaoh makes a face. 'That wasn't one of your prettier "You Should Come to Scotland" pitches, Hector. That was downright bloody horrible.'

'Sorry.'

They stand in silence. McAvoy feels as though there's a weight in his gut: a kernel of something hard; unyielding. He knows what he has to say. Knows that if he doesn't, there'll be no way back. She'll find out – there's no hiding anything from Pharaoh. She tells her officers the same thing whenever they get themselves in trouble. It's burned into the frontal lobes of every officer who has joined her team. *Learn to lie, and lie well, but don't lie to me. I'll protect you, I'll cover for you, I'll lay down in traffic for you, but I need to know everything. Lie to me, and I'll rip your tongue out . . .*

'Laptop's still here at least,' says Pharaoh, pointing at the grubby silver computer that sits open on the wooden table. 'Christ, I think we're about the same age, Hector. Did you see the blood on her chin? I saw some slides at a conference, years back: drug dealers out in banjo country in West Ireland. Had a penchant for taking the tongues of informants. The blood pooled just like that.'

McAvoy feels his phone begin to vibrate. Can't decide whether to silence it and tell her what he must, or thank God for the distraction.

'Paw prints,' says Pharaoh, absently, as she slowly gives the room a once-over. There's a mess of four-pronged imprints around the wreckage of licked-clean feeding bowls. She narrows her eyes. Considers the pile of soiled papers and empty containers that have been raked through by three frantic cats, searching for food. Moves past McAvoy, and peers among the debris. 'Phone,' she says, quietly.

McAvoy does as instructed. Cancels the call from Roisin without even thinking. Passes her the mobile and watches as she reels off several shots. Then she extracts her sunglasses from under the papery hood of the suit, and uses the arm to slide free the colourful square of card deposited among the refuse.

McAvoy swallows, hard. He knows what it will be even before the gaudy colours and tattered edges align themselves into a picture.

It's an Oracle card. A gaudy, blood-soaked specimen from a fortune-telling deck favoured by those with some Gypsy in their blood. There is a hole through its centre, hemmed with dried blood. Despite the destruction, the central image remains clear: a childish depiction of a fluffy black-and-white cat: dazzling eyes and a curling question mark of tail.

'Falseness,' says McAvoy automatically. 'A liar's card.'

Pharaoh looks up at him. Pulls aside her face covering so he can see her piercing blue eyes.

'You know this because of Roisin?' she asks, quietly, lest Grover be listening at the door.

'Sort of, I don't know . . . it's something from before, from when we met – I think . . . look, I should probably tell you this right away . . .' says McAvoy, and the words tumble out in a rush: a disjointed mess.

Pharaoh tries to shush him. To calm him. To get him to make sense.

She is standing with her hands on his forearms when Grover pokes his head into the kitchen. His own face covering is pulled down, and there are two spots of colour on his cheeks. He's out of breath, but whatever it is, can't wait.

'Guv, I've just heard from one of the old boys works in collating at Beverley nick. Word travels fast, doesn't it? Anyway, you'll never guess. Turns out this has happened before.'

Pharaoh gives McAvoy a hard stare. Drops her arms to her sides.

A growl in her voice as she mutters, 'You don't fucking say.'

SEVEN

Twelve years ago

A coal-dark street, pummelled by sharp, slanting rain. Lamplight spilling from tatty bay windows, held captive in a million raindrops, slick atop dirty puddles – shattered glass pixels glittering on the slick metal of cars parked nose to tail.

This is Exmouth Street, at the shabbier end of the Hull neighbourhood that calls itself the Avenues. For the past four months, Aector McAvoy has been living in the bland, brick property at the end of the terrace. It's demonstrably fine. He can think of a better description. That's what he tells the family, when they ask. Says it's all 'fine'. The house, the city, the job, the people he's getting to know. He can think of no better way to put it. This will do, for now. He can't ever imagine calling this place 'home'. He arrived in the city just as austerity was starting to bite chunks out of the police budget. At around the same time as he was being offered the job with the Community Policing Team, Humberside Police was deciding it could no longer afford to maintain accommodation for its officers. He has tried not to take it too personally. He's stumbled into a house share with a colleague, and is pretty confident he can stick it out here for the foreseeable. He doesn't trouble himself unduly with home comforts. He just needs somewhere to sleep, to read, to feed himself, and the rest of the time he can devote to acquainting himself with this rough-hewn, mercurial city.

Were he not concerned with appearing rude, McAvoy would be in his bedroom, upstairs at the end of the bare corridor. He would be sitting in the hard-backed chair, feet on the windowsill, reading by the light of the street lamp. He may even have a big bag of Galaxy Minstrels open on his lap, chocolate adhering to his fingertips and leaving smudges over the neat lined pages of his jotter. He finds peace in such moments, and McAvoy knows that peace is a commodity to be treasured. He is not a man at ease with the world or his place within it. He feels permanently displaced; dislocated – endlessly cast an outsider. He's still the lumbering, red-haired Scotsman who left the family croft at ten years old and has been looking for 'home' ever since. He doesn't know what it is to fit in; doesn't know how it feels to introduce himself and not have somebody laugh and ask him how it's spelled. It's been the same for twenty years. Never one of the lads. He was too poor, too shy, too big, too clever to be part of the in-crowd at boarding school. Had to sit with a teacher when there was a coach trip to an inter-school sporting event, even though the other lads knew he was their best player. Never had anybody in his corner when the school allowed him to participate in amateur boxing. Won every bout to the sound of the polite applause of strangers. He only managed a year and a half at university, quitting when he realized that he'd learned more during the shifts at the little bookshop where he had a part-time job, than in eighteen months of intensive university education. He spent time travelling, teaching rugby, fitness, English as a foreign language. He considered joining the Armed Forces, before the ethics of the whole affair threatened to tie him in knots. The idea of joining the police rather crept up on him. There was no thunderbolt moment. He just wanted to do some good; to help people, to try and stop bad people from getting worse. He's been a copper for six years now and has answered none of his questions about the nature of people; about good and evil, decency and justice. He just bumbles through, trying to only ever do that which he can live with, and hoping that he never again finds himself in a situation where he has to choose between being a good police officer, and a good man.

McAvoy is sitting on the leather-effect sofa in the sitting room of the terraced property. It was already furnished when he moved in, though 'furnished' may be pushing the definition of the term. The sitting room contains a two-seater sofa, a matching armchair, a three-bar electric fire and round metal table and chairs intended for outdoor use. The only 'art' on the wall is an ugly reproduction of something blobby by Matisse, hanging awkwardly against the bright-white chimney breast in a cracked clip-frame. McAvoy's meagre possessions are in his room. Books, photographs, sporting trophies and medals: a leather-bound folder containing his certificates of achievement: a few drawings of animals, of birds, of wildflowers; the landscapes of his childhood in the Western Highlands. He didn't even bring more than a rucksack of clothes when he left Carlisle. He's either in uniform, or makes do with his three or four rugby shirts, and faded, Britpop-era jeans. He's wearing an Arran sweater and some denim shorts this evening. His short red hair sticks up at the back and despite his best efforts, his broad, handsome face looks as though it is covered in four days' growth of stubble. In truth, he shaved this morning. He fancies he could probably grow a biblical beard in about a week. At school, they blamed an excess of testosterone: an accusation that made him blush. He presumes he still suffers from the same problem, though there is no shortage of people who have offered to help him siphon off the excess. Nobody was more surprised than he was when it emerged, during freshers week, that he was considered devilishly handsome by the opposite sex. He's never really made his peace with it. In the company of women he has a tendency to trip over his own feet, or say the wrong thing, or say nothing at all. He can't get the hang of double-entendres and his cheeks burn crimson if anybody is direct with him.

'. . . I mean, it doesn't bother me, but people will, y'know . . .'

McAvoy looks up. Detective Constable Dachman Buller is still talking to him. McAvoy wonders if he's missed anything important. Certainly the presence of his housemate has ruined his enjoyment of the book that he holds in his lap. He's read the same sentence nine times. He's midway through a Ken Bruen novel, quietly delighting in the exploits of crumpled private investigator Jack Taylor. Taylor's his guilty pleasure. He adores his one-liners, his capacity for the drink; the way he takes the pain of others inside him, powerless to stop it metastasizing into violence, into the deaths of those closest to him. There is something of the avenging angel about Taylor, and McAvoy almost envies the poor broken bastard for at least having the freedom to be himself. McAvoy wishes life were that simple. Wishes he had the first clue whether he believes himself to be the last of the good men, or a coward too afraid to do anything other than follow orders.

'Sorry, Dachman,' says McAvoy, inserting his bookmark between the pages. 'Miles away.'

'Hope there was a girl there with you, Jock. Big lump like you – you should be beating them off with a shitty stick.'

McAvoy looks appropriately appalled at the imagery. Manages a smile, so his housemate doesn't think him rude. Gets a mumbled 'for fuck's sake' in reply.

Dachman Buller is a tall, dark, slightly rumpled lad. He's mixed race: half Algerian, half Lancastrian. The people of Hull seem to harbour no grudges about the North African hue to his skin, but the Lancashire accent has caused him one or two scrapes. He's on the highly esteemed CID team run by Detective Superintendent Doug Roper: a slick operator with a reputation for getting the job done. He respects Roper's record, and presumes he must be a good judge of character, though he hasn't observed a great deal about his housemate to imply he deserves a place on an elite unit of detectives. He's disorganized, loud and frequently bone-idle. The only time he seems to get passionate about anything is when Burnley are playing a match that matters to him, or he's arguing with one, or both, of the ex-girlfriends. He has two sons, both around the same age, and both by different mums. He has little to do with the boys, and feels that as a consequence, he should be spared the indignity of paying more than the absolute minimum for their upkeep. McAvoy keeps telling himself to stay out of it: not to pry. He has a habit of getting too involved – of taking other people's pain inside himself. And he presumes that Buller must be in pain – that there is a repressed agony, a secret trauma, that compels him to act with such caddish disregard towards his own flesh and blood. He cannot conceive of any other reason why a person would do anything other than the right thing.

'I was saying, Jock . . . dinner, like. It's really good, like. I mean, I'd pay a good chunk for this in a restaurant. But look, I've said before, don't go thinking you've got to make enough for two, yeah? You do you, I'll do me. I mean, we're housemates, aren't we? But, this coming in to find my tea in the microwave . . . it's like . . .'

McAvoy looks back at the cover of his book, trying to spare Buller the awkwardness of having to meet his eye while he informs him that he's being a bit smothering in his attentiveness. It's not the first time they've had this conversation. Nor is it the first time that McAvoy has struggled to explain the concept of 'being considerate' to other people.

'The butcher on Newland Avenue did us a deal,' said McAvoy, quietly. 'It was as cheap for four pounds of the braising steak as it was for two.'

'And it's not "us", yeah, mate?' says Buller, mopping up the last of his stew-and-dumplings with a slice of buttered brown bread. He has a bottle of beer open in front of him, a pile of papers and printouts piled up at his feet. He's been playing a game on his phone while he's been eating; smacking his lips and making appreciative noises and occasionally allowing his tie to fall in the gravy.

'It's just a figure of speech,' says McAvoy, a little hurt. He wills himself not to blush. He can't understand why everybody

he's lived with has been so peculiar about such things. If he sees
a pile of dishes, he washes them. If the sink needs scrubbing, he
scrubs it. If there's a heap of dirty clothes outside his housemate's
bedroom door, he throws it in the washing machine with his own.
That's considerate, isn't it? That's just basic human decency?
Wouldn't that qualify as the absolute least that one person could
do for another?

'And the bath, Hector,' says Buller, shaking his head and
looking at him as if he might be simple. 'I don't know why, it's
just weird. You don't run a bath for your mate. It's just fucking
odd.'

'You said your back was aching,' protests McAvoy. 'I was
going upstairs anyway . . .'

Buller pushes his plate away, tired of explaining the world to
somebody clearly born in the cold, icy reaches of another solar
system. He gathers up his papers from the floor. Takes a swig
of his beer and stifles a belch.

'Pardon you,' says McAvoy automatically.

'For fuck's sake,' growls Buller, and polishes off the rest of
the beer. He stares into the neck, hoping to refill the bottle with
his eye. When a miracle doesn't occur, he stands up, still snarling,
and carries his dirty plates to the kitchen. Bangs them down
unnecessarily harshly, then stomps out into the little back yard
for a smoke.

McAvoy waits a moment, letting the air in the room regain
some sort of equilibrium. Then, gently, he eases back the curtains.
Shakes his head, sadly, at the huddled shape of his poor, conflicted
associate. He watches, unblinking, as the DC gets comfortable,
tucked in against the back wall, cigarette in one hand, phone in
the other, perfectly shielded from the wild, sideways rain. McAvoy
knows he'll be there for a while. Keeps watching, just to make
sure. Behind him, the tops of the houses start to blend in with
the gathering dark. If he listens carefully, he can hear the sound
of the droplets hammering on the felted roof of the little shed
at the bottom of the yard. The air feels supercharged; static
and thick. There's a crackle to the air; a purplish light seaming
the thick, roiling clouds. A storm is coming. A storm that's going
to hit hard.

McAvoy closes the gap in the curtain, puts his book neatly on the floor, and walks as softly as he can to where Buller has left his case notes. He feels a little furtive, a touch deceitful – as if he might be doing something morally questionable. But he's a police officer, isn't he? They're all on the same side, after all. And he knows he's good at his job – that he sees things that others don't; that he can make connections and read faces and spot a lie like few others. He doesn't say any of this out loud: can't bring himself to blow his own trumpet, but he's been part of big cases before. Acquitted himself admirably. He's stopped bad people doing anything worse and he's helped secure justice for the cruelly bereaved. He might be able to help. He can't see how he can do any harm. He's simply sparing the pair of them the awkwardness of having to ask whether it's OK to look at the case file. He's sure he'd say yes. So sure, it's not even worth putting the question.

The name on the top file, written in black marker, is **Eva-Jayne Puck**.

He already knows the basics from the news bulletins, the snatches of radio traffic, and overheard conversations in the staff canteen. Two days ago, she was brutally murdered in the living room of her low-rent flat overlooking Kingsway in Scunthorpe. Somebody strangled her to the very point of death. Then they drove something hard and sharp through her skin, her fat, her bones, and right into her heart. Her downstairs neighbours were disturbed by the sound of a commotion but didn't call the police until the blood started seeping through the ceiling. When they made their way upstairs, they found a man bleeding in the stairwell. When they made their way to the victim's flat, they found the door wide open. Found Eva-Jayne, a puddle of gory emptiness.

McAvoy looks at the image of the dead woman as she was in life. There's a hastily assembled victim profile, tucked in among the various witness reports and the preliminary forensic findings. McAvoy locks eyes with the dead. She's smiling, in the picture, showing perfect false teeth. There's a gold sovereign on a chain around her neck, and her hair is rainbow-coloured and stuck up haphazardly at the crown and fringe. He thinks he would probably have liked her. There's a knowingness in her eyes: a sense of having endured a lot and gleaned no end of wisdom from her traumas and trials. According to the neighbours downstairs, she was a palmist. Read Oracle and Tarot cards. Had a few gentlemen callers and they regularly saw women leaving her apartment in grateful tears.

McAvoy looks at the crime-scene photos. At what was done to her. He feels an emptiness; a queasy sort of sorrow, like a greasy tuber squirming in his gullet. Looks at the handwritten notes beside the full-colour picture of her ruined mouth. Attempts had been made to cut off her tongue. It has been impossible to discern if this was done post-mortem.

McAvoy checks the door. Pulls his phone from his pocket. It's a new model; the only treat he's afforded himself since the new job started to put some excess in his bank account. It takes photographs: a technological marvel that seems positively space age. He starts taking pictures: page after page, scanning and skimming and absorbing grisly sentences and grainy shots.

He stops when he reads the witness statement. The man on the stairs owned a property in the building and had been calling to hear a resident's complaint about persistent damp. He'd been waiting in the stairwell, wondering whether the occupant had gone out, when a slim girl with dark hair and piercing eyes had leapt past him, plunging down the stairs and clattering into him like a bowling ball into skittles. He'd fallen backwards, taking his weight on his arm, dislocating his shoulder and smacking his head on the hard floor. He'd lost consciousness for a moment, but he'd seen a figure in black, leaping over him, blood dripping from a curve of silvery blade.

McAvoy turns the page. There is a CCTV image of the girl, sprinting through the lobby of the flats, her likeness pixilated but still familiar. He considers eyes that he has not looked into for so long: eyes belonging to a girl he sometimes thinks about with hope, with kindness, with sorrow and regret.

The investigation team don't have a name for her. McAvoy does. She's Roisin Teague. She's an Irish Traveller from Galway. And six years ago he half killed a man to save her from an attack that still chews at his soul.

He closes the file. Makes sure everything is as he left it.

Then he returns to his seat.

Puts his head in his hands.

And knows, all the way through to the centre of himself, that he will not be able to leave this be.

EIGHT

A gleaming Lexus, hugging the corners as it eats up the miles; big halogen lights setting the trees aflame and casting searchlights into the darkness. Heading east, the roads running parallel to the coastline. Signs, glimpsed and gone, pointing back inland to Patrington, Ottringham, Keyingham.

'These place names are making me hungry.'

'Eh?'

'They've all got pissing *ham* in the title.'

Petulant, sulky, Detective Constable Andy Daniells moves the muesli and yoghurt around in his bowl. Tries to remove something from his back teeth. Suffers a surge of memory: for a moment he's a boy again, embarrassed in front of the rest of his classmates, forced to walk up to the teacher and politely request a new pencil, having devoured yet another yellow HB. He endured a lot of tests as a child. Doctors and psychologists wondered whether he might suffer from some terrible disorder. By his mid-teens, people had just accepted he was a hungry boy.

Innate hungriness is the reason for the mélange of rabbit food and effluent that squats, maliciously, in his cereal bowl. His husband, Stefan, is taking his health seriously. He has him on a strict diet, and has laid out an exercise regime that, to Daniells, seems woefully short on rest periods. His ideal rest period would last from now, sitting in the passenger seat of Stefan's swanky Lexus, all the way through to death.

'How does it taste?' asks Stefan, glancing across.

'Tastes like I'd rather be fat,' grumbles Daniells, just as the satnav interrupts to inform them they have arrived at their destination. The information is unnecessary. There are police vehicles parked all the way down the long, desolate road and a variety of uniformed figures are milling around, shivering and trying to look busy. Just beyond the furthest patrol car, he spies the bulk of his sergeant. He's staring off into the distance, out to sea. His body language speaks in soft, sad whispers. Daniells knows this is going to be bad.

'You've barely eaten any of it,' says Stefan, peering at the homemade assortment of raisins and dust. 'How do you know you don't like it, if you don't even try it?'

'Stef, I used to say that to people when I was on the pull in straight bars. Can't I just grab a muffin?'

'Was that their reply?'

Daniells grins. Reaches over and squeezes his husband's hand. Stefan is a doctor, and a few years older than the small, plump detective constable. He's a lot more stylish too. Daniells always wears the same creased blue suit and pale-blue shirt, and usually looks a little clammy, as if he has recently exerted himself. There is a blob of yoghurt on his lapel, which Stefan dutifully wipes away with a wet wipe from the glove box.

'Thanks, Dad.' Daniells grins, leaning over to kiss his tall, tanned, grey-haired partner.

'Don't you bloody dare,' replies Stefan with a smile. He stares through the glass and something about the view seems to sap him of energy. 'Desolate spot, isn't it?'

'Windswept and interesting, I think that's the phrase.'

'A woman, you said?'

'Dymphna Lowell. I've been reading her Facebook page. Nice lady. I think she's got a daughter and a granddaughter. Lots of five-star reviews.'

'And somebody's killed her? Why would anybody do that?'

Daniells shakes his head, a little smile on his face. 'I don't know, love. Maybe the police will find that out.'

Stefan doesn't respond. Just looks out into the slowly evaporating darkness. 'There he is,' says Stefan, approvingly. 'The warrior poet. Hamish McGoldenbollocks. God, he's like a Greek statue, isn't he? It would almost be worth getting murdered just to have him trying to do justice to your memory.'

Daniells gives a mock shiver. 'Don't,' he says, and his voice sounds sharper than he intended. 'He wouldn't like you making fun.'

Stefan laughs, as if at a shared joke. Then his face hardens, as he realizes Daniells is being serious. 'Oh sorry, wouldn't want to offend your hero. Christ, Andy, why don't you write his name on your pencil case and put his poster up in your locker?'

Daniells screws up his face. There are a lot of things he'd like to say to Stefan. A lot of backed-up frustrations that he would like to vent. But he knows they won't make a difference. His husband is the jealous type: an alpha male who automatically needs to compare himself to anybody who might be held in high regard. It puts a strain on what is an otherwise happy union. Daniells, a natural peacemaker, softens his eyes. 'He only has eyes for his wife,' he says, kindly. Then he considers it. 'And maybe the boss. Or maybe not. It's hard to tell. But I don't think I'm his type. And he's not mine. He's just, I dunno . . . good at all this. Just good in general. He's one of those earnest types who don't make you want to vomit. You should get to know him.'

Stefan snorts, as if the idea is ridiculous. Cranes his neck. 'Pharaoh's giving him a roasting, by the looks of it. Finger wagging and all sorts.'

'She'll be hungover,' says Daniells, dismissively. 'She likes shouting at him. I think it's the biggest thrill she gets.'

'He looks so crestfallen,' laughs Stefan. 'Hanging his head like a schoolboy. Oh, here we go – news van up ahead. I'd best let you out. You can go do your thing.'

Daniells sighs. He doesn't really know what his 'thing' is. He's good at his job, he knows that. And the two police officers he rates the highest, rate him in return. He can't help wondering what the sergeant has done to irritate the boss, and how much of a knock-on effect it will have to his day. Usually he's the target of Pharaoh's ire. He doesn't like it when she and McAvoy are at loggerheads – it reminds him of when Mum and Dad used to fight.

A sudden rap on the window startles him. He jerks in his seat. Gathers himself, grinning awkwardly, as he buzzes down the window. A man in a surgical face mask is jogging on the spot; grey hoodie and shorts that show thick, well-muscled legs.

'Help you?'

'Happening?' asks the jogger, gesturing at the scene. 'Somebody hurt?'

'And you are?' asks Daniells, friendly.

'Live over the way,' says the runner, vaguely. There's mud on his legs, sweat on his brow. Above the mask, his blue eyes are hidden beneath thick, dark brows. He's older than Daniells. Maybe late fifties, though it's hard to tell. The Covid-19 outbreak has caused no end of problems for detectives. Face masks are no longer just the preserve of criminals.

'Up with the lark, I see,' observes Daniells, slipping into the role of friendly, unflappable copper. 'They'll want you behind the line, wherever that is. Just arrived myself, as you can see . . .'

'Burglars, was it? Druggies?'

Daniells gives his best smile. 'That a problem around here, Mr . . .?'

'Bad in Withernsea,' he says, pressing his fingers to his neck and counting his pulse. 'Plays merry hell with the house prices. Little sods smashed up half the graves in the cemetery a few years back and it knocked a fifth off the market value. Few headlines like that and a place is done in.'

'Well, as I say, we don't know what's happened here.'

'Burglars, I'll be bound,' he says, again, looking past Daniells to the handsome man in the driving seat. He takes in the cut of the suit; the Chanel Monsieur watch on his wrist. 'Some lovely holiday properties for sale at the moment, perfect time to buy . . .'

'Not just now, sir,' says Daniells, a little more forcefully. He doesn't like being overlooked. Doesn't like being take off-guard.

'Sorry, sorry, I'll leave you be.'

Daniells nods, feeling a little out-of-sorts. He turns back to Stefan, about to apologize for this and that and everything else. Spins back when a thought occurs. 'Excuse me, we'll be . . .' The jogger is already disappearing down the dark road. 'Bugger,' finishes Daniells.

'That was all very exciting,' says Stefan, drily. 'Right. I'll be seeing you when I see you.'

Daniells deposits his breakfast bowl on the dashboard and gathers up his laptop and papers from the floor. As he bends forward, a Twix falls out of his jacket pocket. He gathers it up, rises, and sees Stefan looking at him, hard.

'Twix, Andy?'

Daniells looks at it. Looks at his husband. He feels like he's
in *Sophie's Choice*. Then he gives the chocolate bar to Stefan,
and climbs from the car without another word. His posture speaks
of catastrophic loss.

He watches Stefan drive away. Looks around for any sign that
the uniformed officers have an issue with him being dropped off
by his husband, and is a little irked to find that nobody seems
to care.

Coldly, hungrily, he picks his way through the cars to where
Pharaoh and McAvoy are standing. He notices that Pharaoh has
positioned McAvoy in such a way as to block the wind. She huddles
in the shelter he creates like a lamb behind an oak tree.

Her words carry. He picks up snatches; files them away.

'. . . Jesus, Hector, how do I protect you from this? You have
to talk to her. If it's the same person . . . if this is like it was
before . . . oh, here comes our defective constable . . .'

She turns, face flushed. Beside her, McAvoy, white as a sheet,
gives him a tight little smile.

'Morning all. I just saw the BBC arrive. They're up early,
aren't they? Facebook's buzzing with it. You'll have heard already,
I've no doubt, but there's some serious conspiracy theory shit
going on over at the One Hull of a City page. Do you know
about Eva-Jayne Puck? Scunthorpe, years back. She was a
palmist. Somebody made a right mess of her at those flats off
Kingsway. Anyway, as I say, you'll know . . .'

McAvoy and Pharaoh exchange a look. From behind, comes
the sound of a reporter and a cameraman trying to be charming
to the large police constable who has been given the job of
guarding the hedge, and looks as though he will buckle under
the pressure.

'I can't,' says Pharaoh, quietly. 'I need to be sheep-dipped
before I can go in front of the camera. You do it. You're
presentable.'

McAvoy doesn't look up from his phone. It's buzzing. He
can't seem to bring himself to answer it. Slips it back in his
pocket. Swallows as if it pains him.

'Sure,' he says, drily. 'And then the daughter?'

'Neighbours first,' says Pharaoh, daggers in her gaze. 'Then
Roisin.'

NINE

Twelve years ago

Aector McAvoy, still as a headstone, sitting in the bay window of his sparsely-furnished bedroom; silver moonlight and the gaudy yellow of the streetlamp casting an eerie light into the contours of his face.

On his knee, the laptop computer, wire trickling down to the socket in the skirting board, a black cable spilling over a column of textbooks and neatly transcribed revision files. He passed his sergeant exams just before he applied for the constable job with Humberside Police. Has kept it to himself. Just because he passed with flying colours doesn't mean he considers himself ready to take the step up. He'd hate to be accused of arrogance.

On the screen in front of him, two men are fighting. They're both stripped to the waist, their hands bound in bloodied bandages, their faces pummelled bloody. Around them, a semi-circle of jostling, excitable men, punching the air, yelling encouragement, bawling out 'fair play, fair play' whenever one of the pugilists breaks what passes for the rules. McAvoy leans forward and pauses the video just as the camera spins around the dirty, blubbery back of one of the fighters, and rests for a moment on a man with a drooping moustache, porkpie hat and so many gold sovereign rings he seems to be wearing a knuckle-duster. He snarls. Swats the camera away.

McAvoy purses his lips and breathes out, slowly. Leans forward. Stares into the grainy, pixilated eyes of Padraig 'Papa' Teague.

He opens the other tab on the screen: the archive page of the *Hull Daily Mail*, detailing a court case against Grieg Leeming, his address listed as Wood Hill Traveller site, Cottingham. It is dated November of last year. McAvoy had been part of the unit that carried out the raid on premises rumoured to be in use as a cannabis factory. Although they found plenty of evidence of a major growing operation, somebody had clearly tipped him off and given him opportunity to clear out the premises. All the investigators had found was the set-up for a disbanded pirate radio operation, and an industrial sized DVD printing operation, specializing in borderline illegal entertainment. As well as the more X-rated pornography, there are videos of deaths caught on camera; beheadings filmed in gory detail; CCTV footage of sexual assaults and bloodbath muggings. And fights. Always more money in violence than sex, according to the world-weary chap from trading standards who had assisted with the investigation.

People go mad for the blood-feud stuff, he'd confided, looking baffled. *Treat these clashes like the heavyweight title's on the line. The money they stick on their man is obscene . . .*

McAvoy has done his due diligence. Has watched as many of the scraps as he's been able to find on the new video-sharing platform that everybody's going crazy for. Even glimpsed a familiar face. There's a colossal market for brutality. For bare-knuckle bouts, filmed down back alleys and side streets, waste ground and car parks: men pulverizing each other in the name of honour. The CID unit were able to make a case against Leeming, but the two-year sentence was water off a duck's back to a career criminal like him. He pleaded guilty, told the court he didn't know what was on the footage, and that he was just a businessman supplying a demand. He was pushed for information on how the fights were arranged; whether the participants had received medical attention; whether they took a cut of the proceeds from the video sales. He didn't give away much. Just knew the cameraman, he said – admitting to being 'close pals' with the amateur film-maker who was given permission to film the more high-profile bouts. He had 'Traveller connections', he admitted, at the last. McAvoy, ever-alert to any mention of the clan he had briefly helped, had taken note. Even spoken to Grieg's wife outside Hull Magistrates Court, lighting her cigarette with a forced nonchalance while chatting about this and that and nothing much at all – all the while gathering the courage to ask her if she knew the Teagues, and whether the eldest girl was doing OK. She spared him the agony, in the end. Did a kindness to a copper, in a way that suggested she had put two and two together. She'd even squeezed his forearm. Told her she didn't know anybody, anywhere, but if she did, she'd take some pride in telling him that the girl he mentioned, was flourishing, and the apple of her daddy's eye.

McAvoy pulls his phone from his pocket. Calls up the photographs of his housemate's confidential files. Finds the image of the girl he once knew.

He hadn't doubted it, not really – not deep down – but now he knows for sure. Knows it's Roisin Teague.

McAvoy runs his hand through his hair, chewing his lip. Stares into the screen, and feels the images blur and shift as his focus moves to his own reflection. He sees himself, big and clumsy and ridiculous, frightened of his own shadow and terrified of making a mistake. Sees the man he briefly was, too; sees the creature who emerged when he witnessed the horrors being inflicted upon the girl who'd stood at her daddy's side and peered at his notebook and asked him if he was one of the good coppers, or the same as all the others. He closes his eyes. Different emotions rise up like warring tides, and he feels dizzy as they throw him from side to side. He doesn't know what to do. He thinks his instinct is to contact the murder squad and tell them everything he knows about the person they're seeking, but there's another voice, another impulse, that tells him he is hostage to a different kind of duty. They are connected, he and the girl. He divides his life up into two distinct sections and the events of their brief meeting serve as a dividing line. Everything he thought he knew about himself was dismantled that day. Everything he feared, and believed, and shied away from examining too closely – it all evaporated in a single moment of rage and blood: the absolute clarity that came from stopping something horrific, and dispensing justice in the name of the wronged.

He looks again at the screen. It's a straightener; a grudge match between the best men of two clans. Padraig Teague is serving as 'fair play' man: there to make sure nobody bites or kicks or puts the boot in. The video was uploaded a few weeks back and has been watched 36,000 times. He scans the comments. Reads the ill-typed, pointless missives from armchair experts across the globe.

Two wee lassies throwing handbags . . .
Pikey scumbags, can't throw a decent punch between them
They both got into shape for this one. It's not a human
shape, but it's definitely a shape . . .
Papa Teague as fair play man? Jesus, that's like asking a
fox to look after the chickens . . .

McAvoy bites his lip. Looks down again at Roisin's picture, as
if asking for help.

He reads the little argument that has broken out on
the message board: those with a soft spot for Papa Teague
defending his honour by calling his detractor a lying cunt and
offering to stab him in the eyes. Third parties leap in quickly,
asking one another if they've got a copy of the legendary fight
between Pa Teague and Micky Helden. Ah, that was a
fight. Three and a half hours it lasted. Teague fought half of
it with one of Helden's incisors stuck in his knuckle. Helden,
in turn, got his thumb in one of Teague's cuts, and dragged
with all he had, leaving him with a flap of skin hanging over
his eye like a heavy fringe.

He stops when he finds the name he's been looking for. Clicks
on their profile and finds a link to a cheaply-built website,
offering VHS and DVD recordings from the underground fight
scene. He scrolls down, his eyes flicking over familiar names,
Travellers with blossoming reputations as hard men: McDonagh,
Joyce, Nevin, Teague, Helden . . .

There's a mobile phone number at the very bottom of the site.
An email address too.

He stares through the window, at the damp brick of the little
house across the street. There's a cat sitting on a windowsill,
glaring into the wind and the rain, as if daring it to hit harder.
He chews his cheeks. Checks his watch.

Two birds, one stone, he tells himself. If you do the right thing
and the wrong thing at once, you've got all bases covered.

He sends a message to the number on the screen: an act as
optimistic as prayer.

The girl we both know. How much trouble is she really in? I
can help.

He holds Roisin's gaze for a moment before he puts the phone away. What would she be now? Eighteen? Nineteen? She's beautiful, he can see that much, and there's a fierceness about her: something intelligent – endlessly questioning – about the way she gazes out from the tiny screen and seems to see right through to the words written on his bones.

Then he begins to change into his uniform. If he's going to fuck everything up, he at least wants to be appropriately dressed.

TEN

5.45 a.m.
Hessle Foreshore

Roisin McAvoy: cross-legged on a big plush rug. In her leopard-print dressing gown, a towel wrapping her hair up in an extravagant turban, she looks as though she is riding a magic carpet.

In front of her is an old metal tin: pink and violet, emblazoned with a Forever Friends teddy bear. In it, she keeps her memories, her keepsakes, her precious mementos. It gives off a whiff of wet metal; of stale herbs, of old smoke. The letters and journals within cannot transport her into reminiscences as perfectly as this scent. It tugs at her heart; pricks tears in her eyes – makes her skin tingle as if containing an electrical charge.

She doesn't touch the papers. Just stares into the box as if it were a window. Sees the pressed flower: a pale blue Himalayan poppy, still carrying a trace of perfume. A Valentine's card, received at aged fourteen and written in her own hand. Cinema passes. Receipts. Bus tickets. A yellowing scroll, bound with red. Crystals. Passport photos. Her rosary, in a silk purse. Daddy's ring. An old, police-issue notebook; muddy boot print on the cover. A ragged patch of bloodstained cotton, white and frayed at the edges.

She closes her eyes. Feels memories come. Fights them down. They threaten to bring her a comfort to which she has no right.

There's a pain at the back of her neck, where her soft dark hair meets her warm skin. She yearns for Aector's big pink hands, kneading at her knots, her gristly clumps of tension, moving her head around gently with his thumbs while his fingers raise goose-flesh from her crown to her painted toes. She knows he would offer, were he here. But she doesn't deserve his kindnesses. Can't acquiesce to his kisses, his caresses. She deserves the pain. Deserves to wake rimed in sweat, her fingers in her mouth, probing at the soft and pulpy fruit of her bloodied gums – the last traces of the nightmare rising from her skin like smoke.

It's ridiculously early – not yet six a.m. She tried to get back to sleep after Aector left but her thoughts are too fizzy, too intense, for her to even consider closing her eyes. She has found herself waking some mornings with little horseshoe grooves dug into the soft flesh of her palms. Sometimes her wrists and elbows ache until lunchtime. She sleeps like a toppled pugilist: a Pompeian tragedy. Sees such terrible things in the few snatched moments of unconsciousness. Her whole world feels displaced; skewed. She thinks of herself as a straw in water: dislocated, refracted, broken. Worse, there is nobody to blame. Her lies have created this new reality; her concealments and deceptions. It doesn't matter that she has her reasons. The knowledge of what she is doing to Aector is enough to half kill her with guilt.

She glances up. There is a muddy, purply smudge to the sky above the Humber, casting just enough light to lend silvery peaks to the rippling water. She wonders if he is looking at the same sky. Wonders what he is thinking. Whether he is telling her about what a cold and distant bitch his wife has become these past weeks. Wonders if they'll share a moment. Whether he'll tell her the lot: open up about that night, twelve years ago, when she climbed into his bed and refused to take no for an answer. About the violence that had preceded it, and the bloodshed that came after. She does not begrudge him a friend and confidante. She just wishes that he would choose somebody less like an older, wiser, cleverer version of herself.

There's a creak from upstairs. Fin? Lilah? She prays they go back to sleep – have themselves another hour of peaceful nothingness before they have to get up and deal with the distracted, horrible bitch that their mother has recently become.

She leafs through the papers: dog-eared, folded and unfurled so many times that they carry a jigsaw pattern of creases. There is a whiff of the perfume she used to wear. Joop. She thought it smelled awful, but oddly sophisticated, and she needed him to forget that she was just a girl. She sprayed each letter with a liberal dose of scent, even while her sisters, her mum, her auntie, made well-intentioned fun and shook their heads, despairing of the Pavee girl who had taken it upon herself to fall in love with a policeman. She never posted the letters, of course. Wouldn't know where to send them, or how they would be received. But she enjoyed the act of writing. Adored the thrill that thrummed through her as she sat at the little table in the caravan, and wrote the words *Dear Aector*.

Footsteps, outside. The soft creak of an opening door. Two heads, peering into the soft darkness of the living room, bed-headed and lovely; still half asleep and muzzy with half remembered dreams.

Lilah, seven, is spokeswoman for the pair. She's a fierce little thing: dark hair, blue eyes, a vocabulary that bamboozles her mother most days. She's wearing a Ross County football shirt that stretches down to her ankles. Fixes her mother with an accusing stare.

'You're up early. Why haven't you got your glasses on? The light isn't very good for reading. Did I hear Daddy go out? I had an odd dream. My nose was a button mushroom. And there was a house, and smoke was going in through the windows instead of out, like a fire in reverse, and before he starts, tell Fin that I'm getting the last of the Cheerios because he ate those two Bourbon biscuits last night after I went to sleep and I don't really think that's fair as I had my eye on them and was going to hide them behind the microwave and I don't think I should be blamed for forgetting . . .'

'Lilah, you're doing that thing. Dad spoke to you about this. It's great to talk and we love hearing your enthusiasm, but ask yourself whether some of the things you say might work better as thoughts.'

Lilah punches Fin in the kidney and plods, heavy-footed, into the living room. She plonks herself down by her mum and leans against her, demanding cuddles.

Fin takes an extra moment, hanging back in the doorway lest his presence be unwelcome. He has a self-doubt that his sister does not suffer from. He's every bit as shy as their father; a big, pink-skinned lad with flame-red hair. There's a fleshiness to him that makes him appear soft, and despite being head and shoulders above his peers, it makes him a target for bullies. His soft brown eyes make him look as though he is incapable of causing harm, or fighting back. They pick on him at school. Pick on the lad with the Pikey mum, who does his homework on time, gets top marks in everything, and who has been told to 'just do some reading' in a lot of his classes, having already completed the primary school curriculum.

'Close the door, babes,' says Roisin, raising an arm to indicate her son is very welcome at her side. He does as instructed and she pulls him close. He smells like his dad: warm and clean and laced with some tang of outdoor air. She feels her heart clench.

'Did he go out?' asks Lilah. 'I heard the car start.'

'Yes,' says Roisin, softly. 'A lady's been hurt.'

'Hurt as in dead?' asks Lilah. She is a stranger to the unpleasantness of the world. She knows bad things happen to good people. Her only wish is that it doesn't happen to her daddy.

'I think so,' says Roisin. 'I tried to call him but maybe he hasn't got a signal.'

'Is Auntie Trish with him?' asks Lilah, nosing through the papers in the tin.

Roisin nods. 'He picked her up on the way.'

Lilah sucks her lip. She seems noticeably less worried about her father's welfare when she knows that Pharaoh is with him. She is of the opinion that her Auntie Trish is indestructible. Her father, whom she has seen in too many hospital beds, strikes her as immortal but not invulnerable. She sometimes traces her fingers over his scars, as if able to take them away through sheer force of love.

'Is she settled in?' asks Fin, making conversation. 'The new house, I mean. I bet she's a bit lonely. Sophia off travelling, Poppy on her scholarship, the other two staying with her mum so they can finish their courses. And her husband, of course . . .'

'I'm sure she won't be short of company,' says Roisin, a blade in her voice.

'What's this?' asks Lilah, picking up the scroll wrapped in red.

'Don't touch that!'

Lilah, pretending to slap herself on the wrist, does as instructed, and drops the paper back in the tin. An old photo falls out the end. It's faded, creased – blotchy in places. But it shows the big, earnest face of her father.

'Is that Daddy?'

Roisin snatches up the picture and scroll and slips one back inside the other. She can't stand the thought of them seeing any more. Can imagine the looks on their faces if they saw the words written on the creamy paper; the desperate words of a teenager intensely in love and lust with the shy, square-jawed police officer who saved her from the bad men on the day that changed her life.

She feels Fin vacate the space at her side. He flicks on the TV and navigates to the local news. Turns it down to a considerate volume then makes his way to the kitchen. He sits down at the little table, awaiting breakfast. Lilah follows his lead and sets about sorting bowls, plates and cups. It took their father a long time to become comfortable with certain aspects of her culture. He is a dad who wants to do his share. But Roisin has been raised in an environment where the women look after the men. The house sparkles; the food is always sublime. She will barely let her husband lift a finger. She tells him it is his job to provide, and to protect them. It goes against everything that McAvoy stands for. He's incapable of idleness or indolence; blushes at the very idea of being waited on. But Roisin gets cross whenever he attempts to help around the house, and he finds himself in the bizarre position of not cooking or cleaning lest he upset his partner. Lilah, her mother's apprentice, is not as keen on the set-up. She has taken to printing out suffragette fliers, depositing emancipation and women's lib posters at strategic points in the kitchen.

Roisin gathers up her things. Holds the tin like a teddy bear. Hauls herself upright and returns it to the cupboard under the stairs. Curses herself for the thousandth time. Had she put the spare phone in the tin, Aector would never have found it. He wouldn't have broken her trust by peeking inside something he knows to be private. He's just not capable of such a betrayal. Instead she tucked the phone into the toe of a little-worn pair of shoes. He didn't question her on it, but she knew from his face, from the change in the air around him, that something was wrong. She'd longed to tell him. Would have given anything to take his face in her hands; to press his damp forehead against her cheek, and tell him the truth. Instead she had decided upon silence. The silence turned into moodiness; snappiness; to bad dreams and absences. And he tried so damn hard to be helpful, to be strong, to be better. She rebuffed his every advance, shrugging off his caresses, dismissing his soft words as platitudes. Told him she felt smothered. None of it was true. What she felt was afraid. She knew something he did not, and to share it with him would be to forever change the way he looked at her. And she needs his love like air.

She roots around inside the cupboard, looking for the offending shoe. Rips it upside down and feels it fall into her palm. It had half killed her when she realized that it had been replaced upside down. That it had been discovered, and wordlessly replaced.

She looks at the dead screen. Powers it up, and enters the code. Prays for silence; for an absence of news. This is her morning ritual. Each day, she hopes it will not ring. Each day, she begs the universe to spare her the horror she knows is coming.

Her younger brother, Valentine, is the only member of her family who understands the life she leads with Aector; the concessions and compromises they have both made to allow their relationship to be greater than the sum of its parts. He knows the importance of letting her keep the truth from him until it is absolutely unavoidable. It is Valentine who sent her the phone, and who has vowed to keep her informed. Valentine who has refused to go into hiding with the rest of his clan, while they await the wrath that will soon descend. Valentine who has promised to tell her if it is time to run.

The screen fills with text.

> Grālt'a. Bwikad hu grīson? He got Aidan. Shotgun and slash-hook. Siobhaun saw it all. He'd have done her too if not for a Gardai patrol car. He's getting closer, Ro. You have to tell him. He's coming. For all of us. He deserves it. Deserves his revenge. I love you, Mo gra'ath. xx

She holds in the sobs that threaten to unravel her. Holds the phone like a hot gun. Pictures her cousin, Padraig. Thirty-odd. Big lad with dark hair and a tattoo of the Blessed Virgin on his neck. Thinks of his little girl, Siobhaun, watching as the man who has sworn vengeance on the Teagues took blade and hot metal to her kin.

There is a tapping at the door to the cupboard under the stairs. From the timidity, she knows it is her son. She smears her tears away. Tries a smile. Opens the door and looks into his big worried face.

'Daddy's on the telly,' says Fin, half proud, half concerned. 'He doesn't look right.'

Roisin follows her son to the living room. Looks into the eyes of her husband. Reads his eyes and knows that he has seen something that has scared him to his bones.

Then he is gone, and the screen switches to a news reporter, wrapped up warm, her back to the gathering dawn. Roisin forces herself to listen. To concentrate over the low buzz of panic that fills her skull.

And then she hears the word that makes it all real.

'. . . Unfolding tragedy . . . Dymphna Lowell . . . respected clairvoyant and fortune teller . . . suspected murder . . .'

And very gently, Roisin McAvoy slides to the floor.

ELEVEN

Twelve years ago

The fight had looked like something from an arcade game. She'd watched it in Jackie's caravan, crammed in with every bugger else on the plastic-covered sofa, baby Valentine sticky on her lap and a tin of flat, warm beer in her fist.

The video was jerky, fragmented: a symphony of roars and ugly curses; hard hands striking flesh, splashing blood, breaking bones.

Her cousin, Ruareigh: lean, muscular; his torso a William Morris of elaborate ink; his head shaved down to nothing and a ship's compass inked upon his scalp, the points of east and west encroaching into his bristly beard.

His opponent, a great bouncy castle of a man: blue singlet, grey joggers, a gut that looked like he was trying to steal a bass drum. He chewed on a cigar as they brawled; as they traded punches, grabble and broke, swung and scrapped, for almost two hours.

In the end, it was Ruareigh who had his hand raised: his opponent, Michael 'Blip' Helden, unable to lift his arms to defend himself; his lips swollen, bee-stung, who mumbled to the 'fair play' man that he'd had enough. Ruareigh was too exhausted to raise his hands in celebration. He was there alone, on the halting site in the Kent countryside: his clan, his supporters, half an hour away in the car park of a chain hotel. He'd gone into enemy territory alone, convinced that he'd be treated fairly, that the code would be adhered to. He offered Blip his hand. Told the bigger man he'd fought well; that he'd nothing to be ashamed of. And Blip hit him in the face with such power that Ruareigh was unconscious before he hit the floor. His supporters, peering through a chain-link fence, roared their approval. They declared their man the winner. Blip has beaten the best of the Teagues, and secured the eighty-thousand-pound purse.

Ruareigh was dumped at a roadside, half dead. The injuries he suffered were life-altering. Eight weeks on and he can barely remember his own name, needs two sticks to walk. The Teagues had been willing to accept the Heldens' version of events. Then they saw the video. Somebody had filmed the whole bout: grainy footage, captured through a chain-link fence, showing their beaten man having his hand raised, then falling victim to a sucker punch. Papa Teague half lost his mind. He ordered the boys to go to the Carrowbrowne halting site on the outskirts of Galway and to drag every Helden from their bed. He demanded vengeance. And when the boys could find none of the Heldens' men, he settled for torching the caravan that belonged to one of the older members of the family. The Heldens hit back. Shootings, bombings, abductions; pitched battles down pitted country tracks . . .

Roisin chews her cheek as she thinks upon the endless cycle of threat and counter-threat; slight and rebuttal; the violence upon violence, that has been the background music of her life. She cannot remember a time when some member of her family has not been in training for the latest 'straightener' against a member of their rival clan. Cannot think of a single time when their menfolk have not been healing from the vicious wounds suffered at the last clash. She thinks of Daddy. Of Papa Teague. Sees him on the steps of the caravan: porkpie hat, dark hair; gold bracelets; his rings lined up like bullets on his knee. Sees him now: bare, hairy arms, a waistcoat open over a hairy barrel stomach; his Pancho Villa moustache framing lips that chew upon a cigarette. He's got his hands in a Tupperware box full of petrol, soaking them in the stinking, astringent liquid until the skin turns hard as rock. He sees her looking. Gives her that little smile of his – the one that says he understands her; that this is all a bit silly but he doesn't have a lot of choice. Gives her the smile that says: this life isn't for you. And she lowers her head, and returns to her notebook, and writes another letter to Aector about how she wishes everything were different, even without knowing what 'different' might be.

She jerks awake, unsure if she has been lost in dream or memory. Takes a quick glance at her surroundings. Pictures clamour for attention; scraps of recent recollection forming a tatty collage; feelings, fears, things half glimpsed, faces unseen. She thinks of Eva-Jayne. Of the wound in her chest – the blood at her mouth. Concentrates on the blurry features of the man who had visited such horrors upon her flesh. She can't make herself see. He's just a shape; a hazy blob of darkness. He came after her, she remembers that. Managed to get a hand upon her handbag and yank it from her shoulder. She remembers a moment of impact, of spinning around and driving her knee into some fleshy part of his anatomy, and then they had both been fumbling, fighting, falling, bouncing down the stairs at the end of the corridor. She'd hurt something; heard something inside her break. She'd bit through her tongue. She found her feet before her mind could process what had just occurred, and she'd scrabbled, painfully, towards the glass doors. Had there been another figure? A man, waiting by a red door? She can't picture it. Just ran, and stumbled, and didn't stop until she was halfway up the dual carriageway and there was no strength left in her body.

It's been more than twenty-four hours since she fled the scene. Twenty-four hours of grief and fear. She found some brief shelter beneath the base of a truck-stop café, in a little layby at the top of the busy road. In the damp earth, surrounded by the stink of fried food and spilled diesel, she had heard the police cars scream by; saw their blue lights flickering in the dirty mirrors that gathered in the cracked road. She didn't let herself cry. Hasn't cried since she was a girl, and the bad men took her childhood away in an abandoned farm building.

It's now a little after ten p.m., and Roisin is four miles from the scene of Eva-Jayne's murder. She's taken refuge in an abandoned, timber-framed wood-store, well off the main pathway that leads through this damp, overgrown woodland. She's heard few voices, these past hours. A couple of dog walkers; a middle-aged couple having an angry row; two clandestine lovers coupling wetly against the bark of a maple. None have seemed the right people to ask for help. Not that she'd accept it if it were offered. She was raised to be wary of do-gooders, of outsiders, of country-folk and Gorjas. The idea of going to the police is horrific. She has no doubt they'll be seeking her. Knows that she might even be a suspect. There was probably CCTV in the lobby of the flats, and she left enough personal items to set them on her trail. Were she able, she might do the one thing that she has sought opportunity to do since reaching something close to adulthood. She would contact Aector. Would tell him she needs help. She doesn't doubt he would come to her, she just doesn't know where to find him. Last time she'd checked he was still with Cumbria Police, but she can't imagine how she could track him down, or even how the conversation would start. He might even think she was holding something over him, blackmailing him with the secret she holds in her heart. The thought disgusts her. The thing he did for her was an act of goodness; of mercy. God himself would have struck down those men for what they did.

She shivers. Hugs herself. Blinks tired eyes – grit and eyeliner grimy against her irises. Listens as the rain slaps wetly against the leaves and the rotten timbers and trickles into the damp, dark earth. Considers herself, and what the hell to do. She's still wearing her grimy going-out clothes. Hasn't got a phone, or money, or Daddy's knife. Her heart keeps clenching every time she thinks of the other treasured possessions discarded in her flight. Thinks of all those special, secret words to Aector; the letters and diary entries and pencil sketches. Thinks of the spells – the little scroll, with the private words, and the image she clawed out of his warrant card years before.

There is a sudden growl of painful hunger from her gut. She's barely managed a scrap of food today. There were some dry, unopened bread rolls in the bin by the truck stop where she woke, but trying to swallow them without water made her gag. She had better fortune once she stumbled her way into the forest that hugs the main road. She has spent huge portions of her life sleeping at roadsides and has a natural gift for foraging, for herbalism; for what some might call hedgerow medicine. She feasted upon bitter dandelion leaves; chickweed flowers, the succulent stems of peppery, parsley-tasting cow parsley. She has managed to get enough nutrients into her body, but she's ravenous. Ravenous, and cold, and with no bloody idea what to do next.

She looks around, taking in the bleak surroundings. There are large plastic barrels under a tarpaulin; a rusted buzz-saw sticking up from a grimy, cobwebbed table; coils of chicken wire, barbed wire; old doors, still carrying hinges and nails, propped up beneath the central ceiling joist to support the sagging roof. She's rummaged in every dark corner of the long, low building. Found empty packets, empty tins, broken bottles, condoms and glass.

She shudders at the thought of spending the night here. The long hours waiting for the sky to turn dark have been unbearable. Every car engine, every breaking twig, every raised voice – all have transformed in her skull into the approach of some malevolent force. She hadn't believed Daddy when he told her she was at risk. Why would the Heldens come for her? Why would they send their hired gun after her, when better, more important Teagues were closer to home.

The answer, when it came to her, was brutal in its simplicity.

Because you're his favourite, Roisin. You're Daddy's little princess. You're the one whose picture he carries in his wallet. You're the one whose death would pulverize his heart . . .

She pushes her hair back from her face. Peers out into the wet black air.

Sees . . .

There's something moving. Something slinking, inkily, through
the bare, black trees: a needle moving in and out of thick,
dark threads.

Roisin forces herself to remain still. She becomes aware of
herself – the small, intimate sounds as she shifts, so softly,
upon the damp floor; the drip of water from her wet hair; the
wingbeat flutter of her breath, turning into ghosts on the chill
blackness.

She sees a light: the glaring white circle of a mobile phone's
puny torch. Something jerks, out there, among the trees. She
glimpses two flashing mirrors – black eyes, the white flash of
tail as an animal darts forward, then jerks away.

Roisin chews upon her cheek. Tastes blood; raw liver and iron.
A phone, she tells herself. Whoever it is, they've got a phone.

Softly, she moves her hands to the side, patting the ground in
search of something with which she can protect herself. She can
only see one figure: one blobby black silhouette overlaid on the
ink-dipped canvas of trees and night. If she moved quickly, if
she startled them, if she hit and run.

Another voice, tremulous, imploring: willing her to stay here,
to stay safe.

Who would you call, Roisin? Who would you ask for help?

The answer is a fist in her gut. She has kin – distant, half
remembered outliers of the Teagues' great cobwebbed clan.
Eva-Jayne had mentioned them, early on in her stay. Had crossed
herself, theatrically, as she spoke. Michael and Padua. Half-
brothers. She remembers little about them, save the reputation as
men to fear. Can just about recall two young men in string ties
and loud suits, one fat, one skinny as a stair-rod, drinking orange
juice at a family wedding; shy, unblinking, pleased to be invited
and afraid to mess it up by being themselves. Her mother had
warned her not to talk to them. Padua was bad, according to
Mammy. Half mad. Had served time for doing things no man
worthy of the name should ever do. He was here because his half-
brother doted on him, and because Michael knew enough of the
family's secrets to be afforded the respect of an invitation to
the wedding. Mammy had made the same warning in their hasty
goodbye. Told her that under no circumstances was she to allow
Eva-Jayne to introduce her to the men she referred to as 'cousins'.

Roisin can barely untangle the complex network of familial love knots that make the kin, but here and now, she has nobody else. Eva-Jayne had spoken of a landscape business, felling trees, digging ditches, laying patio. With a phone, she could find them. Could beg for help. Could find a warm place to lay low until she can contact Daddy and tell her that Cromwell came for her, and mutilated the good woman who had offered her sanctuary from the violence wrought by men.

A sudden rasping; a match held up to the drooping tip of a hand-rolled cigarette – the orange flame illuminating a sallow, cadaverous face: deep-set eyes, bristly, pointed chin. She squints. Watches the shapes rearrange themselves. Waterproof clothes, bags over either arm, a collapsible chair clutched in his left hand.

She continues to hold her breath. The fear doesn't vanish completely, but this is none of the people who seek her. Not the Heldens, not Cromwell, not the police. This is a fisherman, up to no good, out after dark and probably as scared as she is.

Silently, swiftly, Roisin rises to her feet. Still barefoot, her soles bleeding, she moves without a sound to where the angler huffs and puffs his way past the far end of the wood-store. Up ahead, a pile of soggy, mossed-over fence-posts; a mosaic of smashed tiles. She waits until he is at the very edge of the wooden building, then sprints forward, placing her feet firmly on the sodden grass. She catches him as he turns. Hits him with her shoulder and watches as he spins; a yelp of surprise erupting from his throat as he slips, tumbles, falls.

Roisin snatches up a slate from the pile by the floor.

'Bastard!' she hisses, spit-flecked venom in every word. She wants to hit him. Christ how she wants to bring the slate down on his exposed scalp. Wants to make this one pay for all that has been done to her by the others. Wants to beat the stranger into the dirt and leave him bloodied: leave him incapable of harm.

She throws the slate away. Puts her wet, mud-streaked sole on his damp face and pushes him over – the weight of his bags, his burdens, causing him to topple all the way over, wrapped like a bird in a mesh of wires.

The phone, still live: a gleaming square a little near-miraculous possibility . . .

She scoops it from the earth. Feels her hand close around it as if she were grasping a rope thrown into pounding, crashing waves.

The woods close around her like a mouth.

TWELVE

7.13 a.m.
Sunk Island

'Some people say it's like Holland, but I don't see it myself. Windmill would take off with the winds we get here. I make myself laugh sometimes, picturing big old wheels of Edam bowling past the front door. That's when you know you've gone mad, isn't it? When you're chuckling about cheese. And I'm not one for clogs – not with my high instep. We had a writer here, reckoned it was like Ullapool but I haven't been to Ullapool so couldn't really say. That your way, is it? I caught some Edinburgh in your accent when you introduced yourself. Wonderful city. What's that sugary fudge they do? Wonderful stuff – like Kendal Mint Cake but you don't end up with jittery fingers. I've a guidebook, somewhere. Here, not Edinburgh, I mean. Odd place, but you sort of fall in love with it. Or you don't. My husband has his fits and starts. You need a strong unit, when there's just the two of you and miles and miles of not a lot . . .'

Mrs Dash is doing a commendable job of masking her grief at the demise of her nearest neighbour. She seems positively effervescent: thoroughly delighted to have a little excitement in her life, and an opportunity to use the good china. She's a small, grey-haired lady with a slightly brittle air, as if she is holding on to the atmosphere all around her and doing her best to keep it a nice, safe bubble where nothing bad can happen. She's wearing a purple dressing gown over flannel pyjamas, and her bare, blue-veined feet are hidden inside fluffy slippers with loose Velcro fastenings around the sides. Behind her, through the bare window, the sun is continuing its torpid ascent into the misty grey sky: a scalded bald head emerging from the neat polar neck of the horizon.

'There's Dundee cake in the tin,' says Mrs Dash, bustling around her little kitchen, opening drawers, retrieving cake forks and pouring milk into a little white jug in the shape of a cow. 'Oh, and biscuits. You'll want biscuits. The lady, she mentioned being a little peckish. There are potatoes in the pan. I've got a good hand whisk. I don't know if a Spanish omelette is really Spanish, but I can do my best . . .'

McAvoy lets his confusion show. 'Spanish?'

'Your partner. She's Spanish, isn't she? Or have I got that wrong? I don't know the rules. Are you allowed to ask? We were in Tunbridge Wells for a wedding and were served by this lovely dark girl and I asked her where she was from and about three people told me off for being rude. I mean, it's a conversation, isn't it? I'm itching to know where you're from, with that lovely accent.'

McAvoy blows on his tea. He can't get his fingers through the handle of the teacup. Holds it between forefinger and thumb, as if taking a leper by the car.

'Detective Superintendent Pharaoh isn't Spanish, to my knowledge,' he says. 'And I should imagine she would be grateful for whatever omelette you made for her, and I have no doubt it would be delicious. As for me, I'm from the Western Highlands. Loch Ewe, if you know. And both she, and I, are quite content with the drinks, thank you. Now, if perhaps . . .'

She stops, unable to think of anything she can do to keep herself busy and avoid focusing on the carnage that has occurred next door. Her husband is in the living room, having taken pills for his angina and a little something of his wife's. He's dozing, fitfully, in an armchair by the fire: adrift in a sea of cat teeth and ripped skin.

'Mrs Dash, perhaps you could sit down for a moment and talk me through what happened, precisely? The initial report said your husband was watching out for a particular bird?'

Her lips become a line. She leans back against the sofa, her whole body stiff. She takes on the appearance of a tuning fork, vibrating at a harsh semi-tone. McAvoy says nothing. Lets her fill the silence. Catches the sound of something fat and frantic buzzing against glass. Remembers a time when he would have been unable to rest until he had freed the captive creature. Wonders what it says about him that these days, he can barely summon the strength.

'He doesn't think I know,' mumbles Mrs Dash, nodding at the living-room door. 'Bit pitiful, isn't it? Bloody Peeping Tom. Do people still say that? Such an old-fashioned phrase, isn't it? Like calling an outfit a "two-piece" or saying "mentally ill" instead of "loony". And me upstairs in bed, willing to pay good money for as much as a kindly glance . . .' She presses her lips harder together, wetness filling her eyes. She sniffs, demurely, against the back of her thin, mottled wrist. Holds back her tears. 'The shine goes off it, after a while. Marriage, I mean. You tell yourself you're happy just to be a unit that works, but then you read books and poems and switch on the TV and people are all pawing at each other as if they're made of chocolate, and you can't help but want some of that for yourself. We were never like that. Maybe we were but I don't remember it. We've got our routine, I suppose . . .'

McAvoy nods, his eyes gentle. 'And his involves a late night look at . . .'

'At her,' says Mrs Dash, gesturing in the general direction of the crime scene. 'Can't even be cross about it now, can I? She won't have known he was there, I've no doubt of that. She wasn't the type to flaunt herself, if you know what I mean. And I suppose, him looking at her like he did . . . I suppose it was helpful in a way, wasn't it? I mean, that's what's brought you all out here.'

McAvoy sips his tea. It's good stuff, from a caddy, and left to mash properly in a pot. He thinks, briefly, of home. Of Dad, telling his lads that anything worth doing were worth doing well. Thinks of Roisin, reading his leaves: the smudge of black pixels that spoke of true love born in fire. He has to snatch back the smile that threatens to grip his features. He pulls out his phone, looking at the growing number of missed calls. He is desperate to speak to her, and yet he cannot make himself answer when she rings. Nor can he make himself ring her. To do so, would be to make his suspicions become something more. He doesn't want to be right. Not this time – not when it means she has done something so much worse than he feared when he awoke in the early hours.

'You were friends?' asks McAvoy, trying to concentrate.

'Acquaintances, I suppose. He's not keen on me getting too chummy with people.' She nods again at the living room. 'But she's an interesting lady. My daughter, she set me up with a Facebook account and I found her on there. Palmist, crystal balls, all that stuff. Was a relief to find out what people were coming to the house for, if I'm honest. I had my suspicions it was a something a bit, well, not very nice, though she didn't give off that kind of air. She was always friendly. Card at Christmas, offered to feed the fish if we were ever away – let us use the phone at her place when we came back from Wales and there'd been a bit of a flood and the electrics had gone. Just a nice, bubbly sort of a lady.' She rubs her hands together, spinning her plain gold wedding ring. 'You're sure somebody's done this to her? It couldn't be an accident or something . . .'

'We're trying to understand that,' says McAvoy, casting an eye around the kitchen. If not for the view, it would be insufferably bland. There's a small ceramic swan on the windowsill and a bland picture of some wildflowers in a frame by the fridge, but it's not a homely space. He feels for her, tucked away at the edge of the map with a man who makes her feel invisible, a man who gets his kicks watching the woman next door. He's glad he doesn't have to talk to Mr Dash. Isn't sure he could stop himself shaking him by the ankle and seeing what secrets fell from his cardigan pockets. Pharaoh is outside, waiting for a call back from a former underling. Wilma Bradley is a DCI with West Mercia Constabulary. McAvoy doubts she's forgotten Eva-Jayne Puck. Hopes to God she's at least forgotten about him.

'I was half tempted to ask for a reading,' confides Mrs Dash, dropping her voice. 'I don't know what I believe, but it's exciting, isn't it? A Lottery win, or a tall handsome stranger – they're something worth getting up for, and even if it's nonsense then it's the kind of nonsense you don't mind hearing.'

McAvoy smiles. Gestures at himself. 'Tall and strange,' he says. 'And I can't promise a Lottery win.'

She nods, grateful that he's being gentle. Refills the kettle, just for something to do.

'You haven't seen anybody coming and going, then?' asks McAvoy, softly. 'Any visitors. Nothing to alarm you?'

'I take no notice,' she says, apologetically. 'I've heard the cats, of course. Sound carries. But if I'd thought there was something horrible going on, well . . .'

McAvoy turns as the door opens and Pharaoh clatters in, flicking her cigarette butt into the back garden. Her hair is damp and plastered to one side of her face. She's got the arm of her sunglasses down her blouse. She gives McAvoy a glare. 'Sergeant. When you've finished eating poor Mrs Dash out of house and home I could use a moment, yes?'

McAvoy feels his cheeks begin to burn. He doesn't know whether she's doing the thing she does to amuse herself by pretending to be mad with him, or whether she really is. He raises his eyebrows, quizzically. She winks, and sits down opposite him, kicking him in the shin.

'You're sure she's not Spanish?' asks Mrs Dash, holding the teapot, somewhat defensively.

'Might be,' says Pharaoh. 'Dark nights in Mexborough. You can only hope the person in the bed next to you is who they say they are. I'd love to learn I was from matador stock. Although I'd have to change the way I have my coffee.'

She looks at her, blankly.

'*Ole*,' she says, smiling. She sags, when nobody responds. '*Au lait* . . .'

'Oh, right, yes, I can make some, there's a nice box upstairs I was sending our Mandy in a hamper . . .'

Pharaoh watches her bustle from the room then leans over to McAvoy. 'You need to speak to Roisin. Or I do. Similarities between next door and what happened in Scunthorpe . . . not just similar, a bloody mirror.'

McAvoy nods. His chest tightens as the here and now blurs with memories, visions, snapshots of recollection bright as wet paint.

'He died,' says McAvoy, to himself. He knows he has to hang on to this thought; this hope. The alternative is too horrible to contemplate.

'And you saw that, did you? Saw a body, felt for a pulse . . .'

McAvoy shakes his head. He'd taken them at their word.

It was over. The bad man was in the ground. Roisin was safe. And he, drunk on love, had shushed every dissenting voice in his head.

'It's been twelve years,' he says. 'Where would he have been? And why her? She's not connected. If he were here for revenge, why some fortune teller in the middle of nowhere? He'd come for a Teague, wouldn't he? He'd come for . . .'

Pharaoh manoeuvres herself to meet his gaze. Watches as he realizes what he's saying. Twelve years ago, a killer came for Roisin. He killed a clairvoyant, butchered her, then set his sights on the target he missed. Wherever the hell he's been, he's just announced himself in grand and bloody fashion. And Roisin, his darling, his everything, has been so damn distant, has been so preoccupied and secretive. What has she known and not told him? Could it be that Daddy and the boys were lying? Could it be that they made a deal with *an deabhil* . . .

McAvoy stands up quickly. He feels light-headed, suddenly. Can smell the burning embers; can feel the blade biting into his skin: Cromwell squatting above him and watching, dispassionately, as the slash hook finds bone.

He stops, one hand on the door. 'If it is him . . . if this is because I did wrong . . .'

Pharaoh stands up. Puts her arms around him. Presses her face to the broad expanse of his back. Something passes between them. Something that takes her strength. She feels him shake, to tremble as though new-born. And she lets him go.

Holds the smell of him, the nearness of him, in her lungs; sparks dancing in her eyes. Watches, through the glass, as he walks to the end of the driveway, and leans his head against a tree. Anybody else would scream into the big grey sky.

McAvoy merely whispers: his lips touching the bark, gentle as a kiss.

'What the hell do I do?'

THIRTEEN

Twelve years ago

McAvoy.
Up the stairs and down the corridor, chewing his cheek as if trying to eat through to his blush. He's changed into uniform. Wants to feel like a police officer, even as he acts like a criminal.

A quick glance at the clock above the doorway. It's 9.58 p.m. In the last couple of hours, his world has shifted on its axis. One image was all it took. The image of the girl he knows as Roisin Teague, and whom the murder squad are failing to identify or locate.

The big rectangular space at the end of the corridor is called the Murder Room by the other men and women who work at Queen's Gardens Police Station. The desk sergeant calls it Roper's Room, in honour of the detective superintendent who occupies it, and who runs his small unit like a medieval baron, demanding loyalty, fealty and absolute respect from those under his command. It seems to work, too. Roper has an almost unbelievable clearance record: brings unexpected confessions and last-minute guilty pleas from suspects against whom the evidence is far from concrete. He's the toast of the police authority and the senior officers leave him to do things his way.

McAvoy pauses, one hand on the door. He knows he shouldn't be here. When he saw Roisin's face in the CCTV image he should have contacted the unit dealing with the Puck murder and told them everything he knows. He could earn himself no shortage of plaudits and add a big tick next to his name in the eyes of the investigators, were he to serve up chapter and verse on the pretty young girl who may be able to get them a swift result. But to do so, he risks everything. These past years he has persuaded himself to stop thinking about what happened in that tumbledown barn off the Brampton Road. The things he did in temper: the pain he inflicted on the bastards who violated a twelve-year-old girl just because her people had parked up on private land and made themselves at home. Images flash in his mind. Scraps of sound. Her, screeching, biting, fighting; telling them what her daddy would do when he found out. And the landowner, laughing in her face, pushing her cheek into the cobwebs and rotten wood of a pile of old palettes. His lads, waiting their turn. McAvoy had hit them so hard that it left his arms numb all the way to the shoulder. Had thrown the biggest of them through the sagging wooden wall and followed him outside to continue pounding him into the earth. He left all three broken, bloodied, pressed into the dirt. He didn't return to himself until he was arriving at the family caravan and handing her over to her family. He didn't know how to tell them what had happened. Papa Teague saw it all in his eyes. Flicked a gaze over the blood on his hands, the sweat soaking his shirt, and knew. Just took his daughter from the rookie police officer and held her like a baby. Then he told McAvoy to go. Said he would take care of it all. He was as good as his word. There was never a police report filed. Months later, McAvoy heard that the three men claimed to have been in a bad car accident. That, at least, accounted for the shattered legs and the terrible scars. McAvoy has never known whether he did the right thing or the wrong thing on that hellish day. But he knows that the Teagues have something over him, and worse, that Roisin has already endured more in her life than anybody should have to. He feels an overwhelming need to see her. To seek her blessing before he betrays her to cops who might see her as nothing more than a no-good thieving Tinker.

He pushes open the door and steps into the cold, grimy light of the murder room. Quiet, despite the urgency of the case. Two civilian members of staff tapping away at computers, and a detective constable talking on the phone, her back to him, gazing through her own reflection into the dark, rain-streaked night.

He takes a moment to scan the room. Empty, dirty desks: paper overspilling, phones set atop mounds of files, printouts, pizza boxes, cans of drink. The bins are empty, suggesting a cleaner has done their best, but the room looks more like a student hall of residence than the home of an elite team of detectives. He shoots a glance towards Roper's office, at the far end of the room. Beside it is the Murder Wall: a big, blue, fabric-covered board, with pictures, printouts, maps and names stuck up like mismatched paving stones.

'Help you?'

The officer has hung up on whoever had her attention and risen from her chair, giving McAvoy the once over. Looks him up, and further up. Smiles, nicely. She seems glad of the interruption. She's a smallish woman in her early thirties, with sensibly bobbed dark hair. In her unremarkable polo neck, dark trousers and walking shoes, she has the look of a teacher taking a bunch of kids away on a residential break.

'PC McAvoy,' he says, stepping over some discarded foil containers and extending his hand. He takes hers in his, and holds her gaze while they shake. He reminds himself, as he always does, that he must treat other people's palms and fingers as if they were a frightened bird, having been chided many times at school and university for leaving people in agony having accidentally crushed their hands like an empty lager can.

'We haven't met,' she says, brightly. 'I'd remember. What are you, six foot six? Seven?'

'Five,' he says, colouring.

'Bollocks. You're bigger than that. My ex was six foot five and you're bigger than him. You'd be bigger still if you stood up straight.'

McAvoy doesn't know how to reply. Just stands, lost, a little awkward, fiddling with his hands.

'I'm Bradley,' she says, suddenly. 'First name is Wilma, but if you use that in earshot of these bastards I may have to kill you. You can imagine what it leads to. So, Bradley works for me.'

'Aector,' says McAvoy, self-consciously.

'Bless you,' says Bradley with a smile, stretching to ease some tension in her back. 'You'll be Scottish.'

'I will. I am.'

'And you want me to say that name, do you?'

'Hector will be fine,' mumbles McAvoy, sweating. 'Or just McAvoy. Call me what you like.'

'Oh, don't give me that kind of permission.' She grins. 'That's carte blanche with me. I'll be up all night thinking of nicknames and I'm bound to cause offence. Anyway, what can I do for you?

Were you after the boss? I think he's off doing his thing, talking to whoever it is he talks to when he slithers away from his desk.'

McAvoy notices the slight look of distaste on her face. 'Slithers?'

'Oh, he's an oily one, that's all,' replies Bradley, nonchalantly. 'Bit greasy. Got that Portillo quality, y'know? You can imagine him sitting in a bath of Vaseline in his leisure time. I'm not one of his, so I can say this stuff. I'm from the other side of the water. Part of a specialist team my proper boss has set up: domestic abuse and incidents of violence against women. Quite a broad brief. But in the eyes of CID, that means I'm available, and I have local knowledge, so they've got me here as office manager.'

'How's it all going?' asks McAvoy, in what he hopes is a chatty manner. 'Post-mortem finished?'

'Not long since,' says Bradley, leaning against a desk and clearly enjoying having somebody to talk to. 'Absolutely horrible. He tried to cut out her tongue, if you can believe that. Cuts all over her face. Half strangled her – more than half, I suppose – then finished her off. No murder weapon found at the scene but it looks like he took a hammer and chisel to her chest.'

McAvoy shakes his head, feeling every wound as if it were his own. 'And the witness?'

She raises her eyebrows. 'You're in that camp, are you? Yeah, me too. But the brains trust that runs things, they've got her down as a suspect. There'll be a general appeal first thing in the morning and the image will be distributed to the press, unless Roper manages to find her tonight. I can't see it myself.'

'What's he got?' asks McAvoy, cautiously.

Bradley shrugs. 'According to a neighbour, Eva-Jayne's had some "gipsy-looking lass" staying with her for a couple of weeks. Spotted her staring out the window a few times, apparently. And Eva-Jayne's got some Traveller connections. Also got a couple of old convictions for fencing stolen goods. Lived there alone. No kids.'

'Clairvoyant?'

'Yeah. The lads reckon she never saw it coming.'

'Rather bad taste,' says McAvoy, wincing.

'Christ, you can tell you're not from around here,' says Bradley with a smile. Then the smile fades. 'Regular clients, by all accounts, but not very good record-keeping and her mobile phone is missing, so it's all going to take some piecing together. Roper reckons the girl lost her temper and did her in. We don't know who she is yet, but it won't be long. I've been looking at the Traveller connection. Apparently she's distantly related to some fearsome clan from out of Galway. Had a chat with a Garda over email and there's some devil of a feud going on over there – tit for tat attacks between this lot and some other. Maybe it's connected. Maybe this girl just got caught up in it. Maybe . . .'

'Maybe she was the intended target,' says McAvoy, softly.

She considers him, liking what she sees. 'My proper boss would love you,' she says, warmly. 'Big and strong, soft as honey, and a brain like a rocket. You married?'

McAvoy lets it all wash over him. He's talking to himself, trying to decide on the 'right' thing to do. He could tell them her name. Bradley seems a decent sort and it won't be long before she'll work out which of the Teague girls the photograph most resembles. He just can't bring himself to do it. He doesn't trust that she'll be fairly treated. He can't say, in full certainty, that she would be right to hand herself in. He suddenly realizes that he's already made up his mind. He has to find her.

'What was it you were wanting, anyway?' asks Bradley, when she notices he's lost in thought.

'My housemate,' he says, thinking on his feet. 'Dachman. I'm just off shift. Wondered if he needed a lift home.'

Bradley scoffs and makes a face. 'Oh, I can't see that working out. Definitely not the type you want to be shacked up with, no matter how bad the rent is. He's already gone, anyway. Probably skulking around a women's toilet somewhere, hoping he gets five minutes free to go sniff the u-bend. Proper prick, that one. No offence.'

McAvoy smiles, pleased to have made a friend. 'I was only being polite,' he says, shrugging. 'I'll probably see him at home.'

'If you do, tell him it's a seven a.m. briefing. Oh, and tell him the samples from the spare room have gone to the lab but there's a god-awful delay, so he needs to focus on her client list.' She stops herself from talking. 'In fact, don't worry about it. I'm going myself in a jiff. Bugger the drive back, I'm taking up the offer of accommodation. I'd planned to fall into a rather wonderful sleep, unless you've got any suggestions what I might do in a strange city until morning . . .'

McAvoy misses the invitation completely. 'The museums are shut at this time,' he says, apologetically. 'But there are some gorgeous views off Sammy's Point, down by The Deep. Closest thing to fresh air you can get. It's good for you. Other than that . . .'

She starts laughing, and he joins in, so as not to appear rude. She shakes her head. 'Wait until I tell Trish about you,' she mumbles, exasperated.

McAvoy doesn't push it. He's got what he came for. Turns back to the door, before a thought stops him dead.

'The Traveller site in Cottingham,' he says. 'Any of the Teague clan up that way?'

'We haven't the manpower to get to that just yet,' says Bradley, with a note of apology. 'If she's there, we'd never find her. Very good at hiding things away, in my experience.'

'But some background might help . . .'

'You know somebody?' asks Bradley, all business.

'Sort of,' he says, half to himself. He shrugs again, not wanting to say any more until he knows what he thinks. 'Maybe. I'll get back to you when I've had a ponder.'

'A ponder?' Bradley smiles. 'Christ, you're a tonic. Can I give you my number?'

She realizes she's talking to empty air.

FOURTEEN

7.54 a.m.
Sunk Island

McAvoy stares up into the broad, black sky. He's never got used to landscapes like this. He was raised in the shelter of the mountains, tucked within the shadow of crags and forests and heather-fringed pools. There's something unnerving about the absolute flatness of the earth. It's as if God ran out of ideas. He feels wrong, here. Feels exposed, as though his head were poking over the top of every fence and boundary line. There is something about the endless nothingness, something that makes him feel as though he is staring through a telescope and seeing another Aector McAvoy waving back. It makes him feel queasy. Vulnerable. Were he sure about his beliefs, he could imagine the giant hand of God flicking him from the flat terrain like a fly from a snooker table. Could picture himself thumbed flat.

He leans back against the trunk of a tree that shields Dymphna Lowell's property from the road, and gazes away into the endless nothing. Tries to centre himself. To breathe. He imagines Roisin's touch, her fingers and thumbs kneading his temple, her soft song at his throat. Pictures Lilah, her little hand in his. Thinks of Fin, and the deep-soul sadness in his big brown eyes. Tells himself to focus on this. On the dead woman in the house. On finding some kind of justice for those bereaved by this cruel, merciless act.

He focuses on the near-empty air. If he squints, he can make out a couple of stick-figures in the distance, making slow, wind-blown progress across the headland, following the curve of the coastline. From time to time, he hears a snatch of birdsong, carried on the cold, saw-toothed wind. He has his back to the other officers, huddled in the protection of the patrol cars and specialist vehicles. He wants to feel this place properly – to stare into the gale and imagine how it must feel to live here, in the final house before the land runs out.

Miles and miles in every direction, empty fields grooved by the teeth and tyres of tractors or neatly parted by old drainage ditches. And the Humber, slapping its brown waters against the mud and sand over at the little horseshoe-shaped bay called Stone Creek. There are fishing boats and pleasure craft moored up out there, he remembers, from a visit, long before. Barely a soul around. A man with murder in his heart could approach from the water. A mile or two of tramping across easy fields and he'd find himself at the rear of Dymphna Lowell's house. He could have left the same way . . .

McAvoy sucks in his lower lip, his hands sunk deep in the pockets of his big woollen overcoat. He's got the collar turned up, the way Roisin likes it. The material rubs at his beard, and slaps him in the face whenever he turns side on to the wind.

'Could have come in from the sea,' says Pharaoh, appearing at his side. She hands him a coffee in a thermal travel-cup. It matches hers. He takes a sip, grateful. It's hot chocolate, with three sugars. He can smell the brandy in Pharaoh's coffee. Chooses not to mention it. 'Local boys say there's been a few burglaries out this way. Farm equipment, stuff taken from washing lines, that sort of thing. Andy had a chat with a jogger who said they're a menace, which is a bit rich coming from a jogger. Tried to sell Stefan on the idea of a holiday home.'

McAvoy, grateful to have something to focus on, pulls out his phone as a thought bubbles up. Changes his position to show the screen to Pharaoh as he navigates his way to a property site and thumbs in the location. 'Three empty on this road, all for sale, and over the way there's plenty to rent. Caravans at Patrington too. Same number. Bit early yet but if it's all one property portfolio . . .'

Pharaoh nods, understanding. 'They might have some security footage – maybe even a chap or two doing the occasional drive-by. If they've got a security system we might get lucky with some CCTV.'

'We can but hope,' says McAvoy. 'I'll chase it up.'

'What's the name of that place?' asks Pharaoh, pointing into the featureless expanse.

'Stone Creek,' says McAvoy, following her gaze out across the shimmering fields to the place where the land bleeds in to the sky.

'Sounds lovely. Poetic, even.'

'Not much there, but nice for a walk. Bleak, but in a good way.'

'Add the owners and skippers to the house-to-house,' says Pharaoh, trying to light a long black cigarette without setting fire to her hair, which whips and coils upon air. 'Sergeant from Withernsea says there's an old World War One battery down the ways, a little. Big blocky things surrounded by a little bit of woodland, and very popular with the teenagers looking for a place to be teenage.'

McAvoy is about to volunteer to do it himself, but stops, aware that Pharaoh no doubt has something else planned for him. He looks down at her. Tries not to loom.

'Could be absolutely no connection at all, of course,' says Pharaoh, grinning triumphantly at the tip of her cigarette as it begins to smoulder. 'And we're going to treat it as such, yes? We're going to brief the team about the similarities to an unsolved case from Scunthorpe a dozen years back, and we're going to be quite clear that's a line of enquiry. But we are not, and I repeat not, going to tell people that there's a good chance you've come into contact with our killer before. And you are sure as shit not going to tell anybody that he's previously tried to kill your bloody precious wife.'

McAvoy feels as though snakes are uncoiling in his gut. He feels clammy. Ill. 'But if it's him, if he's somehow doing this . . .'

'And why would he be, Hector?' she asks, gently. 'He was set upon the Teagues by the Heldens. He missed his chance with Roisin, and took apart a poor woman who happened to make a bit of money reading crystal balls. If this is his handiwork, where has he been? And why target this woman, out here, in the armpit of nowhere? I mean yeah, we might discover a connection to your Roisin's world, but there's literally nothing here to suggest that from the off. More likely we've got a pissed-off punter who didn't like what she read in their tea leaves or saw in her crystal ball.'

'And the injuries?' asks McAvoy. 'I'm not pre-empting anything, but the similarities are . . .'

'Similar, yes,' says Pharaoh, pushing her hair back from her face. She gives a tut of irritation as her phone rings. Pulls out her mobile and gives a sharp, hard-faced laugh at the screen. 'Speak of the devil.'

'Sorry?'

'Your Roisin,' says Pharaoh. 'Wonders if you're in a bad signal zone as she's been trying to call . . .'

McAvoy feels his cheeks flush crimson. 'Sorry,' he mutters. 'I know, I know, I have to talk to her, but the way she's acting, it's as if she already knows. They have a different code, Trish. Their world and everybody else's – sometimes there's no bridge between the two. Her father, her family – they'll already be taking steps, and they still see me more as a police officer than as her husband and they'll just clam up. And if it's all in my head, if I've made connections that aren't there, then I'm going to scare the life out of her and trigger memories that nobody should ever have to see again. And she's tough, Trish. You know that. Tougher than me.' He drops his head, a picture of despair. 'I'll talk to her properly when I know what to say.'

Pharaoh puts her phone away, message unanswered. She takes a glug of coffee. Gives a soft growl of irritation. 'My nana had the sight, or so they say,' admits Pharaoh, staring into the distance. 'Her mum, the one with the links to the music hall, the original Nefertiti . . .'

McAvoy doesn't meet her eye as she talks. Recently, after years of deliberately not asking, Pharaoh had unexpectedly divulged the origins of the family surname. She had a great grandmother who performed in variety shows, under the alluringly mysterious pseudonym of Rosetta Pharaoh, which provided more titillation than the original moniker of Mabel Cartwright. Her son was Thomas Pharaoh, and he married the much younger Glenda just before the war. The name carried on down the generations. When Patricia Pharaoh married, she kept the name. Her daughters have all been warned that they will damn well be doing the same.

'The sight?' asks McAvoy, though he knows exactly what she means.

'To see,' she shrugs. 'To see what's in store for people. Good times, bad times, catastrophes and windfalls. Could tell you if somebody had died in a room, and she'd get these headaches, real killers, thy were – as if there were a hundred different voices all talking to her at once. No wonder she turned to drink. And she told my nan that it was a curse, not a gift. Seeing what fate had in store for people, getting these whispers from the other side . . . I'm not closed-minded, Hector. And I know your Roisin's got the touch of something about her . . .'

McAvoy scratches his beard, wishing they could talk about something else. His head is full of memories. Fears. He hears himself mumbling something about Lilah, sharing a confidence he hadn't planned to divulge.

'She's got more than a touch,' says McAvoy, quietly. 'When she met her grandmother, Ro's mum, it was like they were welcoming some sort of Messiah into the clan. They saw something in her. To you and me, she's a very intelligent, astute little girl. To them, she's got something, sort of . . .'

'Mystical?' asks Pharaoh, not unkindly.

'I don't know,' says McAvoy, his shoulders sagging. 'She can be a bit unnerving, I know that. Even before she was talking in real sentences, she'd babble away having conversations with empty air. She'd draw pictures with her crayons of animals she'd never seen. Sometimes she'd be laughing to herself, all alone in her cot. And now she's bigger, she knows stuff she shouldn't. It's like empathy, but so much more than that. She can meet somebody for the first time and get a feeling from them . . . more than a good vibes, bad vibes thing, and there'll be times when she's talking to you, but not you . . . as if she's seeing something just behind your ear . . .'

Pharaoh nods. 'She's bright as a button, I know that much. Best little girl I haven't given birth to. And yeah, she's got something about her. But, look, you and Roisin, whatever's going on . . . oh shite . . .'

She turns away, answering the phone. Assistant Chief Constable Julie Graves has woken to the news of a murder on her patch, and wants to know why she wasn't informed earlier; ideally, before it happened. Pharaoh switches on her 'talking to the brass' voice, and McAvoy gives her some space, mooching off to go and stare at a different patch of nothing.

He can't help but let the memories come. They arrive as a blur: random scraps of things hidden, buried, concealed. He remembers the fairground graveyard; the great expanse of rusting metal and smashed lights and leering faces grinning out from the side of abandoned circus rides. He remembers the half-brothers, and the man who hurt him. Remembers the empty eyes, the blade cutting him to the bone. And then his mind is full of Roisin, telling him it's over, that the feud is done, the bad man is dead, that they don't ever need to think about it any more. He feels sick as he remembers how easily he let himself be silenced. He'd done as he was bid. Turned his thoughts to the future, to family, to being all he could be. Became the police officer he always hoped he could be, and more importantly, became the kind of man Roisin could love forever.

'You're ringing, sarge.'

McAvoy hadn't heard Daniells approach. Hadn't heard his phone buzzing away in his pocket. He gives Daniells a befuddled

little smile and snatches the phone from his pocket. It slips from
his hand and clatters down onto the grass. Daniells bends to retrieve
it just as McAvoy does the same and there is a clash of heads.

'Oh you fucker!' growls Daniells, clutching his temple and
wincing, stars in his eyes. He thrusts the phone to McAvoy.
Screws up his eyes. Regains his composure. 'Sorry, sarge, just
slipped out . . .'

McAvoy takes the phone, cheeks burning. Answers without
even looking at the screen, a ringing in his ears.

'Aector, that you, pal?'

McAvoy closes his eyes. Forces himself not to swear. Lucas
Barrington is one of the coxswains of Rescue Humber: a private
lifeboat service with its HQ a couple of hundred yards from
McAvoy's front door. The crew have spent the last year trying
to persuade him to sign up for the call-out crew. He's resisted
their overtures but is bitterly regretting giving Lucas his mobile
number. He believes quite fervently that McAvoy should drop
all other investigations and assist him and 'the lads' in finding
out who has been breaking into the boathouse.

'Lucas,' he says, wishing he'd glanced at the caller ID before
answering. 'Not the best moment, I'm afraid . . .'

'Never is, never bloody is,' says Barrington, moodily. 'Saw
you leave this morning. Tried to flag you down but you must
have had your mind on something else.'

'Oh, sorry, Lucas, yes . . . at the crime scene now, actually . . .'

'Just got back from a call-out, as it happened. Rather hoped
you might have waved. An update would be nice.'

'What was the call-out?' asks McAvoy, unthinkingly, as he
tries to come up with something that will placate the nice young
man who has told the other crewmen that his 'friend' will pull
some strings.

'Pleasure cruiser, heading for Rotterdam with a road map,'
says Barrington, tiredly. 'Bought it last Thursday and figured he
could pick up the basics on the way. Silly sod got about as far
as the Forts before he overcooked it. Anyway, all safe and sound.
RNLI lads were busy down Mablethorpe way. Anyway, do you
have anything for us?'

'Not right now, Lucas,' says McAvoy, tactfully. 'As I say, the
CCTV footage picked up nothing at all – the equipment is all

marked with your infra-red so if it's recovered we can match it to you, but I'm afraid it may be that the Uniforms were right when they said it was just bad luck.'

'Happened again, Aector,' says Barrington, brusquely. 'Got back from the call and the door's been jimmied again. Some sod's helped himself. Food from the fridge, been through the cupboards, took themselves a first aid kit and an oilskin. We're doing an inventory. Shall I see you here? Fifteen minutes, twenty . . .'

McAvoy pinches the bridge of his nose. 'Lucas, I'm at a crime scene right now. Can I give you a call back when I've got my thoughts together . . .'

'Sarge, the boss said you were phoning the estate agent – wants to know if you've done it already – anyway, I just called him myself, no answer, I'll ask him to ring you not me, yeah . . . is that OK . . . sorry about the "fucker" thing, like I said . . .'

McAvoy holds up a hand. His brain feels as though it's exploding. 'Me, you, whoever you like,' he mutters.

'Sorry, Aector?' asks Barrington, in his ear.

'I can't deal with this,' says McAvoy, to himself. He feels as though his brain is pouring out of his ears.

'I've got to go . . .' he says.

'Sarge?'

'Aector!'

'For fuck's sake!' he shouts, and throws the phone like a weapon. White-faced, he spins around, faces Daniells, who's recoiling in surprise. Perhaps even in fright.

'Sarge, what's wrong?'

McAvoy shakes his head. Turns his back. Stomps away in the direction he had flung the phone, collar up over his ears. He runs his hands through his hair. When he examines his palms, he sees a dozen grey hairs, each wrenched free at the root.

'You're losing your fucking mind,' he hisses at himself, as he bends down and starts rummaging in the grass. Finds the phone and picks it up. Is unsurprised to learn that Barrington is still talking.

'Go on,' he says, with a sigh. 'I'm listening.'

FIFTEEN

He moves quickly. Wriggles from the little pocket of fallen trees and moves through the dead leaves with barely a sound.

The mud has dried upon him. It keeps him warm. He feels like an unbaked golem, something half formed, incomplete. Were the sun to shine he would bake hard as clay.

Up ahead, angry voices. Men in wetsuits and life vests, grumbling as they wheel out the big orange dinghy from the brick boathouse up ahead.

He lays flat. Listens, holding his breath.

'Can't bloody get in again, Lucas . . .'

'Taking it too seriously mate . . .'

'Be nothing, I promise you – a log in the pissing water . . .'

'And then she told me it was normal at my age, and just to wash more often, and . . .'

'It was a good cup of tea that one. Just right. Not the same in a thermos, is it?'

'Close it. Keys. I'm not having it, though I swear, it might be for the best . . .'

He presses his face to the earth. The ground smells musky. Meaty perhaps, as if blood were spilled here, seeping into the earth and feeding the high trees and the fruit-rich bramble bushes with its thick, red goodness.

Voices, nearby. Children, now. Children laughing, running forward towards the damp, puddle-pocked little swing park. Slides, roundabouts, a red rope climbing frame, bright against the wall of trees that mark the entryway to the little wood.

He wriggles forward. Feels a surge of pain: the hot, metallic grinding of bone biting down on unprotected bone. Smothers his gasp and reaches into the pocket of his mud-calked trousers. Fumbles at the little dimple packet of medication. Stuffs a muddy, bitter handful into his dry mouth and swallows them like sweets.

Feels the numbness take effect almost at once. Feels his body
expand and soften, puddling into the earth.

He wriggles forward. Sights the pile of red-gold corruption;
the great pile of leaves and sticks and brambles gathered up
by the railings like a wall of thorns.

Looks beyond it, to the sea, to the distant pin-prick of the
disappearing boat.

Feels the familiar, comforting bulge of the hammer and nails;
the plastic and metal and tape of the taser.

Wriggles forward, to the place where the McAvoy children
come to play.

SIXTEEN

M cAvoy and his thoughts: alone at last.
He shivers, as if a breeze from an unlocked crypt
were playing with his hair. He'd wanted time to think.
Needed somewhere out of the wind, and away from prying eyes.

'Fuck,' he mumbles, chewing at his lip. 'There's no way . . .
no way . . .'

Realizes he has mooched down the little side path around the
property and found himself in the tatty back garden at the rear
of the cottage. There's little to no barrier between the garden and
the great swathe of empty farmland beyond. The concrete posts
sunk into the ground more than a century ago are hanging crook-
edly; rusting wire sagging around clumps of damp grass and
tangled weeds. Even somebody with limited physical ability could
get through this excuse for a fence. He thinks again of the water's
edge at Stone Creek. Could it be significant? Could somebody
have come in from the water and wreaked bloody havoc at the
first house they saw? McAvoy has been present at murder scenes
where every potential motive came to nought when the culprit
was eventually found. Some people killed because they liked the
feeling. To some, the victim's death was so much more important
than their life.

He stands with his hands in his pockets, looking around. Big

plant pots, packed with nothing but dirt. Wind chimes, knotted
around one another in the shelter of a low, mortar-free wall
where the dead stalks of flowers and plants stick out from grey
earth. The grass is overgrown, sticking up in irregular peaks
where the wind has whipped in off the water. He angles his head,
examining the jumble of rotten wood and chicken wire bundled
up at the very end of the garden. An animal run? Chicken coop?
It certainly hasn't been used for a long time. It shields a little of
the sagging fence from view: the concrete post leaning up against
it, loose twists of rusty wire sticking up like the teeth of a snare.

McAvoy moves through the long, damp grass, wincing into
the damp gale. Peers past the clump of tumbledown wood and
wire. If their killer came from the water, this would be where
they had scaled the fragile fence; putting their feet down on the
pile of rotting planks, hopping down onto the bed-spring coils
of chicken wire. He changes position. Peers low at the impres-
sions in the long grass. Makes out the faintest of indentations.
Stands straight, arching his back, looking back towards the
windows of the house, then left, to the home of Mr and Mrs
Dash. A larger, sturdier-looking wall encircles their property,
made more formidable by the screen of tall, rain-blackened trees.
The other direction offers nothing save for a swathe of farmland,
which disappears into a sharp-edged ditch. He imagines the scene
from above and gets his bearings. Cautiously, hitching up trousers
and coat, he sidesteps over the wire of the fence. Feels his boot
sink into damp soil. Awkwardly, trying not to step on anything
that might later prove useful, he walks lightly away from the
house, heading up to where the drainage ditch slashes through
the earth like a perfect wound.

To his left, the rising sun gives off a weak, watery light. He
squints as he places his feet, trying to keep to rocks, to patches
of hogweed and twisted grass.

There's a little smudge of privet, off to his right: an ancient
boundary marker picking out the edge of one field and the beginning of another. He stops, peering past the hedgerow towards the
footpath that leads in from the water's edge and circles back
towards the main road. He feels dizzy, as though the landscape
is turning and twisting around him. He ducks under the spindly
edges of the privet, eyes still fixed on the drainage ditch, pushing

his hand out to stop the spiky, spindly branches slapping at his face.

Sees a glint of silver: a flash of something metal glinting among the spindly twigs and curled-in leaves.

He peers at it, easing the other twigs aside to better examine the curious little flash of silver. A memory rises: crickets and butterflies, skewered onto sharp sticks; a larder of twitching near-cadavers; a feast for the bird who impaled them with sick accuracy that their suffering would endure long after it had begun to feed.

'A shrike,' he mumbles, as the silvery shape delineates into a shape he recognizes.

It's a silver charm. A gypsy wagon, dangling from a silver ring. It belongs on a charm bracelet. An antique, French-made charm bracelet. A bracelet that entwined the slender wrists of the young Roisin Teague.

McAvoy's feet slip on the wet earth. Sharp branches rip at his face: claws scoring trenches into the cold, wind-kissed flesh of his cheekbone. In the periphery of his vision, the jewelled haze of crimson blood.

He's pulling his phone from his pocket as he starts to run.

Over the sound of his thudding heart, the mechanical arpeggio.

Three notes.

Call failed.

SEVENTEEN

Twelve years ago

This is the Fair Maid, set back from a quiet road near the centre of Cottingham, on the northerly reaches of Hull. It calls itself a village, but it's the size of a decent town. It's popular with the self-made crowd: plumbers, builders, structural engineers, all proud to have invested in property at the right time; revelling in their grand five- and six-bedroomed properties that line the wide roads – bay windows reflecting long, landscaped gardens built around Audis and the wife's weekend convertible. It's got an edge, has Cottingham – a certain toxicity to the air in certain pubs, once the casual drinkers have gone and the regulars can reel off their lengthy checklist of prejudices: the wife, the darkies, the young. And the Travellers. The families up at the halting site, squashed in between the Indian restaurant and the golf club. Hundreds of them, now. Caravans, mobile homes, lodges, bungalows: a proper little community that routinely enrages the locals.

McAvoy's sitting outside at a little wooden table, drawing stick figures in spilled beer. He's drinking something tropical and sticky, and which would benefit from being frozen around a stick, and licked on sunny days.

He checks his watch. Almost eleven p.m. He's heard them call last orders. He's starting to think he asked too much of her . . .

A blue hatchback careers too fast into the car park and swings into a parking space for the disabled, sending up a spray of muddy water. The door swings open in an instant, and the driver yanks the keys from the ignition as she hauls herself from the vehicle. She stomps across the puddle-patterned car park: a vision in rubber sandals, pyjama trousers and a puffer-style gilet over bare arms. Her name is Donna, but people call her 'Red', in respect of her frizzy, sun-kissed hair. She's tall, broad-shouldered, and has the names of several children and former lovers tattooed in various styles down her left forearm, as if trying to select a favourite font.

'I got you a drink,' says McAvoy, quietly, rising from his chair like a gentleman receiving a lady of rank. He nods at the Bacardi Breezer on the table. 'Didn't know you'd be driving.'

'Expected me to run, did you?' she demands, coming to a stop in front of him and picking up the bottle. She takes a swig. Shakes her head at him in the exasperated way he is beginning to become familiar with. 'It'll have to be quick. He thinks I'm pricing up a Gonfalon.'

McAvoy furrows his brow. 'That's a flag, isn't it? A Spanish military banner?'

'Is it?' asks Red, sitting down in the damp wooden chair. 'I dunno. Made up a word and he's too much of a know-it-all to ask what it means.'

Despite the thoughts and fears fizzing around inside him,

McAvoy laughs. He likes Red. Should he ever make it into CID, he plans to register her as an official informant. For now, their relationship is anything but official. She's a thief and a fence and has been known to throw her fists when the situation calls for it. She's also the long-term girlfriend of a perennial drug-pusher, part-time armed robber and video-nasty purveyor by the name of Grieg Leeming.

'He's out, then?'

'Austerity, innit?' Red shrugs. 'Prisons are full. They're looking for any excuse to let people out. And our Grieg's no bother to anybody.'

McAvoy looks away, lest his look of incredulity sour the mood.

'You've guessed, I presume,' says McAvoy, quietly. 'Why I got in touch . . .'

'You're a silly bollocks,' growls Red, shaking her head. 'That number on the website – nine times out of ten he'd answer it. Wouldn't have had a clue what you were talking about. You must have a charmed life.'

McAvoy stares into his orange juice, wondering how a cursed existence would play out differently. He isn't sure how to get the best out of somebody like Red. Isn't sure how to get the best out of anybody. Can never make up his mind about himself – whether he's good at his job, or a bumbling incompetent, hideously out of his depth. He supposed it depends on who's doing the judging.

'Did you know her?' asks McAvoy, quietly. 'Eva-Jayne?'

'Never heard of her,' says Red, half-heartedly crossing herself. 'Clairvoyant, wasn't she? No, meant nowt to me, or to Grieg. The talk weren't about her this morning, although half the *gossens* on the site reckoned they knew every gory detail. No, it was her houseguest that had the tongues wagging, if you'll excuse the pun.'

'The pun?'

'Cut her tongue out, didn't he?' asks Red, lighting a fresh cigarette from the tip of her last one. 'That's what I heard, anyway. Reckon she was a grass? Speak no evil, kind of a deal? Or maybe it's just Cromwell enjoying himself. Either way, poor lass.'

'And the girl?' he prompts. Manages to say her name, cheeks burning. 'Roisin.'

Red chews her lip, eyeing him up. She fiddles with a gold medallion on a chain, as if asking the saints for guidance. 'I got the full story, after we met,' she says, quietly. 'Heard the rumours, of course, but it's not the sort of thing a family wants everybody knowing. Eldest daughter, treated like that. Just a girl. And her daddy, such a strong man, and not there when she needed him. Left it to some bloody copper – no offence – and them as did it still able to draw breath? An ugly business. She'd have made a good mammy, from what I've heard.'

McAvoy stares at her, his palms face down on the table, the lights overhead adding an intensity to his gaze. 'Would have?'

'She'll not get a husband, will she? A man wants his wife, shall we say, untainted . . .'

McAvoy lets his disgust show. 'The things that were done to her . . . what she suffered . . . people judge her on that?'

She shrugs, implying that the world is nothing if not horribly unfair. 'Nobody knows where she is, before you ask,' says Red, directly. 'Didn't know she was with that lady in Scunthorpe until we got wind of what had happened. I don't know if the coppers have put two and two together yet but it won't be long. Couldn't have happened at a worse time. Her daddy must have been scared as all hell if he sent her over here in the first place. And now, well . . . if he gets her . . .' She looks away, as if whatever she is imagining is painful.

'He?'

Red shrugs, trying to make light of it. 'You know they're at war again, yeah? Heldens and the Teagues? Fifty odd years of it now and I can't see it ending. But this time, the Heldens want to put it to bed for good. Only good Teague is a dead Teague, or so they say. Nothing's out of bounds any more. And after bringing Cromwell in, well, that mess in the flat in Scunthorpe, that's what you're going to get.'

'Slow down,' says McAvoy, pushing his hand through his wet hair. 'Cromwell?'

'Killer,' says Red, matter-of-factly. 'Loyal to whoever pays his butcher bill. Papa Helden's set him loose. That's why the Teagues are in hiding. They can handle a lot, they're good brave lads, but Cromwell, if the stories are to be believed – he's merciless. An artist. Can do things to a body that even the Inquisition didn't dream up. Doesn't stop. You kill him, or he kills you. And nobody's killed him yet. If he came for Roisin and she got away . . .'

'And you think he did?'

'He wouldn't have gone there for Eva-Jayne,' says Red with a shrug, flicking a glance at her watch. 'Roisin's her daddy's favourite. He must have thought this was the safest place for her. Nobody would have thought to come to some shitty flat in Scunthorpe to find his princess. My Grieg spoke to the half-brothers and they didn't even know she was in the area. A bit offended, I reckon, though you can never tell with those weird bastards.'

'Half-brothers?'

'Some distant connection to Padraig,' explains Red, shrugging. 'They'll claim that, anyway. They're not Travellers, but they're connected. Family, but not blood, if you'll understand the difference. Bad lads. Wouldn't let either of them within a mile of my family, but then, I'm not desperate, am I?' She begins to rise from her chair. She's given him more than intended.

'Local to here?'

'Out Epworth way,' says Red, grinding out her cigarette in the ashtray. Out of habit, she pockets the butt.

'Could she have contacted them? If she were able?'

'She'd have to be in a hell of a way to think about that,' muses Red. 'Padua – he's done time for rape. His brother, he's the real fucking nutter. But they're handy people. And to answer your next question, she'd be a bloody fool to come to the halting site. As many loyal to the Heldens as the Teagues, and most with no fucking idea about any of it. There's a curse on that girl, I swear to the Blessed Virgin. Always a touch of the sight about her, according to her ma.'

'Could you not stay another five minutes?' asks McAvoy, his mind racing. He can feel the tug of responsibility; the need to do something that he really doesn't want to. 'Names?' he asks. 'The half-brothers . . . and Cromwell? What's his real name?'

Red pauses. Considers. '*An diabhal*,' she says, then crosses herself. 'That's to us. Other languages, other names.'

McAvoy looks at her, confused.

'The devil,' she says, quietly, then turns and walks away.

EIGHTEEN

'What do you mean he headbutted you, Andy? I know we have a policy of believing the victim, but the fact that you're alive and still have a head suggests that there may be bits missing from this story.'

Daniells looks up at Pharaoh, grimacing in advance of what he knows will be a difficult exchange. 'I didn't say he headbutted me, I said we clashed heads. He was all jittery. You know, distracted, a bit all over the place.'

'He's McAvoy,' says Pharaoh, her mouth turning down at the corners and her nostrils starting to flare. Her officers have grown used to reading such subtle indicators when trying to gauge her mood. Right now, she's frustrated, and getting cross. When her lower teeth protrude past the top row, the team know that it's time to run.

'Boss?'

'He's always jittery. It comes with being ten feet tall and suffering from the only physical deformity that people are still allowed to make fun of!'

'The big hands?' asks Daniells, grasping.

'The ginger!' growls Pharaoh, pulling her half finished cigarette from her mouth and tossing it into the long grass. 'Get somebody to pick that up before Forensics bag it,' she growls, shaking her head.

'Look, he went past me like he had a rugby ball under his arm. Took the car and shot off. I'm telling you so I don't have to worry about it anymore.'

Pharaoh runs her hands through her hair. They come away damp. She can't tell if it's rain or sweat.

'Not sure if you need to hear this, but the dad of that anarchist – the one who's missing – he was on Radio Humberside last bulletin, saying you weren't doing enough, that you didn't care . . .'

'Of course he was,' says Pharaoh, softly. 'His boy's missing. It might be useful in jogging some memories, getting some witnesses forward. Remind me later to tell them to keep an eye on the message forums on that urban explorer site, would you? They all know each other, though they've got daft bloody names and talk like they're about to start a revolution by breaking into old buildings. He was into all that, from what I remember.'

'Sure thing,' says Daniells, making a note. 'I tried that estate agent. Left a message. He'll call the sarge, but maybe I should ring back and take that on myself, for now . . .'

Pharaoh nods. Licks dry lips.

'All OK with you two?' asks Daniells, with the facial expression of one who knows they are walking on thin ice. 'You and the sarge, I mean?'

'Peachy,' she says, stuffing her hands in the pockets of her leather jacket. Behind her sunglasses, the pupils in her blue eyes have shrunk down to tiny pinpricks. Beneath her dress, it feels as though tiny insects are biting at her skin. She feels over-whelmed suddenly, and Pharaoh isn't somebody who ever believes she has taken on too much. There just aren't enough officers any more. Too much crime and not enough people to deal with it all. And she, as a very senior officer, constantly being told to do more with less. Of course her officers are cracking. Of course they're quitting in droves. Of course they're running from a crime scene without so much as a word. She's started to expect it. But not from him. Not Aector.

'Should I get that?' asks Daniells, helpfully, gesturing at the light shining from her pocket.

'Another coffee would be nice,' says Pharaoh, taking the call and turning away. Daniells, accepting the closest thing he'll ever receive to an apology, hurries away.

'Boss, I got a message to ring . . .'

Pharaoh tries to gather her thoughts. She may as well be using a fishing net.

'Trish?'

'Sorry, Wilma – staffing issues. If I commit murder, can you provide a character reference?'

'My pleasure,' says DCI Wilma Bradley, in her ear. 'Cool, calm, composed, not the sort to push somebody's eyeballs into their head with her thumbs . . .'

'I've told you, it was an ugly rumour. One eyeball, just one . . .'

Pharaoh forces herself to relax. To concentrate on the job in hand. Turns to face the wind and lets it cool her flushed skin. 'Case you were on,' she says, lighting another cigarette. 'Eva-Jayne Puck. I've requested all the files but I thought you could give me a precis. I was with the Met for that god-awful eight months – first job back after my last lot of maternity leave. I barely remember.'

There's a pause, as Pharaoh's former colleague gets herself comfortable. 'This to do with our mutual friend?' she asks, quietly.

'Sorry?'

'Your big friendly giant, I mean. Scottish chap. Muscles like piglets in a pop sock. Blushes. Did for Roper and nearly got himself killed. In hospital more often than he's not . . .'

'I know who you're referring to,' says Pharaoh, testily. 'I just don't follow.'

'It'll be in the file,' says Bradley, taking a slurp of something hot. 'The witness. Briefly a suspect. He married her not more than a few weeks after it all happened.'

Pharaoh stays silent. Sucks on her cigarette. Considers for a moment.

'Trish?'

'That's an oddly specific thing to remember, Wilma,' says Pharaoh, at last. 'I've got a good memory myself, but you knowing that, it's a bit uncanny.'

Bradley laughs, a pleasant enough sound. 'I took the statement that she gave after it was all done and dusted. Nice girl. Very pretty. He wasn't part of the investigation. Hadn't long since arrived. Bit of a surprise when I heard he'd got hitched to a Gypsy.'

'Irish Traveller,' corrects Pharaoh, automatically.

'Aye, whatever. None of our business though. I'd only been there on secondment and was glad to get out before Roper turned me into one of them. No, I only remember because I was in charge of exhibits and I gave him back some of his new wife's things.'

'Go on.'

Bradley pauses. 'Look, I know you two are close. Maybe you should just read this.'

'Wilma, get on with it.'

'There were some personal items,' says Bradley. 'A journal she'd written. A spell, if that doesn't make you spit your cigarette out. A love spell, to make him fall in love with her. It was all lovey-dovey stuff. Sweet, y'know. Like, they'd known each other a long time. And I was a bit surprised when I put the pieces together, because when he came into CID that night, he didn't say he knew her. And if I'm honest, I've always thought there were unanswered questions on the whole case. I mean, the Garda I spoke to gave me a lot of stuff about some stone-cold contract killer and a big feud about the bare-knuckle world, but Roper was very good at making little problems like that go away. There were two brothers – half-brothers, now I think on it – went missing not long after and Roper very much pointed the finger that way. He was a bad man. Wouldn't wish it on many people, but he got what he deserved.'

Pharaoh sucks her teeth. Chews the tip of her cigarette. 'The clairvoyant,' she says, at last. 'Any foreign objects . . .'

'Labradorite,' says Bradley, at once. 'Did my research there. Said to ward off evil.'

Pharaoh glares at the tip of her cigarette. Blows on the glowing red ember. Thinks of the ruined body, lying empty and maimed in the little house beyond the trees. Shakes her head.

'Didn't fucking work.'

NINETEEN

Twelve years ago

'I slipped. Fell. Sorry . . . forgot my . . . I just need . . .'

Roisin stumbles over her words. Gabbles, the way she's seen the English do. Makes a show of herself. Gives just enough away to guarantee that the young woman in the T-shirt and leggings holds the door for her. Doesn't give her chance to

second-guess herself, or ask difficult questions. She ducks under
the outstretched arm, her hand to her face, briars and mud in her
hair. She's soaked through. Shivering. Tired to the bone.

A voice behind her: the woman recovering herself, remem-
bering, trying to do things properly.

'Which room are you in, please? Which room – it's members
. . . members only . . .'

'Thanks,' she shouts, over her shoulder.

The voice fades as Roisin hurries into the warm, menthol-
scented air of the health spa. The hotel had appeared like
a mirage: a grand affair with gleaming glass frontage and a
golf course beyond the tree-lined car park. Dripping, sucking
down urgent breaths, she'd sidled down the back of the hotel
and followed the smell of chlorine and peppermint oil. Her
daddy always told her not to ask for permission. Told her to
take what she wanted, and then ask the Lord for forgiveness.
She's taking now, jogging briskly past a darkened nail bar,
past a reception area for beauty treatments and massages. By
God's grace she finds the door to the changing rooms
unlocked, held open by a yellow plastic triangle declaring
'cleaning in progress'.

The lights flick into life as she ducks inside, She finds herself
in the big cool cathedral of a long changing room: wooden doors
and banks of clean, well-maintained lockers. There's a smell of
soap and sweat; the high, bright tang of disinfectant. She puts
the stolen mobile phone into a bin for dirty towels. Glances
at the clock on the wall. They'll be here, soon. Here to
collect her. To put things back together.

One wall is entirely mirrored. She sees herself. Sees something
half drowned; bedraggled and broken down. There's dirt smudging
her cheek. Mud and blood on her wrist. She peers at the graze
on her skin as if the wound belongs to somebody else. She has
a flash of memory; of the charm bracelet digging into her skin,
snagging, snapping: her silver treasures tumbling into Eva-Jayne's
blood.

She watches dispassionately as the girl in the mirror begins
to sob: silvery tears charting tracks in the dirt. Turns her back
on the image, hoping she can leave the weak, snivelling creature
in the mirror and move forward unimpeded by tears. She will

grieve for Eva-Jayne in her own time and in her own way. She'll tell Daddy, and Daddy will put the man who did it in the dirt.

Alert for any sounds, her senses cat-like in their keenness, she hurries past the lockers to the showers. Slips inside an open cubicle and presses her palm to the fat button set into the neat mosaic of tiles. Strips as glorious clean hot water cascades from the shower head. She finds soap in a plastic container bolted to the wall and squeezes great dollops into her palm. She has never been in a place like this. Has showered in cold water as often as hot. She soaps her clothes first, scrubbing the dirty fabric against itself, until her feet stand in a swirl of brown water. Scrubs herself next, under her nails, behind her ears, removing every trace of Eva-Jayne's flat, and her night and day hunkered down in the forest.

She steps from the shower. Wrings out her clothes. Climbs back into them, wincing at the touch of wet fabric. There's hairdryers by the row of sinks and Roisin would love nothing more than to blast hot air onto her damp clothes and skin, but she has no doubt that the sound would bring somebody running and she doesn't have the strength for confrontation.

She walks past the mirror and back into the hallway. There's a glass fire door to her left but she doesn't want to trigger any alarms so she leaves the same way she came in. The same young woman is manning the reception area, playing with her phone and looking generally bored. Roisin taps on the glass and she's buzzed through into the brightly lit lobby of the spa. Glances at racks of sportswear: golfing jerseys, waterproof coats: swimming costumes stretched over elegant mannequins.

'You forgot to sign in . . .'

And Roisin is moving quickly again, passing down a corridor and through the double doors, back into the darkness and the swirl of rain. She shivers. Hears her teeth chatter. Moves quickly past the warm yellow light of a ground-floor hotel room, a flash of skin and bed linen; the insinuation of naked flesh as she darts back to the treeline.

Into the car park now. Mercedes, Lexus, Audi, parked side by side or nose to nose, raindrops glinting on expensive metal.

Lights flash, at the furthest recess of the car park. She runs towards them. Feels her breath trip in her throat as she sees them.

Michael and Padua. Sitting in the front of the blue van, still as cardboard cut-outs.

She hadn't been sure they'd come. Michael had told her they had been hoping to hear from her sooner. Made no mention of whether he knew about the murder of their shared kin. Just told her to head for the posh hotel on the roundabout. They'd be there soon.

A door slides open. Roisin's breath comes in short, static bursts. She's frozen all the way through. Doesn't know whether she's safe here, with the men who her family told her to avoid, or should take her chances in the woods. But she needs food. Needs to find a way to contact her father. And the van offers something close to warmth and shelter.

'Roisin Teague, as I live and breathe. Will you look at yourself, dripping like a poacher's pocket, so you are. Come in, girl. We've towels. Got the blowers on . . .'

A welcoming voice, accent scarcely credible: a mix of Johnny Cash and Daniel O'Donnell, and neither imitation any good. She looks into gold teeth and bright eyes and sees a whole wall of used cigarette packets lining the lower half of the windscreen. Beside him, smaller, rounder, balder, baby-faced, denim jacket over white T-shirt and a silver steer pendant on a string.

She runs to the passenger side, and takes the hand of the younger, smaller man. Padua. His palm is cold and clammy – a dead fish between her fingers. He yanks her upwards and into a space that stinks of Lucky strike cigarettes, fried food and dead animals. Makes space for her on the torn leather. Fixes his eyes on the floor.

In the driver's seat, his brother Michael, all smiles and twinkle. Big curly head of hair and a line across the bridge of his nose where the doctors removed a splinter of crushed cartilage. He's wearing a suede jacket, with tassels. In the footwell, his red leather boots catch the light.

'Padua, say howdy to your cousin . . .'

Padua mumbles something she can't decipher. Shoves up towards his brother and makes room for her.

'Towel, Padua . . .'

The other man does as he is bid. Reaches behind him and pulls out a dry, rough towel, a Thermos of coffee and a big padded lumberjack shirt.

'Thank you,' says Roisin, her voice weak. 'Honestly, I didn't know if you'd come, whether you'd even know who I was . . .'

She unscrews the lid of the Thermos. Pours hot coffee into the plastic cup and takes a swig, enjoying the scald to her lips and tongue. Drains it and takes another. She can barely taste it but she relishes the sweetness. Can even stomach that bitter, chemical tang which lingers even after she's swallowed down three cupfulls.

Michael grins, watching as she towels her hair and wriggles herself through the sleeves of the quilted jacket. Her damp top rides up, exposing the jewel in her belly button and a stretch of smooth, tanned skin.

Padua takes a packet of cigarettes from his shirt pocket. Lights one, then hands it to Roisin. She hesitates, then takes, it, gratefully. Sucks the smoke into her lungs and feels the warmth of it. Her limbs feel heavy, suddenly. There's a delicious warmth to the air, swaddling her, bringing in a soft darkness at the edges of her vision. She shakes her head. Sees Michael grinning at her. Tries to return it and can't seem to make her mouth work. Her lips seem to tingle, as though she's been smacked in the mouth. She can hear something, close up and far away, a high ringing, like metal wire pulled tight and plucked with a nail.

'Eyes down, Padua,' intones Michael, firmly. He gives a nod, his eyes on hers. 'And don't you be worrying, girl. We've already spoken to your father. Fair worried, so he is, though a hard knacker like him wouldn't let himself show it. We've to get you somewhere safe and cosy while he takes care of things. You'll take my condolences, I hope. Never had much to do with her, your Eva-Jayne, but she had a few drops of our blood and we've got some of hers, or so I'm told. And the bastard will pay for what he's done to ours. Blood's blood, yeah. We're not Pavee, not Traveller, you knows that. But we're the next best thing. You're safe. Right hand to God, you're safe.'

Roisin gives the faintest of nods. 'Thank you . . .' she begins.

Mikey stamps on the accelerator as if trying to kill a venomous spider, and they lurch forward in a spray of dirty rain. The radio roars into life.

'Oh you'll fucking love this one,' shouts Mikey, eyes wide,

gold teeth glinting in his smile. 'Live from Folsom Prison. Oh
to have been there, eh, Padua?'

The man beside her keeps his eyes on the floor. His big hand,
bristled with arachnoid black hairs, clutches at the material of
his trousers, scoring grooves in the dirty denim. He's fighting
with himself. Fighting with something he doesn't ever want to
let out again.

Roisin wraps herself in the damp towel. Tucks a fold of her huge
shirt between her head and the window. She's exhausted: bone-
weary. She can't think straight. Can't remember where they said
they were taking her, or how Daddy is going to find her. Her tongue
feels too big for her mouth: thick, furred. Helpless, she gives in.
Closes her eyes and drifts into a fitful sleep: diesel and dog hair in
her nostrils; peacock feathers and dirty snow in her dreams.

When he's sure she's asleep, Padua raises his head. Looks
at her profile, the slender angles of her jawline, the elegant
narrowness of her neck.

'Padua . . .'

Chastened, he looks away. Rests his head on his big brother's
arm.

When both of his passengers are asleep, the driver pulls the
slim mobile phone from his pocket, and types a short text message,
both eyes on the rain-speckled blackness of the motorway.

We have her. The bidding opens at dawn.

He smiles to himself, as he mentally composes a postscript.

So does she . . .

TWENTY

8.06 a.m.
Hessle Foreshore

'You don't have to come. Fin can take me.'
        'You'll get filthy.'
        'No I won't. I've got a technique.'
'It's the park, you always get dirty . . .'

'Mammy, don't act like that bothers you. I've gone to school with a whole slice of pizza in my cardigan pocket before now.'

'That was your snack for break . . .'

'And you tried to colour in Fin's white sock with a black marker when you couldn't find any that matched . . .'

'Lilah-Rose, you are treating me with no respect . . .'

'That's not true. I respect you, like, totally! I respect you as a free spirit. A Bohemian. An independent woman. I respect you as the kind of Mammy who will let their favourite daughter pop to the swings before school . . .'

Roisin knew she was beaten before she began. Lilah is relentless. She's the cleverest person in any room and is also acutely aware of the fact that she's funny, charming and beautiful. She's not arrogant, but she does possess the self-assuredness of somebody who knows they are always right. She doesn't so much argue with people, as outline her case, and wait for them to agree with her, or permit them to continue to be wrong. She's been going on about the park for half an hour now and Roisin has reached the 'going through the motions' stage.

Roisin glances again at the clock on the mantelpiece. It's not even eight a.m. They don't have to leave for school for at least half an hour, and that's only if they decide that today is one of the days when they will endeavour to be vaguely punctual. Roisin feels a bit unwell, truth be told: her bones seem shaky; her stomach is griping. She can't seem to swallow without it feeling as though there is an obstruction in her chest. Her vision seems hazy, blurred. Were she to allow herself to focus on the memory, she could be back in the van. She could be unconscious, slumped beside the half-brothers; a chemical tang on her tongue and ugly hallucinations behind her eyes. It feels as though twelve years could fall away like snow.

'Mammy, I have a feral soul. A Traveller's essence. You are being a barrier to my journey of cultural self-discovery. It's an act of cruelty to keep me in this cage.'

'Oh for feck's sake, Lilah.'

Roisin would love to agree. The children love the park and she loves it when they're happy. But the air isn't right. She can feel echoes from long ago. Can feel him, out there. Even the name makes her shudder. *Cromwell*. The name is a stab wound into the meat of her brain.

She closes her eyes, trying to work out what the hell to do. She can feel Lilah hovering nearby, hoping to change her mind. She ignores her, lays her head back and feels overcome by a sudden wave of tiredness. She's so damn tired. Needs to wake herself up so she can make sense of things. She doesn't know the dead woman out at Spurn Point but she still needs to check with her younger brother. She hates coincidences, and the death of a fortune teller, this close to home, at a time when the Teagues and Heldens are united in fear . . . she needs to talk to somebody who understands. And then she can tell Aector everything. She should have done so from the start, she knows that now, but the thought of him thinking poorly of her; of the pain in his big mournful eyes – the inevitable realization that he had played a part in a blood-laced lie . . . she had fought to spare him that.

Everything becomes faint. Muddled. Her head feels thick with exhaustion. Her thoughts are a mess of wire wool and damp paper. She wills herself awake, half noticing the sound of a door quietly closing somewhere nearby. She dismisses it, drifting gently into the darkness of sleep.

She jerks awake, teetering in a place between sleep and consciousness. Glances around her, looking for the children. Shouts their names. Shouts louder. A primal, serpentine fear uncoils in her gut. No, she thinks. No, they wouldn't have . . .

She shouts their names again. Peers through the open curtains towards the bridge. It's only a five-minute walk to the play area, which serves as an elaborate entrance to the dense woodland of the country park. She flicks her gaze up to the concrete underbelly of the Humber Bridge. She still can't decide if it's beautiful. It's just there: as much a part of the landscape now as the murky brown water, the strip of shingly beach, and the damp green grass across the silent expanse of Cliff Road.

'No,' she says, aloud, and crosses herself, frantic now, kissing her crucifix, blinking back tears. 'No, please . . .'

She can feel her heart beating hard. Places her palm upon her chest and realizes her skin is clammy. Shivers, violently. She tells herself she's panicking about nothing – it's just the result of feeling so paranoid and jittery. She's been sleeping badly.

Waking from the same damn dream and sitting at the window like a sailor's widow staring out to sea. Things will be OK again soon, she knows that. And their 'OK' is better than most. Aector has been home more these past few months. There have been investigations, he's worked as hard as he ever has, but he hasn't had to bleed for the dead since Pharaoh came back from Iceland, all loved up and dribbling about some gorgeous Aector-doppelganger. They've talked about different types of future. For the first time since they fell for one another, she has wafted the idea of travel beneath his nose. Has spoken of a world in which he is not a police officer. She doesn't know what that world would look like, but she cannot help but smile when she imagines an open road and Aector's hand in hers. The kids are clever enough to miss some school. She left education at twelve and she's never felt any the worse for it, and Aector's education could have been completed in a fraction of the time if they'd just left him alone in the library.

She is thinking upon this, and more, when she closes her fingers around the phone. She is in such a frenzy that she doesn't even register that it is ringing until she has raised it to her ear and said 'hello'.

'Roisin, it's me. Valentine. It's definite, sis – not just us, the Heldens too. They tried to call him off and he opened up Packy Ratcliffe's chest like it was an umbrella. Left him on the roof of Papa Helden's caravan. Weren't found until the police helicopter spotted it. Dogs had been yapping but nobody saw. Jaysus, Roisin, he's said he's coming for the lot of us. You've got to tell him. Get yourself safe, or at least prepared. He won't stop, and by Christ he deserves his revenge . . .'

Roisin can barely untangle the words. She has never heard her brash, impulsive brother so rattled. She shivers again, violently, as though somebody were blowing cold air against the skin of her neck.

Pulls open the door, and starts to run.

TWENTY-ONE

Twelve years ago

Twenty miles west of Scunthorpe, a mile or so back from the motorway, screened by a line of trees and a wall of rotting hay bales, is the funfair cemetery. It's primarily a scrapyard, but it specializes in showground memorabilia. This is a place where derelict dodgems and rusted-up rollercoasters can be abandoned to slowly sink in upon themselves: a video-game city, built of great rusting metal towers and smashed, multicoloured glass. An area the size of a football pitch is covered in the rusting hulks of showground wagons, their sides patterned with lurid, leering faces – chassis sinking into oily dirt and their insides long since disembowelled for their still-useful parts.

The land belongs to the father of Michael Fitz and Padua McAteer. He's been dead eight years now, but nobody's asked any questions of importance and the brothers see no reason to stop claiming his pension or signing documents on his behalf. As the brothers see it, he owes them. He carried on with both their mammies, smoked cigars and drove a Cadillac while they were being dragged up in damp flats or being dumped in foster homes. His occasional visits were treated like a Papal deputation. They grew up thinking of their father as something approaching a deity: remote, unavailable, but demanding veneration. It struck both as ironic that he took religion, late in life. Stopped pretending to worship the Lord and actually started to do so. Repented for the man he was and decided he would use his twilight years making amends for his past misdeeds. He brought his sons together. Told them they were brothers; they were blood. Told them that whatever happened, they were family and needed to put one another, and the Lord, before all else. It is a time Padua remembers with something approaching fondness. For a handful of years, he and his dad and his brother ran the scrapyard. Michael had the brains for it all. Reached out to men in Ireland whom

his father called 'the cousins' and set up a side business exporting
crushed and cubed metal to their contacts in the west of Ireland,
where men loyal to Papa Teague would disentangle the twisted
squares and excavate their true cargo. False documents, fake
invoices, European prescription pads. He knew forgers from his
time inside. In return, he received ketamine from horse trainers
and cash-strapped stable-hands, which he and Padua were able
to flog to the recreational users in Sheffield, Doncaster, Rotherham
– even as far as Nottingham before they pissed off the Yardies.
They branched out, both on the legitimate side of things, and in
the scope of their ambition. Ran a landscape business on the
side, tarmacked the odd drive, and did some breakdown work in
the backwaters round about. They put a few bodies under the
patios of the nice, middle-class people willing to pay cash in
hand for a landscaping and paving job. Life was briefly rather
nice. That Padua was a sex offender was something that didn't
matter to his brother, but it weighed heavily on Daddy's mind.
He kept apologizing to him for not being there, for not setting
the right example, for not giving him the love, or the whippings,
that would have kept him on the righteous path. It became too
much to endure. Padua had worked hard on himself. He took the
medicine the doctors gave him and tolerated the nausea and
the hallucinations and the weight-gain. He kept himself in his
trousers and went to every therapy session his probation officer
decreed. He believes he would have kept getting better had the
girl simply had the good sense to walk away from him. He still
can't forgive her for that. Can still see her, sitting on the top step
of the dirty, glass-filled wagon, drinking orange pop from a bottle,
laughing at his awkwardness, telling him he was her hero for
rescuing her and her stupid little car from the roadside. Thanking
him, again and again, for letting her charge her phone and get
her head together before ringing a friend to come and pick her
up. She must have seen the way he was looking at her. He cannot
imagine why she did not see the threat radiating off him like
sweat. When he grabbed her, pinned her down, hurt her, she'd
thought he was joking. Had laughed, bits of pastry in her teeth,
sweet syrup in the warm wet cave of her mouth – and then Daddy
had been there, shouting and screaming and telling him he was
an animal, a monster, and Padua had had no bloody choice but

to pick up the rusting car battery from the pile by the wheel arches, and bludgeon his father until his head was nothing but chunks of gory bone. The girl had had to die too, of course. Padua hadn't thought himself equal to the task, but Michael had shown him how. He'd returned home to a scene of bloody carnage. Saw an opportunity, and took it. Buried both bodies beneath a great rusting wall of twisted metal and plastic: waltzers and spinning teacups and a great half built log-flume serving as a gaudy monument for the bodies beneath.

These memories, and more, flicker through the mind of Padua McAteer, as the van bumps over the potholed, rain-filled track and swings through the great leering mouth of a carnival sign: mad clown eyes and svelte disco girls peering down from the endless process of wagon walls and sunken carnival rides. A snarl of trees has enveloped some of the older specimens in the yard and to approach the area they think of as 'home' they have to pass a long stretch of overgrown wilderness dotted with curiosities. Padua sees the gleam of the red metal blood pressure machine peeking out from behind a tree; multicoloured arcade games laid out like a stone circle, toppled and tangled up with ivy and wire; a hulk of gaudily-patterned riverboat; an ironmonger's cart wedged up against one side; milk churns and metal bathtubs hanging from the bare branches of the trees that reach out like claws.

'He could be here,' says Padua, quietly, jerking left then right as the van bounces over the potholes. 'We should have a dog.'

'I hate dogs,' says Michael, holding his cigarette butt between his teeth. He glances sidelong at his brother, then at the unconscious form of Roisin Teague. Padua feels something a little like regret take his face in its grasp, but he shakes it away and replaces it with a grin. 'Don't need a dog, do I, boyo? Got a little terrier by my side.'

Padua looks down at the floor. He's never been much of a talker. Always been shy. Michael looks after him. Takes care of him. Accepts him for who he is. He owes Michael, and if Michael believes this is the right way to do things, he won't raise any objections. He'll keep his worries to himself. Will deal with his own guilty conscience somewhere down the line.

'Any luck, she'll sleep til morning,' says Michael, leaning

across and considering the girl. She's breathing OK, but she keeps jerking in her sleep, as if something is trying to hurt her in the world behind her closed eyelids. Padua sympathizes. He has always suffered from bad dreams. Most nights he sleeps with his brother, curled up behind him on the stinking mattress in the old bowtop wagon behind the mound of discarded bumper cars. If Michael thinks there is anything strange in it, he doesn't say so. As far as Padua can tell, his love is genuine. Pure, even. He wishes the world were different, even as he prospers from the ghastly way it is.

They come to a halt in a patch of cleared ground: oil barrels full of rainwater and cold ash marking a vague circle. Inside, two sodden armchairs, grass growing from their waterlogged covers. There are smashed glass bottles and empty tins discarded in a great pile to the left of a patch of black earth where the tea-kettle hangs on an iron spit. The brothers like to sit here, of an evening. They like to play with air rifles. Shoot at bottles and lights and cans. If they are lucky, a rat will scuttle past. Padua is the best at catching them. It's Michael who comes up with the ideas as to what to do next.

'I can hear your thoughts,' says Michael, killing the engine and looking at his brother. 'I know you're worrying.'

'I said nothing, brother . . .'

'You're thinking that the Teagues are kin, aren't you? That we're on their side, and that the thing to do is to get Papa his daughter back, aren't you?'

Padua nods, chewing his lip. He feels ashamed.

'And you're right to think those things, so you are,' says Michael, stubbing out his cigarette against the glass of the window. 'It speaks well of you. Speaks of a man with a good heart. But you've too soft a heart, that's the thing of it, boy. Don't let yourself think of the other stuff, do you? Like, why didn't Papa ask us to babysit her from the off, eh? Why send her to some silly gobshite in a shitty flat in Scunthorpe? Why keep it from us? It's because they've got no real love for us, Padua. Not the way we have tried to love them. They use us, brother. The things they say . . .'

'About what, Michael?' asks Padua, looking up, his big moon face reflecting back in the glass.

'About you, boy. About your affliction.'

'Do they, Michael? Do they say that?'

'They do, boy. And then they don't even give us a how-do-you-do when the feud begins afresh? Good enough to get them what they want but not to bring into the fold.'

Padua looks at Roisin. 'She's gorgeous, brother,' he says, softly.

'Aye, that'll not be in dispute. But you leave her be, boy. There'll be more than broken bones if she goes back home with her honour gone.'

Padua looks puzzled. 'You told me she'd been spoiled, Michael. You said . . .'

'You said, you said . . .' laughs Michael, eyes dazzling. He looks down at his phone. 'Oh there's a cat among the pigeons, boy. Papa's frothing at the mouth.'

Padua looks again at Roisin. Michael has been waiting for an opportunity like this. He'd been disgusted to learn that Roisin Teague had been staying in the care of a fat witch in Scunthorpe these past days and weeks. Had said a whole rosary of prayers, begging the Good Lord to bring her to him for protection. Had chewed his knuckles bloody when he learned of what happened to Eva-Jayne. And then Roisin had called them. Said that the bad man had come for her and she'd managed to get away. Said they were kin, and that she needed somewhere to stay and a way to contact her father. Michael had already made up his mind before he hung up the phone. He'd give her back to Papa Teague, but not for free. And he'd give Papa Helden the chance to outbid his rival. He'd had the good grace to look a little sheepish about it, but the way he saw it, this was an opportunity too good to pass up.

'What about Cromwell?' asks Padua, quietly.

Michael rolls his eyes. Sucks spit through his teeth. 'Fucking fantasy, boy,' he says, scornfully. 'I don't know a soul who's seen him in the flesh. And Papa Helden doesn't need outside help, the ruthless bastard.'

'She's seen him,' says Padua, apologetically. He doesn't like to disagree with Michael. His brother rarely gets cross, but when he does, Padua hurts for days.

'Has she?' Michael shrugs. 'We don't know, do we? She saw somebody killing Eva-Jayne but if it were this *deabhil* that's got everybody vexed, she'd be in pieces by now, don't you think?'

'Yes, Michael . . .'

The phone trills again. Michael grins at the screen. 'Helden. Says he doesn't want the girl. Lying bastard. Trying to play me! Don't you worry, boy, they'll pay.'

Padua stares at Roisin. There's something about the way her hair falls across her features that makes him want to touch her, to drape the tress of inky-blackness upon his knuckles and tuck it behind her ear. He wants to touch her softly, as if she were made of rose petals. He hopes her daddy offers a sensible sum. Michael is a man of his word, and if Daddy doesn't get him a six-figure thank you, he will, with great regret, allow Padua to play with her. And Padua knows that she won't enjoy that one bit.

'There'll be blood, whatever happens,' says Padua, quietly. 'If either one pays, they'll not forget what we've done.'

'And what have we done? Come to the rescue! Saved a girl, lost in the woods. We're just getting a little thank you that should have been offered before I had to start making threats . . .'

Padua jerks his head to the left as a shadow passes in front of the van. The headlights are still gleaming and for a fraction of a second there was a patch of darkness, out there: a flicker of silk.

'You OK, my little terrier?'

Padua looks at his brother, one finger raised to stop him saying any more. He peers into the near-distance: rain, reflection, metal, shadow . . .

Michael sees it too, the sudden shift in the quality of the light – the surging adrenaline charge. Michael is peering forward. Padua, at his side, squints into the light and the dark, searching, fear forming a tight knot in his gut.

A sound, from behind.

And then a curved blade, sharp as honed wire.

A moment of hot, burning understanding.

Then his vision is a spray of hot blood, and his head is falling forward on the gaping mouth of his thorax, and in his dying moments he is watching as Michael kicks, bucking like a wild horse, as the long spike of sharpened steel emerges from his ribcage, again, again: a beak pecking through a shell.

When the bodies stop moving, the man in the rear of the van climbs out through the rear doors. Slowly, a master of his craft, he drags the half-brothers into the dirt. Pats them both down, takes wallets, the change in their pockets. Takes Michael's mobile phone. He drags both bodies towards the bowtop wagon. Over the course of two tiring hours, he arranges the brothers as he wishes them to be found. His employers did not specify what should be done with the two men, but he has made it a point of honour not to allow those to live who would be better served by death. He keeps the tableau simple. When they are found, the scene will speak of a vicious fight. They killed each other – Padua attacking Michael, and the taller man using his last breath to slit his brother's throat before succumbing to his injuries. Any questions the investigators may have will go unanswered: the answers consumed by the flames.

He walks back to the van. Smokes one of the dead man's cigarettes. It's foul. He pockets the butt, and lights one of his own. It's a brand called Jin Ling: a yellow packet, designed to resemble Camels, and pumped out in their millions by Russian counterfeiters. They don't conform to any regulations: each stick a popsicle of poisons, rat-droppings, feathers, mites and pesticides. They have a tendency to stay lit, and start fires. They're fresh off the boat. The aroma is distinctive: chemical and pungent. They are his one indulgence.

He puffs grey smoke into the air. Stretches his back. He grew uncomfortable in the journey back from the hotel, but it did not impede him. He sometimes wishes he knew anybody well enough to brag to. He killed one brother with his left hand – the other with his right. He is not so humble as to detest praise for his accomplishments.

A creak, to his left.

The low groan of a young woman waking up in pain . . .

And ahead. Lights. The soft yellow lights of a car making its way up an unfamiliar path.

An deabhil allows himself a smile, bares his teeth around the cigarette.

He hadn't expected them so quickly. Before the dawn he will have the remainder of his money. The Heldens will have their prize. The Teagues, well . . . that was for another day . . .

The car comes to a halt. The engine fades to nothing. Then a big man steps out of the unremarkable car.

'Hi,' comes a voice: soft, shy, scared. 'I'm Aector. I'm a police officer . . .'

And *an deabhil's* smile glints like the edge of his blade.

TWENTY-TWO

8.24 a.m.
Hessle Foreshore

'I have these spots. Do you think they are chicken pox? Why do you think they are called pox and not chicken spots? Do you get it actually from chickens? Do you think the first time a person got it they had eaten a spotty chicken? I suppose you wouldn't be able to tell until you plucked its feathers and so it could be poorly and you wouldn't know . . .'

Fin listens as his sister talks. Very little else is required of him. She's very clever, is Lilah. Fin's teachers say he's very clever too, but he can't help feeling they're just being nice. He's OK at stuff, and he works hard, but he knows himself to be somebody who's largely unremarkable. He's OK with it. He's luckier than some people, who seem to get dealt a decidedly raw deal by the Fates. But Lilah, well, she's got a mind like a rocket. Always half a dozen steps ahead. And fearless too. Bright and brave and sharp as a knife. She reminds him a little bit of Auntie Trish, though he'd never say as much. Fin knows that of his limited qualities is an ability to keep his mouth shut whenever there is a risk of putting his foot in it. Of the things he has learned from his dad, this is the one for which he is most grateful.

'I'll go on the spider frame. I mean, it's not really a spider frame, is it – it's a pyramid made of ropes, but that isn't really right either. Maybe there's a word for it and I just don't know it. Or we could make one up. The Germans will have a word for that. Do you know the Germans have a word that means being pleased when somebody you like fails at something? I think it's *schnecktopopple*, but that might be a drink I had at the service station on the way to Liverpool . . .'

Fin leans on the railings by the park. Watches his sister, all white socks and dark skin, clambering underneath a length of red, soggy rope. Sees her climbing, giggly, gleeful, up into the top reaches of the big climbing frame.

'That's great, Lilah. You're so good at that!'

'I know!' comes the reply, as she dangles upside down from a rope, skirt falling down over her head.

Fin stares past her. Stares past the black brick of the old windmill. Imagines the little guesthouse just beyond the treeline. He doesn't remember it very clearly but he knows he and his dad were resident there for a time, back when people were trying to hurt Mammy. Lilah had been tiny then. Wasn't even talking. He feels a mild pang of nostalgia.

'Are you coming up? I bet I can hang for longer than you. I bet . . . oh, poot.'

Fin looks up. A pocket calculator has slipped from Lilah's coat, bouncing and clattering down among the ropes and skittering off into the mound of dead leaves.

'Fin,' she says, apologetically. 'You know you're the best brother ever . . .'

Fin doesn't mind. He's a caring lad. Loves his sister and knows it's his job to keep her safe enough to be whatever brilliant thing she's going to be.

'Don't worry,' he shouts up, breathing in deeply as the wind carries in a bright, briny aroma of the sea. Leaves lift off from the pile, dancing away into the darkness of the wood.

'You look funny upside down, Fin. Did I tell you about the people in that book I read? The one in the jungle, with the people who hang by their feet because it's the only way the world makes sense, and I thought to myself that would be OK but you'd get an awful headache and the indigestion would be awful and that got me thinking about how bats poop, and . . .'

Fin starts to rummage in the leaves. Rakes his hands through the mulch: earth and conker-cases, sticks and thorns. Swallows down the smell of disturbed earth, of onion skins and sweat and the wormy gristle of maggot-chewed roots . . .

His hand touches something hard.

Something firm.

Something flesh.

And then the leaves are rising, tumbling down from the black-clad limbs of some dark, mud-caked thing, rising from the ground, squirming upright like a corpse being born . . .

Pain, suddenly. The sensation of teeth upon bone. The momentary stench of his own burning skin, as the metal incisors of the stun gun jab into his unprotected flesh.

Lilah's voice.

Lilah's scream.

And a black, leathery glove upon his mouth, forcing him into the earth, prey to be devoured by the thing that yanks him down and down into the dark.

TWENTY-THREE

Lilah McAvoy is standing on the doorstep, shivering as if pulled from the sea. There is blood on both knees. Dirt on her face. A livid red patch on one cheek. One hand, a crimson glove, dripping red onto the carpet.

'Lilah?' Her voice a prayer.

'A man,' says Lilah.

'What man, Lilah? What man . . .?' Roisin stops herself. Looks into the empty spaces behind and beside her daughter. 'Where's Fin . . .?'

Lilah raises her hand. Nailed to her palm is an Oracle card; its cheerful colours already saturated with blood.

'He took him,' says Lilah.

She looks at her hand. Smiles, as if the whole thing is rather silly.

Then the tears come.

She falls in on herself, tears and snot and blood.

In her head, Mammy's screams: loud enough to wake the dead.

TWENTY-FOUR

McAvoy, heading west, stamping on the accelerator as if grinding his boot on a scorpion. He's ignored every red light and speed camera, tyres screaming around the curve of road where the road through Hull becomes the road out of it: the abandoned warehouses and crumbling docks passing in a blur of grey and brown.

'Pick up,' he's hissing, teeth gritted, phone wedged between his shoulder and cheek. 'Roisin, pick up the phone . . .'

The ringtone taunts him, as it has these last, god-awful miles. He's tried consoling himself with simple explanations. She's taken the kids to school; got chatting in the playground; popped in to the shops and left her phone in the car. None has done him any good. He cannot drag himself from the visions that plague him: paranoid imaginings of his wife taken, hurt, tortured, maimed. Cannot stop himself from thinking of her damp eyes; blood running in prison bars down her teeth as she opens her mouth and screams for help that will not come.

He ends the call. Pulls into the outside lane and overtakes a lorry; the driver taking the time to call him a 'fucking headcase' and lean heavily on the horn. He slaloms through the traffic. Faces flash past the window, mouths open, angry eyes; the rain on the glass turning the other motorists into hazy, half finished things: wax effigies left too close to the heat.

On the passenger seat, the phone trills. Pharaoh, again. He's ignored her last three calls. He needs to keep the line open for Roisin.

Swings the car left, roaring up the slip road that leads off the dual carriageway and towards the car showrooms and offices and supermarkets that cluster together on the edge of Hassle. Left again, down the side road that follows the line of the river. Fewer cars here. He stamps on the accelerator. Makes a decision without even acknowledging it.

'Trish . . .' he says, breathlessly, the phone hot against his ear.

'Hector, where the fuck . . . I've been calling . . . what's going on? You were there and then . . .'

'Trish, please, I'll explain later – something I found, something from before . . .' He can't seem to find the right words to explain himself. Takes a hand from the wheel to pinch the bridge of his nose. Sweat is running into his eyes. He can't seem to get his fingers to do what he wants them to do. Every cell in his body seems to be exploding and reforming – his bones feeling too big for his flesh.

'Hector, slow down, slow down,' she says, her voice soothing. She's comforted plenty of hysterical people over the years. She's good at calming people down.

'She's not answering . . . one of her charms, her bracelet, I mean. Out in the field at the back of the house – it doesn't make sense, he was supposed to be dead – but if he wasn't . . . and I mean, maybe I knew, deep down, but I didn't want to know, because if I knew, what would that make her? And what would it make me? And how could I make sense of it all? Trish, I'm so fucking scared . . . why won't she answer . . .?'

He stops, unsure of what he has said and what he still needs to explain. Glances at the clock on the dashboard. Swings the car past the derelict restaurant and the grimy, rain-streaked scrapyard, sitting either side of the muddy stretch of water where the River Hull meets the Humber. He's nearly home. Half a mile, maybe. Half a mile, and he'll know.

'Hector, please, just slow down. Whatever you think is happening, we can solve it together. You're my sergeant, my friend, my best officer, and you need to be all those things right now. I've had several urgent messages from the ACC, they need us in – they need to talk to you. Where are you? Tell me what's happening.'

Her voice breaks up, the line dropping in and out. He can picture her, face furious despite the gentleness of her tone. Can see her glaring into the hard wind at the crime scene in Holderness, finger in her ear, sunglasses damp with rain, black cigarette moving up and down like a dog's tail.

A beeping, in his ear. Another call, coming through. He hangs up on Pharaoh without another word.

'Ro . . .' he begins, without looking at the screen.

'Is that Sergeant McAvoy? Hello, yes, I received a message
. . . asking me to contact you – I own the property at Stone
Creek, you wanted to talk to me about a tenant, I believe. Um,
how can I . . .?'

'Christ, not now . . .!' spits McAvoy, ending the call and
slamming down the phone. Then, to nobody in particular, he
prays, a roar, so loud it hurts his throat: 'Please!'

His heart is beating so fast it's turning the world into a blur
of indecipherable patterns and colours. Woodland, to his left.
The brown-and-silver surface of the estuary beyond. Playing
fields and barbed wire and allotments to his right. The rugby
club. Houses now. Grand affairs, hidden behind trees and red
brick walls. Big Victorian mansion houses, chopped into flats
and barnacled with satellite dishes.

In front, the soggy grass that runs down to the dirty sand and
slimy rocks of the shoreline. There should be an ice-cream van
parked up, opposite the neat, newish houses that shelter beneath
the perfect curve of the Humber Bridge. It's not there today. He
takes it as somehow symbolic – a bad omen.

Turns right. Sights home. A row of white fishermen's cottages.
A hanging basket outside his own – a splash of red against the
chalky paleness of the terrace.

It takes a moment to make sense of what he is seeing. To turn
the familiar scene from a memory into its new reality.

The door stands wide open. At the window of the neighbouring
property, worried faces, peering out to see what is happening.
Two doors down, another open door; a mother and son framed
in the rectangle of light, faces angled towards the open mouth
of Aector and Roisin's home.

He glances past his own front door – down to the lifeboat
station and the play park and the great mass of the woods beyond.

Sees her. Black hair. Barefoot. Dressing gown and pyjamas.
Lilah, in her arms, holding on, ape-like. She's running up the
road towards home.

McAvoy screeches to a halt outside his own front door.
Boots the door open and stumbles onto the pavement, running
towards his wife; dirt on his knees, his palms – relief flooding
him. She's here. She's safe. She's well . . .

Twenty yards away her face comes into focus. He sees fear.

Wild primal horror scored into the set of her eyes, the anguished line of her jaw.

Ten yards away, he sees his daughter's crimson hand.

Five yards away, he thinks: *Fin.*

And then she is in his arms, dissolving in tears and rage, saying his name; the name of their son; and Lilah is holding up her gory palm, and the police officer within him is closing down, fading, becoming nought but air, as something else, something other, begins to take possession of his flesh.

'No,' he says, again and again and again. 'No.'

She gasps, as if coming back to life. Takes his face in her hands, fingertips like teeth. 'He took him!' she screams, spit and snot popping on her lips. 'Cromwell. Did this to Lilah . . .'

'No . . .'

'Daddy kept him alive. He escaped. He's come back for us. I didn't know. I swear, I didn't know until a few weeks ago. I was so scared – so scared. And I couldn't tell you. And I should . . . sweet Jesus, Aector, he came for Fin . . . he took Fin!'

McAvoy's eyes darken. The clamour in his skull falls silent. For a moment, there is just the sound of the rain and the sensation of his wife and his daughter, pressing themselves damply against the great mass of his chest.

He scoops them up. Carries them into the house. Kicks the door shut behind him. The flowerpot swings on its hook. Catches the wind. Clatters free and plunges down.

An explosion of reds and browns.

Then there is just the sight of crimson petals, falling soft as snow.

PART TWO

PART TWO

TWENTY-FIVE

'**D**o they pay you extra to listen to this?' asks Pharaoh, closing her eyes and wishing, not for the first time, that evolution had seen fit to provide the human ear with protective lids.

'". . . and the sunlight hits the daffodils like milk . . . sourness in my gut, my thighs are rippling silk . . ."'

'Fucking hell,' mutters Pharaoh. She's not a fan of wistful acoustic folk-jazz. She hadn't known it existed until she walked in to the coffee shop. She envies her former self her blissful ignorance.

'Not a fan?' asks the barista, a little snippily. 'We don't get any complaints.'

'I don't doubt it. They're probably too busy attacking their wrists with a spork. Got to get themselves down to the waterfront and jump in the river.'

'Sorry?'

'I should bloody hope so.'

She taps an unlit cigarette against her teeth. Considers taking a bite. She needs a nicotine hit. She finds vaping machines ridiculous and patches only work if she puts them over her eyes and asks the kids to hide her fags.

'Come on, Wilma,' she grumbles, flicking her eyes to her phone. She's got plenty of missed calls but none from anybody she wants to speak to. The assistant chief constable's secretary has left three increasingly irritated voicemails, but Pharaoh wants to have a cover story in place should word have reached him that her number two did a runner from the crime scene.

One finger in her ear, she replays the last voicemail. It's the ACC herself, voice terse. 'Trish, I know you're up to your eyeballs but this really is important. We need to speak to Sergeant McAvoy.

There's a notice to be served. The legal representative will be here for eleven thirty and I'll pencil you in for attendance. I need to know that you've got this. It's a TTL issue. An Osman. I can't go into detail. This has all been rather dropped on us . . .'

Pharaoh closes her eyes. A TTL is a Threat to Life warning: something that used to be known as an 'Osman' warning. It is served on named individuals when intelligence is received by a police service or a security force somewhere within the European Union, which indicates somebody is at immediate risk of serious harm. Pharaoh has received several herself. McAvoy is no stranger to physical threat. She has no doubt that it's some administrative box-ticking exercise rather than a genuine reason to worry, but it's something else for her to mull over when she's supposed to be solving a murder and overseeing half a dozen other active cases.

Her heart clenches like a fist as she thinks of him. He never ignores her calls. Always replies to her texts the moment Roisin pops out of the room. When he's out of contact she feels rudderless; adrift. She sometimes wonders when the balance of power shifted: when their relationship went from being that of mentor and apprentice, to this eerie, symbiotic thing. She feels wrong without him. Scared for him. And fear makes her angry.

'Bloody ring, will you?' she hisses at the phone. It's taking the brunt of her rage. Her hair's wet, and she's sweaty beneath her damp clothes. The doctor recently hinted she may be having problems with menopause. She'd stopped him after the first syllable. As far as she's concerned, the irritability, hot flushes and occasional emotional breakdowns are all the result of people not doing things properly. She takes great umbrage at words like 'hormonal' and 'imbalance' and likes them even less when they are used in the same sentence. She's been told there are herbal remedies that might help, but unless she can sprinkle them into a fat cigarette and inhale, she'd rather keep the rage.

Opening her eyes again, she gives her barista a once-over. 'And do they pay you to look like that? Do you apply, and they give you a how-to manual, or is it that you dress a certain way and then look for an employer who doesn't mind?'

He switches off the coffee machine. Looks at her over his round glasses. 'Sorry, I didn't catch that.'

'I'm sure you didn't,' grumbles Pharaoh, shaking her head at him. She doesn't have particularly strong opinions on music, but there's something about acoustic ballads delivered in syrupy whispers that sets her teeth on edge – especially turned up to eleven and competing with the sound of the big brass coffee machine.

'That'll be four twenty, please,' says the man behind the counter. His name tag declares that his name is 'Boz', and Pharaoh will admit he rather suits it. He's short and stocky, with brawny, tattooed forearms and some impressive neo-traditional inkwork climbing up his neck and into the rhododendron of his beard. His moustache is waxed into tips and his skull is shaved so close that if he were to buy a sharper blade, he'd hit bone. With braces, badges and two big tunnels in his earlobes, he's quite the visual spectacle. She can't help thinking that as and when he commits a crime, he's going to be shitting himself come the identity parade. They won't need an artist so much as a cartoonist.

'Fuck off, Boz,' says Pharaoh, laughing. 'How much really?'

He looks briefly pained. 'Sorry,' he says. 'It's Colombian.'

'What is?' asks Pharaoh.

'The coffee.'

'Am I paying for its flight?' asks Pharaoh, incredulous. She looks behind her, optimistic that somebody else in the queue will share her in an eye-roll and a generalized whinge. Growls, under her breath, as she considers the only other customer. She's got pink hair and is wearing a multicoloured chunky-knit cardigan over a T-shirt that declares: VGN PWR. Pharaoh, once she's confirmed that there isn't an A missing from the end of the first word, fancies that she'll be on Boz's side.

'Bollocks to it,' says Pharaoh, swiping her card against the machine. She snatches the takeaway cup from Boz's outstretched hand. 'I pay less for my Brazilian,' she mutters, turning away and heading to the door. Stops when she sees the weather. It's still raining out. The sky is an ugly swirl of grey water and black clouds; a fine rain hanging in the air and making everything seem damp and dirty. She can't face going outside and her enthusiasm for walking back to the office has waned. Daniells dropped her off on Alfred Gelder Street twenty minutes ago, following a somewhat fraught journey in from Holderness.

He'd heard every word of her conversation with McAvoy. Watched her grind her teeth like a horse with a sugar cube. Saw the way the colour in her cheeks turned from a wind-slapped red to the slate grey of somebody who needs a drink and a lie down. She'd nearly instructed him to take her to an off-licence. Instead, she demanded he drop her at the tobac-conists near the old Victorian arcade. From there, she's stomped her way down to the old fruit market, and into the area where the hipsters have taken up residence. The building in which she finds herself used to be a warehouse and a ship's chandlers. The narrow snicket opposite had run straight to the water and the waiting vessels. Now, the high-ceilinged old building is a symbol of 'regeneration' – a word that always makes Pharaoh deeply uneasy. Humber Street is the jewel in Hull's cultural crown. The old warehouses that used to make up the old fruit market have been transformed into restaurants, galleries and bars. It's a place of chocolatiers and jewellery-makers, barber's shops and antique dealers. The air smells of craft beer and fresh brewed coffee: the shopfronts all bright graffiti and exposed brick. There's usually live music and most of the shopkeepers feel obligated to invest in a resident pug or French bulldog. They're only a stone's throw from the marina – pleasure craft sitting glumly on freezing grey water, ice sparkling on their peeling paint and their chocolate-coloured timbers. This is where the city's tourism bosses bring visitors.

'Fuck it, I'm staying,' says Pharaoh, pulling up a wooden barrel and taking a seat at a table that appears to be made of old packing crates and a brass radiator. She flashes a look at Boz. Dares him to tell her there's a surcharge for sitting in. Feels momentarily aggrieved that he's not remotely interested in arguing. Looks away when she accidentally catches a glimpse of her reflection, peeking back at her through the leaves of a huge bouquet of arum lilies, and a curious copper still draped in rustic coffee sacks.

She sips her coffee. Swears. It's really fucking good.

'Oh thank Christ,' she mutters, as the phone rings in her hand. It's not who she was expecting, but it's the next best thing. 'Helen,' she says, warmly.

'Trish,' says her former officer – her Grimsby accent slightly tempered by the restraining influence of London life. 'What's he done?'

Pharaoh laughs. Shrugs out of her coat and gets as comfy as she can on the awkward stool. 'Why do you presume he's done anything?'

'I'm a senior investigator with the National Crime Agency, Trish,' she says, a smile in her voice. 'That means I have experience and instinct to draw upon. Also, I've met him.'

Pharaoh flicks her hair behind her ears. It falls forward again immediately. 'Not guilty this time,' she says, staring through the rain-streaked glass. 'Obviously he's due a severe Chinese burn just for being McAvoy, but no, I was rather hoping you'd be able to speed up a request. Proper channels are so bloody congested, and I thought to myself, what's the point of having all this dirt on Helen Tremberg if you don't use it to jump the queue.'

Pharaoh hears a sigh, exaggerated to show she had been expecting as much. In truth, Pharaoh knows enough about Tremberg's past indiscretions to see her lose her job and serve ten years inside, but she would die before she ever shared it. Tremberg is one of the best officers she's ever had.

'It's for Wilma Bradley as much as for me,' says Pharaoh, laying it on thick. 'You remember Wilma – she was heading south just as you were thinking about coming over from Uniform. Good lady, done well, wouldn't object to a little help from some-body who knows how hard it is to get on when you've got no balls to scratch . . .'

'Fine, fine, what can I do?' says Tremberg, raising her voice over the sound of an argument nearby. It does nothing to change Pharaoh's opinion of London: a place where the soundtrack seems to be car horns and angry voices.

'You have any pals in the Serious Crime Analysis Section?' she asks, lowering her voice.

'We're all pals here, Trish. You'd bloody hate it.'

'We've got a nasty one. Lady killed out at Sunk Island, right on the edge of the world. PME hasn't even been started yet but there's enough weird shit to suggest that it's not your ordinary house burglary gone wrong. Cause of death is hard to ascertain but there's a crystal shard sticking out of her ribcage. It's got some similarities to—'

'Fortune teller, was she?' interrupts Tremberg, speaking fast. 'There was a case like that in Scunthorpe, years back. And if you're asking whether we're familiar with any other cases, let me ask you something first. Was there a Tarot card at the scene?'

'Tarot cards everywhere, Helen,' confirms Pharaoh. 'Enough to suggest she was giving a reading and somebody didn't like what the future had in store. Why?'

'SCAS, like you said. We don't get anywhere near enough officers taking the time to fill in the database correctly, but it's right up their alley.'

'What a thought,' says Pharaoh with a smile, pulling a pad and pen from her pocket. She puts the unlit cigarette to her mouth. Talks around it. 'There are injuries to the mouth. Somebody may have been trying to cut her tongue off, which implies she's talked about something she shouldn't have.'

'Perhaps,' says Tremberg. 'I remember the one in Scunthorpe pretty well. You'll have been down here at the time, swanning around with the Met, but my old sergeant, Ken Cullen – he used to talk about the injuries to test out the stomachs of the young PCs. She was Traveller stock, as I recall. Unsolved, if I remember rightly, but word was that two lads who owned a scrapyard out towards Doncaster had something to do with it. It was when Roper was boss of CID, so draw your own conclusion. And if you're asking if it has some similarities to other active cases, I can tell you that yes, it bloody does. Can I get back to you when I've gone and kicked some geeks in the shins?'

'The sooner the better,' says Pharaoh, drumming her fingers on the tabletop.

Tremberg seems about to say goodbye. Instead, she pauses, clearly taking her time with a memory. 'There was a girl,' she says. 'The case in Scunthorpe. A witness, at first. There were Traveller connections. Irish Traveller . . .'

Pharaoh gives a little grunt, confirming the unasked question. 'We'll be having a chat,' she says, pointedly. 'Once I know what I need to know.'

'Jesus, Trish. He's like a bloody great vacuum for trouble, isn't he?'

'Quick as you can please, Helen,' she says, and ends the call.

Pharaoh sits for a time, watching the rain. Occasionally her phone bleeps, as a report or an update drops into her inbox. McAvoy doesn't call. She sends an email to Wilma Bradley, asking for information on what happened to the men who were prime suspects in the Scunthorpe killing twelve years before. Pops outside for a cigarette, and smokes it with her face turned into the rain, defying the gale.

Eventually, she orders another coffee. Boz raises his eyebrows.

'Not a fucking word,' says Pharaoh, and returns to her seat. On the table, her phone is buzzing. It's the Grimsby CID office: direct line to DI Tony Blake. She has a vision of a thin, grey, bookish man, perfectly bald on top with a ring of yellow-grey hair starting just above his ears. He always makes Pharaoh think of an egg stopped halfway out of a chicken's cloaca.

'Tony,' she says, brightly. 'Tell me something good, please. I'm near the water and the only reason I haven't jumped in is because I haven't got enough money in my pockets to weigh me down . . .'

'Good and bad, boss,' says Blake, without preamble. 'Good news is, the missing urban explorer isn't missing any more.'

'No? Well that's—'

'Bad news is he's dead.'

'Oh for fuck's sake, Tony.'

'Body washed up at the nudist beach down Mablethorpe. You know the one.'

'Professionally speaking, yes . . .' says Pharaoh, through gritted teeth.

'Lincolnshire Police but they checked against missing persons. Not confirmed yet, but it's your missing anarchist.'

'His father's going to go to pieces,' says Pharaoh, closing her eyes. She wishes she could find the time to go and deliver the news personally. As senior officer, she hates having to delegate the awful duty to somebody else. As far as she's concerned, doing the horrible jobs is one of the duties that comes with seniority. 'Suspicious?'

'He's been in the water a few days. Hard to say whether the injuries were done before or after.'

'Any early indications?'

'Head wound, that much is clear. Poor sod, eh? No age to go.'

'Thanks, Tony,' says Pharaoh, and hangs up. She sips her

coffee, the caffeine starting to make her feel jittery and wired. She checks the phone again. 'Call me back, you bastard,' she mutters, grinding her teeth. 'It's going to be OK. Whatever she's done, or you've done, we can make it work. I'm on your bloody side . . .'

The phone bleeps again. Sophia, her daughter.

'Not the best time, love—' begins Pharaoh.

'Mum,' says Sophia, breathless, urgent. 'She said not to tell you, and I wouldn't normally, and I hate being put in these positions, but I know you'd never forgive me if I didn't, and it looks proper nasty, so I thought . . .'

Pharaoh changes her posture, her voice: becomes a mum. 'It's OK, sweetheart, whatever it is, I'm here for you—'

'Roisin's just dropped Lilah off with me. She said she had to get back home – barely spoke. Asked me to watch her and didn't say when she'd be back or what was going on. She'd been crying. And Lilah's barely talking. I think she needs a doctor. There's an awful wound on her hand and I think she's had a bump to the head as well. I mean, I can take her to the doctor but who do I say I am? And where's Aector? She seemed really scared, Mum, and I've never seen her scared before. She's like you – she does stuff and you'd never know she wasn't in control . . .'

The stool falls with a clatter as Pharaoh jumps up, pulling on her coat.

Out the door and into the rain, heart thudding, thoughts biting like flies.

'On my way . . .'

TWENTY-SIX

Twelve years ago

McAvoy winces, holding up a hand in a lazy salute, trying to shield his eye from the glare of the van's too-bright lights.

'Sorry about the hour . . .'

Stops himself. Squints. He can make out the glow of a lit cigarette, the rippling blackness of a figure, motionless by the van door.

'Excuse me, sir, I'm . . .'

He stops. Shivers. Feels so far out of his depth that he can't remember the shore. Stands damp and mute, watching the rain fall in hard diagonal streaks: a surge of silver necklaces plunging through the square of harsh yellow light. He's had the heater on in the car. He doesn't normally feel the cold, having grown up in an environment cold as revenge, but he isn't himself tonight. He's nervous. Jittery. Can't seem to get his hands to do what he wants them to. He's thinking of her. Of Roisin Teague. Of where she might be and what she may have done. His mind is a clutter of disparate images: past, present – even some scraps of things that are yet to come. He feels as though he's out of his body, looking down. He can't quite believe he's here, in this rotting fun fair, surrounded by great towers of rusting metal and fluorescent paints; a Poundland Mount Rushmore of grinning clowns and leering harlequins.

'Bit late, isn't it?'

The voice drifts across to McAvoy on a damp gust of wind. An accent, perhaps. A touch of the West Country to the vowels. He wonders which of the half-brothers he is addressing. Wonders, again, whether the signs declaring the presence of a guard dog are just for show.

'Humberside Police,' says McAvoy, trying again. 'I'm rather hoping to speak to Michael or Padua. Or both.'

'This would be official business, would it? In the middle of the night? On your own.'

There's scorn to the stranger's words – the suggestion that he's already caught him out in a lie. McAvoy stands still, wishing he had the strength of character to cross to the van and simply extend a hand. He knows himself to be good at calming down volatile situations and has always been good at calming down those ready for a fight, but such actions have always been cloaked in the officialdom of his uniform. He's done what the job has required. Here, now, he feels like a fraud.

'If we could perhaps have a chat . . .'

'If I could perhaps shoot you where you stand.'

This time there's no room for doubt. It's a direct threat; the tone of voice absolute. This is a man used to giving orders and having people do as instructed. This is a man quite willing to make good on a threat.

'My name is Aector McAvoy,' he says, allowing a little steel to enter his own voice. 'I'm here looking for a missing girl. Roisin Teague. I'm told you're family.'

There's silence, for a time. Rain falls on metal, on glass, upon the earth. McAvoy shifts his position as a chain of cold rain dribbles down his neck. His eyes have started to better make shapes from the complex slabs of darkness. He can just about make out the man who stands at the side of the big van. Can almost decipher the shape of the slumped, small figure in the passenger seat.

'You really a copper?'

'I promise,' says McAvoy, and for a moment he experiences a real surge of hope. He's made a connection. Stood his ground. Been firm but fair. This man will invite him to come in out of the rain. He will see the sincerity in McAvoy's eyes and decide he is a man to trust. He will allow him into his confidence and he will take him to where Roisin is safe and dry and blameless. And all will be well. He'll have done the right thing. He'll be a good man and a good police officer, and he'll have learned how to do so in perpetuity.

'A police constable, yes, and I'm sorry for the rather unorthodox circumstances, but it's really very important that we talk . . .'

The quality of the air seems to change. One moment, McAvoy's words are being whipped away like paper gulls. The next they collide with something solid: damp clothing, flesh, bone.

And then there is a face inches from his own. A man with a pale face and dark eyes and a putrid-smelling cigarette clamped between crooked white teeth: a gleaming smile of silver arcing down towards him from out of the wet black air.

McAvoy raises his hand to protect himself from the blow. Expects to feel metal slice through his skin like wire through rotten meat. Feels the thud of the other man's hand instead: fist and handle thumping against the bone of his wrist. Pain shoots up to his shoulder and his fingers burn as if encased in hot lead.

A blow to the gut now; fist striking him fast, hard, below the ribs. He feels his breath rush into the air, the tightness in his lungs, the sudden pain as the smaller, faster man slams his head

against his chin, once, twice, three times,. His feet slip on the
sodden earth and he grabs forward, both hands around his
attacker's head, holding himself up, eyes swivelling around,
desperately searching for the knife, kicking out, adrenaline
sprinting through him like flame.

A sharp, sudden pain in his belly: the slash hook carving a
smile into his stomach. He feels his strength leave him; hot blood
running onto his thighs. Clatters back, landing hard, the man on
top of him, pushing the bloody blade against his cheekbone,
pressing down, teeth bared, the metal touching bone; the pain a
white light; a scream of crimson agony.

McAvoy locks eyes with the man who is killing him. Wonders,
as the darkness rushes in, what people will say when he is found.
Wonders what will happen to Roisin. Whether there's been any
point to any of it. Whether Mum and Dad will argue about where
his ashes are to be scattered.

He thrusts his right hand up, his palm catching the other man
below the chin. His head snacks up like a lid on a hinge. Hits
him again with his muddied, bloodied left hand. Pushes him up
as if trapped beneath soggy timbers. Holds him, arms braced,
staring into his eyes and seeing nothing. No fear, no rage. Just
an endless blackness: two obsidian holes in the universe.

Then the roar. The throaty growl of thunder; of gravel churned
by spinning wheels. And then the van is smashing into the pair
of them and McAvoy is pushing himself into the soft earth, hands
to his face, trying to throw the other man clear, and all is just
metal and heat and tyres and sound.

And then the blessed blackness of oblivion.

Roisin Teague climbs down from the driver's seat. She's
groggy. Her mouth is dry and her head pounds as if full of
ungreased pistons. She walks unsteadily to where the figure lies,
sprawled in the mud and blood and glass. One leg is bent the
wrong way at the knee. Steam rises from his chest as if from
compost. There's blood all over his face and it is caved in where
the van struck him hard enough to crack the glass.

She turns back. Walks on jelly legs to the van. Crouches
down. Sees the big man sandwiched between the damp earth
and the rusting metal of the chassis. Smells blood and churned
earth.

A groan, suddenly. The shudder of waking into pain. The soft, rasping whisper.

'I'm a police officer . . . I'm looking for . . . looking . . .'

Roisin thrusts her hand under the van. Grabs a fistful of sodden coat, bloodied hair. Pulls at him as if he were sliding into the earth.

Watches as he raises his head, turns his face. Looks into her, as if reading words from her bones.

His face, a bloodied full moon; gouts of crimson spilling into one staring eye.

She raises her hands to her mouth. Inhales the scent of him; mud and earth and the iron reek of blood. Licks rain and blood from her lips: a gory communion; blood mingling on her tongue.

Breathes his name, as the eye starts to close. Stares into him with the ferocity of a wild animal defending her young.

'Aector . . .'

The eye turns dark. Closes.

'Aector. I'm here. You came for me. Saved me. Saved me again . . .'

A flicker of life; a sliver of eye, stark as the bone that winks through the trench in his cheek. A voice, half lost to the earth.

'Roisin . . .'

She reaches into the dark space beneath the van. Rummages past the soggy fabric, the ragged gash in his gut. Takes his big cold hand in her warm, soft fingers.

'Stay,' she whispers, worming her way under the van. 'Stay strong. I'll get help . . .'

She feels him squeeze her hand. Feels the bulk of him, the great mass of arms and back and shoulders, pressed against her own fragile skeleton. Wishes she could wrap him in strips of herself – bandage him, cosset him, in the twists of her own being.

Takes her other hand, and makes a blade of her fingers. Paws at the earth. Claws a great trench into the ground around them. Keeps going long after her fingers tear and her nails are pulled from her skin.

And all the while she sings, her lips at his ear, her prayer into his heart.

'You don't die. You can't die. You fight. You matter. You have a duty. You have my heart . . .'

TWENTY-SEVEN

Hessle Foreshore

McAvoy sits on the damp grass, his back pressed up against the peeling white paint and rotten wood of the little fishing boat. He has his back to the water. There's little sun today, but the shadow cast by the Humber Bridge bathes him in a cold, bitter darkness.

Home is a couple of hundred yards away, back down Cliff Road. He can't bring himself to be there alone. There are drops of Lilah's blood on the carpet. Roisin's blood on the wall. She punched the chimney breast until the skin was gone from her knuckles. A bruise was already forming on her forehead when she left; an ugly swollen patch of livid flesh. She hurt herself badly when Lilah came home. Had turned all her rage and fear and guilt upon herself and smacked her bleeding fist into her own temple until Lilah grabbed her hands and begged her to stop. Her questions came out in a torrent. Lilah, through the tears, through the pain, told her all she could. Told her about the man with the stick who'd risen from a pile of earth and leaves and dragged her brother into the earth.

'He was a monster,' said Lilah, over and over. 'He just appeared. And then he was squeezing Fin's throat with his stick, and I screamed, and tried to help, to fight him, but he pushed me down, and then his weight was on me and it all just went dark. And I woke up, like this. With this . . . what's he done, Mammy, where did he take Fin . . . where was Daddy – I screamed for him, and nobody came, nobody came . . .'

Roisin pressed her forehead to her daughter's as she slid her palm free of the nail. There was little blood. The pain was hot and intense, but the nail had passed between the tendons and caused no obvious damage. Roisin cleaned the wound. Dressed it. Wrapped a bandage around her palm and thumb. Checked her for other injuries. She complained of a sore throat; an ache at the back of her neck. A tingle in her fingers.

Only when her daughter's wounds were tended did she allow herself to go to pieces. Her son, her firstborn, her little prince. A bad man had come for him. Cromwell. The very devil. A man she thought was dead, and who had come for her boy because he was blood of the clan who had exacted such a terrible penance for his sins.

She and Lilah had run back to the scene. Scrabbled through the pile of leaves and dirt. Held one another, sobbing and desperate. Neither had spoken of calling the police. Both had known that an evil had entered their lives. Fin had been gathered up by something grotesque. He would be found, of that both were certain. But not before the spilling of blood.

McAvoy had pulled up just as they arrived home. White-faced, glaring through a haze of tears, he listened as his wife and daughter told him everything. Tears had tumbled down his cheeks as he looked at the wound on Lilah's palm. Something had died inside him as Roisin held his hands and looked up at him imploringly, her palms together as if in prayer, begging him to believe her. She'd known he was alive. She'd known he was free. She'd known they were at risk. And she hadn't told him, for fear of his thinking terrible things about her. And now Fin was missing, and another woman was dead, and it was all her fault, all her fucking fault . . .

McAvoy sits in the shelter of the little fishing boat, and thinks of his son. This is their favourite spot. Neither of them knows who the little vessel belongs to, but it's got a jolly look about it and they like climbing inside and pretending to be adventurers or pirates or spies.

Unthinking, McAvoy reaches out and rubs his hand against the peeling paint. Whispers, softly. It's not a prayer, not even a wish – it's an offer, made to whichever force or deity might care to listen.

Keep him safe. Keep him safe and you can have me. Whatever you want, I'll do. But protect him. Please . . .

He pushes his hair back from his face. Breathes in the salt and diesel of the water's edge; the wet grass and newly fallen leaves. He stares past the big square of overgrown grass to the dark smudge of woodland that becomes the country park. Remembers the pain of metal cutting through flesh, through bone. Thinks of the man who

survived so many years below ground, and who climbed free to
wreak vengeance on the blood of Papa Teague.

A pain in his hand. He looks down. He'd forgotten he was
holding the mobile phone. Has squeezed it so hard that the glass
has cracked and a shard had punctured his skin. He stares at it.
Leaves it. Watches a tiny trickle of red snake down to his wrist.

He thinks again of Valentine's voice: the sheer bloody sorrow
and regret.

'I can be there by the morning,' he'd said. 'We all can. Turn
over every rock and stone until we find him. Say the word, Aector,
I'll talk to Daddy, whatever you need . . .'

McAvoy had ended the call without a word. Had told Roisin
to take Lilah somewhere safe. Hadn't been able to take his hands
from his pockets to return her embraces – her desperate clutches
at his clothes, his skin. Hadn't been able to look at her. Stared,
wordlessly, at the water while she threw clothes in a bag and
begged him to tell her what he was going to do. She'd begged
him to call Trish. To ring Helen Tremberg in London. To use
every single person who owes him a kindness to do whatever
was in their power to find their boy. She'd begun talking in her
own native tongue: dark prayers and promises and vows of bloody
vengeance. He'd kept himself still and straight-backed until she
bundled Lilah out the door and into his car. She'd hesitated,
desperate to come back in and search his eyes for some sign of
hope; of love. At the window, he'd given the tiniest shake of his
head. And then she was gone. Only then did he allow himself
to disintegrate. He came apart as if made of tiny pixels: a portrait
in pointillism. Just lay on the living-room floor, wrapped up in
his coat, and thought about his son. Reached out with his mind,
trying to project words of comfort, or promise, into the air.
Begged for strength. It took every ounce of energy he had to get
himself upright.

He pulls his phone from his pocket. Looks at all the missed
calls. Plays back the most recent message from the assistant chief
constable.

'Sergeant, I'm expecting you here at eleven thirty for receipt
of the Osman warning and I'm concerned that neither yourself
nor Trish have returned my numerous calls. It's a matter of great
importance and I . . .'

He ends the call. He's not time for bureaucratic box-ticking nonsense now. He's a police officer – there's always a threat to his life.

'Aector, is that you skulking . . .'

McAvoy doesn't register the voice. Can barely drag himself out of the pit of his thoughts. Doesn't look up until Lucas Barrington is standing beside him, a puzzled look on his face.

McAvoy tries to draw the right file from his memory. He's the coxswain of the lifeboat. There have been break-ins. He wants McAvoy to do something about it.

'Lucas,' he says, though his throat is so dry it comes out as a croak.

'Thought that was you,' he says, failing to read the mood. 'I often see your lad sitting there, your little girl doing the whole *Titanic* thing at the stern . . .'

'Just taking a moment,' says McAvoy, rubbing his hands across his cheeks. He leaves a smear of blood in his beard. Catches the scent of it: iron and old keys.

'Were you popping into the boatshed? Bit of good news, for a change. Took a bit of advice after the last time – being pro-active, and all that . . .'

McAvoy tunes him out. Climbs unsteadily to his feet. He's soaked through. There are blades of grass and dead leaves stuck to his coat. He's taken his tie off. Can't seem to breathe with it on.

The other man takes a step back as McAvoy hauls himself upright. Stops talking. McAvoy is about to offer some half-hearted platitude about getting to it when he has a chance, but he can't even find the enthusiasm for the lie. His son is missing. If he tells his colleagues, they'll know what Roisin was a party to years before. They'll know that he covered up her family's involvement in several deaths. He is willing to take whatever punishment comes his way, but he needs to get his son back first. Needs to make sure that those he loves are never again placed in harm's way. He doesn't think he will be a police officer for very much longer and he won't use the precious hours that he has left on trying to catch a burglar.

'Look, Lucas, my brain's all over the place, I don't . . .'

McAvoy stares past the younger man's pinched, puzzled face. Parked up outside the row of white houses, is a Ford Cougar.

2002. Bottle green. It's the same vehicle that he glimpsed in the rear-view mirror on the way out to Sunk Island. The same vehicle that nosed backwards down the track towards Stone Creek. He narrows his eyes. The fog lights are on, glinting yellowy through the cold and murky air.

'Walk with me,' says McAvoy, quietly. 'At my side. Back towards my house.'

'Sorry, what's happening?' asks the coxswain, confused. 'Look, I just wanted to tell you that . . .'

McAvoy turns him around, roughly. Takes a hold of his sleeve. Half drags him along as he walks briskly back towards his house, trying to look casual while keeping his eye on the parked vehicle.

'Sorry, sergeant, what the bloody hell do you think you're doing?'

'Quicker,' says McAvoy. 'Don't let him know we've noticed, don't let him know . . .'

'Who? Noticed what . . .?'

When they're forty yards from the vehicle, McAvoy watches in horror as the rear lights flare into life. He hears the sound of an engine revving. The sudden squeal of tyres on a damp road.

'No,' says McAvoy, and pushes the coxswain to the ground, listening to a riot of curses as he tumbles into the wet grass.

McAvoy sprints forward as the vehicle shrieks backwards around the corner, smoke and steam swirling up from the exhaust and the threadbare rubber. His boots hammer down as he sprints, arms pumping like pistons, to the very rear of the vehicle. Lunges forward, his fingertips touching cold metal. Clatters forward, hitting the road hard. Scrabbles upwards just as the driver finds the right gear and lurches forward.

McAvoy throws himself forward, grabbing for the wing mirror. Feels his feet momentarily leave the ground. The window is partway open and through the space in the tinted glass he sees a face. Fifties. Swarthy. Dark hair and thick lips.

A thud: the crunch of metal, and then McAvoy is slamming back onto the road, rolling and tumbling on the wet tarmac, feeling the skin across his shoulders tear; thumping his head. He's up again in moments. Stumbles to where the car has come to a stop, the bonnet wedged into the back of a parked Audi.

McAvoy doesn't even think. Doesn't slow his walk. Pulls the

sleeve of his coat over his right hand and smashes his fist into the window with all the strength he can muster. The glass shatters. Skin tears as his fist carries in through into the car; jagged glass clawing at his skin. He feels nothing. Closes his hand around the shirt front of the driver and yanks him forward towards the shattered glass. His head smacks into the broken window. Glass falls like hard snow.

'Where is he?' hisses McAvoy, grabbing the driver through the open window, teeth locked, spit frothing. 'Where's my son?'

'Gardai!' screams the driver, through bloodied lips. 'I'm a guard!'

'I don't give a fuck what you are!' screams McAvoy, drawing back his bloodied hand.

'A guard. A police officer! Please, I'm a police officer!'

McAvoy stops. Feels the strength leave him. Feels the blood upon his face. Watches the crimson trickles cascade down his arm and over his hands, dripping to the floor as if he were squeezing fruit.

'You're Gardai . . .' he mumbles. Leaning against the car. 'You were following me. You started to drive away . . .'

On the floor, the officer spits blood. Drags himself up. 'I was sent to warn you,' he says, groggily. 'I'm Daragh Kincaid. I'm here to warn you that he's coming.'

McAvoy closes his eyes. Shakes his head.

'You're too fucking late.'

TWENTY-EIGHT

Pharaoh glances at the clock as she barrels through reception. It's 11.04 a.m. She's been awake for not far off eight hours. She can't help thinking that she, and the world in general, would have been better served if she'd taken an extra sleeping pill and ignored the ringing phone.

'Message for you, superintendent!' shouts the desk sergeant, as she clatters up the stairs.

She stops, hair tangled in her earrings, fingerprints on her sunglasses, lipstick smudge on the lid of her coffee cup, papers spilling from the bag she carries like a cudgel. Gives him a look that implies she is willing to do serious prison time rather than go back down the stairs.

'Burn it, would you, Frank?'

She gets a grin in return. The reception area of HQ is thoroughly modern, but the desk sergeant is decidedly old school. There are coffee shops, gyms and chain stores within five minutes of the front door, but she admires people who still bring a flask to work and who save a few quid each day by knocking together a meat-paste sandwich at home. He's a bit of an anachronism here, in the shiny openness of Clough Road nick. It feels more like a hotel than a police station. No cigarette smoke in the air, no takeaway food or damp carpet or spilled celebratory ale. It's hard to be a copper in a building like this. It makes her feel old. Obsolete. Past her prime.

She boots the double doors at the top of the flight of stairs. Pushes through into the corridor. Stomps her way down to the little office at the far end of the hall. The PA she shares with two other senior officers has an office larger than she does. Pharaoh's only got an office here because she's been strong-armed into accepting overall responsibility for Major Crime across the Humberside Police region. She's been head of the Serious and Organized Unit for eight years, and has fought tooth and claw to stop it being swallowed up by the bigger body of CID. She fancies it's a losing battle. Do more with less has been the mantra of every chief constable she's served under, and there's no doubt her elite little unit is expensive. During her last appraisal she was told that there was some ill-feeling among the larger portion of CID: accusations that her team of officers were cherry-picking the best jobs and that she showed undue favouritism to her unit in particular, and her sergeant in particular. She'd lost her temper. Challenged the ACC to find anybody who had given more to the job than McAvoy. She'd done such a good job of explaining his worth that the ACC had suggested putting him in charge of cold cases and raising him to the rank of inspector. Pharaoh had performed a swift U-turn after that. She liked him where he was.

'Boss!'

Andy Daniells is hustling his way down the corridor, laptop under one arm and a sheaf of papers in his fist. Pharaoh notices, with a motherly gaze, that he has a chocolate smear on his shirt.

'If he sees you've been eating that he'll have your guts for garters,' Pharaoh says with a smile, crossing to her desk and siting down heavily at her cluttered desk. She stands up again immediately and opens the window. Plonks herself back down on the seat and indicates to Daniells that he should remove the pile of papers on the chair opposite and endeavour to make himself comfortable.

'Any sign of him?' he asks, licking his finger and turning the chocolate stain into a smear.

'Doing his thing,' mutters Pharaoh, hoping this will be enough to stave off further enquiries. She opens the bottom drawer of her desk and removes a plastic bottle. A hard white straw has been belted into an aperture at the neck. It looks a lot like a very simplistic bong. She rummages in her bag, finds her cigarettes. Lights up. When her lungs are full, she blows the smoke down the tube and into the bottle, where it swirls, briefly, like the ghost of a nightmare. She keeps the pad of her finger pressed over the straw. When she first started in the police, she truly never would have believed that the life of a smoker would come to this.

'She was seeing somebody,' says Daniells, flicking through the papers. 'Nothing serious. Chap called Keith Bennett. Forty-four. Lives in one of the caravans at Patrington Haven. An on-off thing, apparently. Sophie Kirkland is with him now. Says he was shocked but not emotional. Sometimes it takes a while to sink in, doesn't it? Anyway, hasn't heard from her for over a week, but that's not unusual apparently. He'd sent her a couple of messages but when she didn't reply he didn't push it. Hadn't even started to worry.'

'And the daughter?'

'Same,' says Daniells. 'Grant broke the news. Again, she says Mum valued her privacy and was pretty independent. Liked her own space. She had Facebook friends. Very busy on different forums and didn't seem lonely. Loved her cats.'

'Feeling was mutual, I'm sure,' says Pharaoh, crossing to the window and freeing the captive smoke into the cold air. She turns back to Daniells. 'I can see you've got something else to tell me, Andy. Don't build up your part, son, just spit.'

Daniells smiles, wide. 'Found this,' he says, handing across a printout of a newspaper report from the *Hexham Courant*, dated

April, 2015. The headline reads: VILLAGE STUNNED BY
'SENSELESS' SLAYING. 'Rachael Gladstone,' says Daniells,
while Pharaoh scans the article. 'Aged fifty-eight. Lived in a tiny
little place in Weardale, which I've never even heard of. Village
called Edmundbyers. Nearest place of any size is Consett, but it
really is the middle of nowhere. She was attacked in her own home.
Little cottage on the outskirts of the village. Article doesn't say the
cause of death but I've requested the case files from the locals.'

'Says "stabbed to death" here,' mutters Pharaoh, finishing
the article. She swallows, a nasty taste in her mouth. Scowls.

'You saw?' asks Daniells, cautiously.

'Yes, Andy, I've mastered the art of reading, thank you.'

'Sorry, boss.'

She chews on her lower lip. Looks at the picture that accom-
panies the article. Small, dark-haired, bright blue eyes full of
sparkle. Considers Rachael Gladstone and mulls over the snippets
of information offered up by the article. She was a mother of
three grown-up children. She worked in child protection, prior
to early retirement. Was active in the community. And she was
a fortune teller. Attended local spiritual fairs, offering Tarot readings and palmistry. Offered phone consultations and occasionally
performed readings from her home. At the time of the newspaper
article, police were asking witnesses to come forward.

'Follow-up,' says Daniells, handing her another piece of paper.
The photo is the same. 'CID spokesman repeating the call for
witnesses. It happened the Friday before – some time between
eleven a.m. and four p.m. Broad daylight. That's why the copper
said—'

'That the assailant would have been covered in blood, yes,'
reads Pharaoh. She hands the paper back to Daniells. 'Helen is
pulling some strings for me,' she says, briskly. 'She can liaise
with you. Call her up and tell her about this, see if it matches
the other active investigations . . .'

Daniells nods. 'She knows about the Scunthorpe one, yes?'

Pharaoh glares at him. 'Yes, Andy. And yes, you are absolutely
right to be thinking what you're thinking. But for now, let's keep
it all as "thoughts" rather than "words", yes?'

Daniells nods. Pulls a face that says 'rather you than me'.

'Anything else?' she asks, tiredness in her voice. She'd like a nap, and a cuddle, and maybe a cheeseburger washed down with a Pinot Noir.

'House was going up for rent,' says Daniells, looking at his notes. 'Sign wasn't up yet but according to her daughter the cold was getting too much for her. Gave her notice a week or so before. She had arthritis. Didn't have anywhere lined up to go but her search history shows retirement villages in Spain and Portugal, and also a couple of cheap properties in Bulgaria.'

'Can't say I blame her,' muses Pharaoh. 'You spoke to the estate agent then?'

'One of the office staff. Offices at Withernsea.'

Pharaoh puts out her hand for Daniells' sheaf of papers. Takes them and stuffs them in her bag. On her desk, the phone rings. She picks it up like a sharpshooter going for their gun. 'Hector?'

'Trish, you're due with the assistant chief . . .'

'Aw bollocks,' mutters Pharaoh, and slams the phone down in its cradle. Looks up at Daniells. 'If I were to just walk out, and go home, and email my resignation letter, do you think people would accept it and leave me alone?'

Daniells smiles. 'You'd miss us. And we need you.'

'You're a tonic,' says Pharaoh, wistfully. 'Trouble is, you're not gin.'

The phone rings again. Daniells picks it up this time. 'I'm sorry, this is a terrible line, I'm afraid the detective superintendent just stepped out . . .'

'You're a good lad,' says Pharaoh sitting back in her chair and closing her eyes.

'Sorry, boss, it's reception.'

'Go on,' mutters Pharaoh, opening an eye.

Daniells winces in advance. 'There's a lady called Roisin to see you.'

A slow smile spreads across Pharaoh's face. She cracks her knuckles.

'Tell them I'll be right down.'

TWENTY-NINE

Twelve years ago

McAvoy feels the song beneath him. Feels the warmth of it; the soft, insistent tug. He finds himself bobbing in black water, the push-and-pull of small, silver-tipped waves turning him, carrying him. He lets himself be borne aloft. Has no strength with which to fight. There is just the dizziness, the empty, bled-white sensation of being steered by another's will.

Words, now. The gentle, siren melody, soft as rabbit fur. Notes, ascending, a lilting glissando, breathy against his neck.

Pain. Tightness, in his cheek; frailty in his bones. The all-over ache of fever.

Delirium. Moments of nothingness, then the heat and colour and shades and shapes; voices raised and hushed; soft pressure upon his brow, his neck, his lips

The song. At his ear. At his throat. The sensation of nearness. Of warm skin upon his own.

> 'Oh, won't you come along with me a small piece of
>   the road
> To see my father's dwelling and place of abode?'
> He knew by her look and her languishing eye
> He was the young man she had cherished most high . . .

Closes his eyes. Falls back into the warm, safe dark.

Jerks awake.

Sees *her*.

Dark. Beautiful. Eyes closed. Curled up beside him, clasped hands a cushion beneath her cheek. Her lips pout a little as she sleeps. Her breath, when it comes, is warm against his mouth.

He looks down the length of himself. There is a bandage around his stomach. Beneath a white sheet and a colourful woollen blanket, he is naked. She, atop the sheets, is wrapped in a black, embroidered shawl.

He shifts position, painfully. Hears a long, drawn-out creak, and the earth seems to shift beneath him. He jerks his head around, trying to make sense of his surroundings. He's laid out on a thin mattress which seems unfeasibly high from the ground, but which is nevertheless close to the ceiling of a rickety wooden ceiling. The light comes from a flickering oil lamp, throwing golden light onto green cupboards patterned with flowers. Squinting, he can make out a small window framed by red curtains, held back by a gold tasselled cord. In the shadow darkness beyond the edge of the bed, he can make out a black stove, its glass window glowing red. A copper kettle throws muddled reflections of green tiles and ceramic ornaments; plates stacked in racks along one wall; a small transistor radio, aerial extended, hangs in a net above a tiny pull-down table. There is a sensation of cosiness, comfort; warmth.

'Morning, handsome . . .'

And she is looking at him. Reaching out and stroking the ruched fabric of his face. Her eyes reflect his. He sees the tiny stitches, seaming the edge of an unfamiliar beard.

'I heard singing,' he says, his voice a croak.

She smiles. Looks into him. He feels no urge to look away. Feels as though this place, this now, is somewhere he doesn't wish to spoil. He wonders whether he is dreaming. Whether he's in a hospital bed somewhere, sedated and hallucinating. He has no wish to make sense of this. Wants to just lie here, and look at her, and hear her song.

'It's an old one. You were upset in your sleep. It seemed to soothe you.'

McAvoy licks his dry lips. His head is pounding. He takes a breath. Catches that scent. She smells of the outdoors. Or the air after a storm. Of honeysuckle and elderflower and clothes dried in damp rooms. She pushes herself up and her hair shimmers, an inky waterfall cascading onto her bare shoulder.

Memories rush in: wine poured from an amphora into an open throat. Hears himself gasp as his mind floods with pictures. There had been a man. He had tried to kill him. An impact. The sensation of falling, of pain. And then hands in his, and the blackness of oblivion. He screws up his face, the stitches in his cheek puckering painfully. He'd been seeking Roisin Teague. There had been a death. A murder. She was in trouble; had gone to family, and he had bumbled along after . . .

He squirms upright, pain gripping him in a dozen places at once. 'Roisin,' he says, and he cannot quite believe that she is here. That she is looking at him as if they are already lovers. A great tendril of guilt climbs up his throat, causing him to gag. He pulls the covers around himself, gasping for air. Pushes himself back against the headboard as if trying to avoid a rising tide. He thinks again of the hands upon him. The soft warmth. The song that brought him back to consciousness on inky black swells of pure pleasure.

'What happened?' he begs, even as she smiles at him, the corners of her mouth jerking upwards, tongue wetting her lips. 'The man . . . you . . . I mean, where . . .?'

'Aector,' she says, and takes such delight in saying it, she repeats the word. She reaches forward to put her hand upon his cheek. Startled, he jerks back, hitting his head on the brass birdcage that dangles above the bed.

'Are you OK?' he asks, his head spinning. 'I went to see your cousins, well . . . sort of cousins . . . I saw your picture – there were people looking for you . . . a feud, something terrible happened . . . the lady, and you were there, and they thought . . .' He stops himself, aware he is gabbling. 'Where am I?' he asks, daring to meet her eye.

'Drink, Aector,' she says, turning onto her side and reaching out one bare, tanned arm to grasp a beaker. She turns back, her eyes seeking his. Tips it to his lips. 'It'll help.'

He tastes honey. Cinnamon. Something deeper. Earthier. Something that warms him, spreading out from his stomach like molten gold.

Already he yearns to sleep – to drift back into that safe, dark place. He has too many questions. Too much pain.

'He's dead,' says Roisin, quietly. 'The man who killed Eva-Jayne. He hurt the half-brothers too, but bugger them because they drugged me and would have sold me to the Heldens. He'd have done to me what he did to Eva-Jayne if you hadn't turned up. You fought him. I drove the van at him when I saw what was

happening. You'd already been hurt. I managed to get you out.
Phoned Daddy's man. They came. Helped me with you. You
scared me. But I looked after you. Took care of you. Sang to
you . . .'

'How long?' begs McAvoy, scratching at his beard.

'Six days, now.'

'And the man. Cromwell . . .'

Roisin looks apologetic. 'Daddy's man took care of him. The
brothers too. They're in the ground.'

McAvoy screws up his eyes. 'But there's an ongoing investigation . . . a murder enquiry . . . people will be looking for
me . . .'

Roisin shakes her head. 'I've been to the station. Made a
statement about what I saw. They're happy with it all. Phoned
your station and said you'd had a family emergency and wouldn't
be in for a few days. Nobody seemed concerned.'

McAvoy's face twists in anguish. He looks round, not quite
believing where he is, who he's with, what he's being expected to
accept. 'And the feud?' he asks. 'Are you safe? Your family? The
Heldens . . .?'

'They were disgusted that their man would go for family. Do
the things he did to Eva-Jayne. What he was willing to do to
me. The man was a fecking monster. They should never have let
him out of his cage. Daddy and the boys have come to an agree-
ment. It's OK. Look on YouTube, you'll see them all preaching
peace and sharing fecking cigars.'

McAvoy feels the warmth of the honey-liquid seeping through
him. His thoughts are heavy, his limbs barely responding to his
command. And yet the nearness of her, the warmth of her. He
feels enchanted; spellbound.

'Roisin,' he begins.

She puts her fingers to his lips. Kisses his cheek. His eyelids.
The tip of his nose. Kisses his mouth, warmly, wetly. Her tongue
snakes over his pained, cracked lips. Finds his. Smiles into his
mouth. Sings.

'No, we can't . . .'

'We already have.'

She lifts the covers. Climbs in beside him, still wrapped in
the shawl. Feels her reach up and touch the dark smudge of

stubble upon his face. Raises his hand and encases her wrist, gently bringing her fingers to his eyeline. The skin is crusted, swollen; the nails missing, as if pulled out by pincers. Without planning to, a surprise even to himself, he puts the fingertips to his lips. Kisses them, softly, one at a time. Looks down at her, curled inside the great plaited top of his arm, looking up at him with that bright-eyed, faraway look. He feels a newness inside himself; a pressure in his chest that feels like a living thing: something fragile and perfect and bigger than any sensation he has ever known.

Her lips upon his. His upon hers.

'I don't want to go anywhere,' she whispers, against his skin. 'I want to be with you. Always with you . . .'

'Your people,' he says, as her song floods him; as he runs his hands through the mane of hair and holds it in his fingers as if enchanted. 'My life . . . your life . . . I'm a police officer, you're a Traveller . . .'

'You've saved me twice. Daddy would build you a statue made of gold . . .'

'You saved me, Roisin. You don't need saving. And you're so young. Too young. Don't saddle yourself to somebody . . . not now, you can be anything . . .'

'I still can. But I can be beside you.'

'Roisin, we don't know each other . . .'

'And yet you love me. I know you do.'

'Roisin . . .'

'Roisin McAvoy,' she says, smiling wide. She nips his lip with her teeth. Strokes her fingers along the line of his chin. Puts her hands in his hair. 'Say it for me. Say it, please . . .'

The smile is fleeing: an animal darting out on a country road. 'I feel like I'm going mad. This doesn't happen. Not to real people. Not to me . . .'

'Say it . . .'

'Will you marry . . .'

'Of course I fecking will.'

THIRTY

'You've nothing stronger have you?' asks Constable Garda Daragh Kincaid, taking the mug of tea in a shaking hand. He's a swarthy sort, thick lips, leathery skin, dark eyebrows that meet in the middle when he's asking a question. He looks as though he needs to shave himself again within twenty minutes of putting his razor away.

'No,' says McAvoy, bluntly.

'My nerves,' he adds, as the tea sloshes over the lip of the cup. 'And by Christ, my fecking head.'

McAvoy feels nothing. No whiff of sympathy, no spark of compassion. Just glares at the guard as he raises the mug to his mouth and then curses as he scalds his split lip.

'I'll just be pottering,' says Barrington, quietly. 'Outside, if you need me . . .'

It was Barrington who suggested they adjourn to the boathouse. Barrington who gently coerced the two big, bleeding men off the street and down Cliff Road and behind the metal shutters and red brick of the lifeboat station. Barrington who led them into the kitchen and made tea and offered both men a damp washcloth and a mirror.

'Get yourself right, then tell me everything,' says McAvoy.

The guard nods. Wraps both big meaty hands around the mug. 'By Christ but you scared me,' he says, offering a weak smile. 'Always thought I was good at surveillance. Twenty-three years a guard! What was it? When did you . . .?'

'I used to have a Ford Cougar,' growls McAvoy, impatient. 'Now, why did you drive off? Why were you following me? I swear, if you're wasting my time when I should be out searching . . .'

Kincaid pats at the air. Takes a breath. 'There's a Threat to Life notice being delivered through the official channels,' he says, his voice pure Dublin. 'Last I heard, you still hadn't signed for it.'

'I've been busy,' mutters McAvoy. Angrily, he snatches up his own mug of tea. Takes a sip. Scowls. It's not sweet enough.

'You'll be regretting that, if I'm any judge,' says Kincaid, sympathetically. 'I was at your crime scene this morning. Bad business.'

'I saw you,' mutters McAvoy, leaning back against the wooden counter and staring into his mug as if it might contain answers.

'Similarities to a certain case,' says Kincaid, smiling. 'Bringing back memories, I shouldn't wonder.'

McAvoy is too angry to blush. Too angry to offer an explanation. 'Dymphna Lowell,' he says, flatly.

'There's a name from the past,' says Kincaid, still smiling. 'Bet you wish you didn't know it, eh? Brought you nowt but trouble.'

McAvoy doesn't reply. Just glares at Kincaid until he looks away.

'Your wife,' he says, with something close to sympathy. 'A strong woman, I've no doubt. Worth all the heartache, I'm sure. But that family . . .'

'My family too,' says McAvoy, loyally. 'I don't want to hear any of your prejudices, Constable Kincaid.'

Kincaid smiles at that. 'By Christ but you're not like I imagined you! Scared of his own shadow but fierce when he's riled – that's what your father-in-law calls you. You do know that he mentions you a lot, don't you? Sweetens business deals, offers incentives, gets away with murder because he's got a highly decorated English policeman on his payroll.'

'Scottish,' corrects McAvoy. 'And no, I don't know that.'

'I'm with the Gardai,' says Kincaid, as some colour returns to his cheeks. 'A place where you have friends, it seems.'

'This way you have of talking . . .' growls McAvoy. 'It's grating on me. Tell me what you came here to say or I'm going.'

'There's people who know your name, that's what I'm saying,' snaps Kincaid, looking put upon. 'You did a good thing when you went to America. Helped make sure a popular man came home alive.'

'Brishen Ayres?'

'Well it wouldn't be Valentine Teague, would it?'

'Valentine's got a good heart,' says McAvoy, wrapping his

arms around himself. He feels cold, as though chill water has seeped into his skin.

'The Heldens and the Teagues have been fighting for years,' says Kincaid, finishing his drink. 'That's normal. The truces don't last long. We don't tend to get involved unless civilians are hurt, or if there's a camera nearby that brings it to the public eye. Nobody thanks us for getting too involved in Tinker scuffles.'

'Don't say that word,' snaps McAvoy. 'Ever.'

'Fine. Traveller. Pavee. Whatever. The scraps don't matter. What matters is their wholesale illegal acts. The smuggling. The armed robberies. The drugs.'

'They're not involved in drugs,' says McAvoy, automatically.

'Bet they're not involved in guns either,' says Kincaid with a smile. 'But look, Papa Teague knows the score. He takes risks and if he's caught he does his time. He lives as he chooses. He doesn't ask us for special treatment and he'd never mention your name in a police interview or in court. But we've got intelligence on him – a file as thick as your arm. And he'll be going away, sergeant. I can promise you that. He put a bullet in the head of one of the top men in the Helden family. And once he's inside, I very much doubt he'll survive to finish his sentence. I'd advise your wife to buy a mourning dress. I don't say that with any malice – I'm just outlining things as they stand.'

McAvoy looks down at the floor. There are shards of glass on the hems of his trousers and the laces of his boots. He brushes at them. Cuts his fingers. Sucks them and tastes blood. Thinks of Papa Teague and wonders whether he'll be welcome at the funeral. Whether he'll grieve for the man for whom he has a solid feeling of respect. He knows his father-in-law to be a criminal and former convict, but he takes care of his family. He's loyal. He loves fiercely. He'd die before letting harm come to those who matter to him. He's a good man, in his way.

'Why are you here, Kincaid?' asks McAvoy, wearily. 'My son,' he says again, and hot pincers grab at his throat. 'Fin.'

'We thought you were the target,' says Kincaid, apologetically. 'My inspector is at your HQ waiting to serve the TTL notice. I saw the sense in tagging along and keeping a watchful eye. Call it professional courtesy.'

'You mean you didn't know if I was somebody to be trusted,' says McAvoy, teeth clenched.

'Aye, that too. Look, sergeant, I'm part of a unit that's investigating a string of murders committed between 1996 and 2008. Nine, in total. All people involved in the drugs trade, arms trade or having recently fallen foul of somebody with deep pockets. All professional hits.'

McAvoy swallows, his throat agony. 'And?'

'And I wouldn't advise you to play poker with a blush like that. You know exactly who I'm referring to, and if you want to see your boy I suggest you admit it.'

McAvoy snaps his head up, eyes like the barrel of a gun. 'What did you say to me?'

'His name is Aeron Slevin,' says Kincaid, looking at McAvoy for any sign of recognition. 'Story goes, he was born in a hospital. Bernie's. You might have heard of it. Horror movie of a place. Whoever his real mammy was, he was raised by Shonagh and Gideon Slevin. Settled Tinkers . . . sorry, Travellers . . . gunsmiths. Used to do their best work for the IRA but weren't fussy about taking on other contracts. Young Aeron was about as well-adjusted as you'd expect given his start in life. Welfare people only ever went out to the house once – great ugly barn of a place out on the islands. Found a boy with incredible intelligence, but emotionally stunted. Didn't like touching. Parents did their best by him but he was broken from the beginning. Investigative, too. An enquiring mind. Loved nothing more than capturing the seabirds and seeing how long he could keep them alive. Plucked their feathers, clipped their wings, blinded them . . .'

'Stop,' hisses McAvoy.

'Grew up to be a very dangerous man. And once he proved himself useful, he became the person that you set upon your enemies, if you could afford him.'

Despite his best efforts, McAvoy thinks of the moment, a dozen years before, when the strong, dark-eyed man had knocked him to the ground and pushed a slash hook through his skin and touched bone. Thinks of the moment when the van struck him, and the way he came apart as if made of damp cardboard. He was dead. Even now, he cannot believe the man who fought him, who came for Roisin and killed Eva-Jayne Puck; he cannot quite believe he is alive. Alive, and in possession of his son.

'Last time the Teagues and the Heldens fell out, the Heldens broke the bank to put an end to it. Set him on their enemies . . .'

'Eva-Jayne,' mumbles McAvoy. 'Roisin.'

'Depends what you believe,' answers Kincaid with a smile. 'There are those who still say your wife killed her auntie. Don't shoot the messenger, sergeant, it's true. Heldens swear blind they never sent their man until after she was already dead. They got a call from two half-brothers from the locality, promising to hand-deliver Roisin Teague. Pure luck of the Irish that their man was already on the mainland.'

McAvoy shakes his head. 'She saw him. Saw him doing those things to her aunt.'

Kincaid shrugs. 'All sounds a bit vague to me. Bet you never pushed it, did you? After you got yourself loved up, I bet you swallowed whatever she gave you.' He grins, foully. 'Bet she did too . . .'

McAvoy is across the space between them in a heartbeat, his fists closing on the scruffs of the other man's shirt, lifting him off the ground. Furious, he pushes his forehead against the other man's, feels him squirm and writhe in his grasp. 'What did you say? What did you fucking say?'

'Listen,' says Kincaid, desperately. 'Just listen . . .'

Daddy, that's not my life now. I don't want to be involved. I don't let myself think about it – I've talked myself into believing what you told me . . .

McAvoy drops him. Hears his wife's voice: small, far-away, but unmistakable.

Jaysus, whatever you did, you know I'll never tell a soul. They can send whoever they like. What you did to him, where you put him – I know it was the right thing to do. I'd have torn the skin from his bones if it were me . . .

McAvoy shakes his head. 'No. No, you've done something.'

'We've had traces on their phones for months. Got three men in their organization. Got two Heldens wearing wires for us. And we've got him.'

'Him?'

'Aeron. The one they call Cromwell. Who do you think got

him out of the ground? Two years he did under there. Flood almost did him in. Roof collapsed, earth caved in, but he clawed himself out. Walked miles, mud-soaked, newborn. Local Garda picked him up. Prints matched. Several open cases, on the books of my little team. We kept it all silent as the grave. We had it on good authority he was dead, and there's no better asset to have on your side than a ghost, is there? We thought we could flip him. Offer a deal and get him to testify on the people who paid him to pull the trigger.'

McAvoy pushes his hands through his hair. 'He wouldn't break?'

'Gave us just enough for us to get him well. To take care of him. To get him his medical treatment and feed him up and get him what he wanted. As soon as it came to the formal stuff, he gave us the slip.'

'The slip? What do you mean?'

Kincaid looks pained. 'We think he had help. But the safe house wasn't as safe as we thought. Left two bodies and a Tarot card.'

McAvoy shakes his head. 'How long ago?'

'This was '05. We have intelligence that he spent time abroad, killing in Eastern Europe.'

'So why come after the Teagues now? Why come after Fin? Why the fortune tellers?'

Kincaid busies himself with his phone. Finds the right recording.

'. . . the devil doesn't forget. He takes you when you're most comfortable – when you're fat and drunk and holding your loved ones close. That's when he reminds you what you owe and reaches into your heart and rips out your soul. Holds the faces of your loved ones up in front of your eyes and rips their flesh like paper. Goes to work on you until you don't know whether you're in Hell or somewhere worse, and you're just a scream, boy – just a fucking scream that echoes forever. You've got too comfortable. And I'm on my way to meet Satan. Seems only right I should bring some company . . .'

'Jesus,' mutters McAvoy.

'He'll do it too,' says Kincaid. '"Hit him where it hurts the most. Nothing matters to Teague more than family".'

McAvoy rolls his thoughts around, trying to think like a police officer. 'You have him,' he says, at last. 'You've got him in custody.'

Kincaid nods. 'Partly for his own protection. He can't do what Aeron wants because he's on suicide watch. And he can't get a message to his kin. If it weren't for his bellyaching about his police officer son-in-law – his blood over the water – we wouldn't have had to institute a TTL. I'm not saying we were in two minds, because that would suggest we're proper bastards, but suffice to say there were some dissenting voices. An operation like this, it's easy to fuck it up. Thankfully, as I say, you've got friends.'

McAvoy rubs his forehead, smearing blood on his brow as if anointing himself for violence. 'So he's here. You know where he is. Where Fin is . . .'

Kincaid holds up his hands, palms towards the heavens. 'I think I've given you quite a lot, matey. Time for something in return.'

'No,' says McAvoy, shaking his head. 'You don't barter with my boy's life. Tell me what you know.'

'He's here,' says Kincaid, slowly, considering his options. 'Mobile phone traced to this locality.' He looks around him. 'Could well be to this actual building, if I've got my bearings. It was my bright idea to check the satellite tower against your address. That led the boss to book his flight, and me to make the rather daft suggestion that I come too.'

'But where is he now?' asks McAvoy, urgently. 'Where's he taken him?' His thoughts smack against the inside of his skull like drumsticks on a timpani. He has so many questions, but none of the answers matter save for the whereabouts of his boy.

'I wish I had the answers,' says Kincaid, and seems to mean it. 'He came over on a fishing boat, we know that much. Stole a vehicle from a dock in North Wales. Changed cars and rang home not far off Sheffield. Spent a night on a houseboat on the Ouse at Goole. Then this place. Couple of nights at least. Time to find himself a bolthole – somewhere he could take his time.'

McAvoy stares at Kincaid, the last of the colour draining from his face. 'Take his time with my son?'

Kincaid has the sense to look ashamed of himself. 'He knows you're a police officer. Can't be sure what you will do. He might have demands he wants you to meet but nothing about him suggests that to be true. I think he'll use him as leverage. Maybe get you to do some of the dirty work for him. Maybe drive him in to the Teague compound and let him open fire. I don't know. But he's a psychopath and a murderer, sergeant. And I'm sorry this warning came too late . . .'

'There have been break-ins,' mutters McAvoy, looking around. 'The calls from here – the missing equipment – the way he appeared and vanished again. He must be on the water. Must be somewhere by the shore.'

'That doesn't narrow it down,' says Kincaid, apologetically.

McAvoy kicks a bin. Squats down, fists at his hairline, holding himself tightly. He can feel his heart thudding against his ribs. Can feel his blood moving in his veins.

'I wasn't eavesdropping,' comes a voice from the door.

McAvoy looks up. Sees Lucas Barrington, hovering nervously in the doorway. 'I think we've found your intruder,' McAvoy says, though his voice barely rises above a whisper.

'I don't think I managed to get the words out,' says Barrington, nervously. 'After the break-on. The first one. Um . . .'

'Not now, eh?' says Kincaid, tactfully.

'It's just, like I tried to explain – I had trackers fitted. The sea canoe. The radio. The all-weather gear. Spent my own money, but, well, if it's the same person, we can pinpoint his location almost exactly. Would you like me to show you?'

Kincaid offers McAvoy his hand. Hauls him to his feet as he takes it. McAvoy closes his eyes. The room is spinning, his head full of hopes and desperate fears. 'Please,' he mumbles. 'Please.'

'Still on the water,' says Barrington, coming back in, staring at his laptop. He glances over the top of the screen. Sees McAvoy's wide, pleading eyes. Glances back at the screen. Gives a little laugh. 'Passed there this morning,' he says, chattily. 'Good spot to hide away, provided you don't get any urban explorers knocking on your door.'

McAvoy takes the laptop from his hands. Looks at the flashing red dot on the screen, half a mile out to sea, where the Humber estuary becomes the sea.

'Haile Sands Fort,' he says, quietly. He looks at the coxswain. 'You said you passed there . . .'

'Body found down towards Mablethorpe. Bit of a trek for us but, well, that missing lad . . .'

McAvoy nods. Licks dry lips.

'Do you want me to call 999?' asks Barrington, quietly.

McAvoy stares into the computer screen. Calls up a memory of the great grey military tower, standing on metal legs in the middle of the water. Stops himself before he imagines his way inside, and fills his head with horrors at the thought of his Fin, captive and afraid.

'No,' says McAvoy, shaking his head. 'I want you to take me there.'

'Steady, sergeant,' says Kincaid. 'Come on, from what I've heard you're the guy who does thing properly. By the book, so they say. I need to call my boss, tell him you've accepted the TTL verbally, absolved us of responsibility. You need tactical support, you need to know what you're dealing with . . .'

McAvoy shoots out a hand and closes his fist around Kincaid's face. Squeezes his mouth shut. Drags him close, eyeball to swivelling eyeball.

'Get in the fucking boat.'

THIRTY-ONE

Twelve years ago

Hard rain and sticky skin; the air pungent, thick.

McAvoy crouches on the shingle and sludge and watches Roisin surface, her dark hair breaking the surface of the ale-coloured water like a shark's fin. She treads water, getting her bearings, squirting out a rainbow of water in McAvoy's direction when she sights him. She's ten yards away, treading water, steam rising from her goose-pimpled flesh.

'Warm rain,' she shouts, making her way towards him. Her voice is almost lost above the sound of the rain striking the water, striking the leaves of the trees that overhang the little pool. 'If I hold up a teabag do you think we'd get a decent brew?'

She rises from the water. Stands, naked, head tipped back, catching the rain on her tongue. McAvoy blushes. Looks away, bashful, then chides himself for being so bloody stupid and swivels his gaze back to where she stands. He's dressed in sodden jeans and a linen shirt, which clings to his body like bubble gum. He has his arms wrapped around her clothes, protecting her garments like a carrion bird protecting a meal. The wound on his face has healed well but there is still a noticeable crevice down his cheek, cutting through the edge of his beard. It gives him a somewhat piratical look that Roisin delights in, even though his big sad-cow eyes betray his gentleness up close.

'Wild garlic,' she says, sniffing the air. Barefoot, she crosses the stones. Squats down and kisses him, hungrily, her mouth all cigarettes and rain. 'I love that smell. Makes you feel all sort of dozy – like the air's a bit heavier and you could snuggle down under it.'

McAvoy opens his arms. She sits between his legs, wrapped up in him. He drops his chin to the crown of her head. Kisses her lightly, at the temples, the cheek.

'I love your words,' he says, softly. 'You should write poetry.'

She grins. Slaps him on his forearms. 'Me? Poetry? I just talk. Just say what I see.'

'That's what poetry is. Just a description of feelings. Of things. But in a language that, I don't know . . . speaks to your marrow. To the places inside you. It's like music at a very specific frequency.'

'It's one of the things I got right,' says Roisin, the rain running down her shoulders. She wrinkles her nose, enjoying the sensation. 'I knew you'd read poetry. I could just tell.'

'I've never studied it,' says McAvoy, apologetically. 'I just like the way some poems make me feel.'

'How do you study poetry?' asks Roisin, baffled. 'You read it. You like it or you don't. Who's that one you keep mentioning?'

'Heaney,' says McAvoy. 'In your accent, it would be sublime.'

She squirms in his grasp, looks back up at him. 'Sublime? I don't know anybody who uses that word. I like it.'

'If we're making Hull our home you might like Larkin. Bit gloomy and some of the sensibilities have changed a little, but he understands people better than most.'

'Sensibilities,' she says, trying out the word and liking it. She adopts a sibilant hiss, moves her head, snakelike. '*Thenthibilitieth* . . .'

They sit in silence for a time. Taste the air. Hold one another. Watch the rain create countless overlapping circles on the surface of the water. On the other bank, hidden among the bracken and nettles, the sap of the birch tree oozes through the metal cylinder and into the small glass container. Over the last few weeks, the pair have made numerous trips to remote parts of the countryside. Seeking out specific hedgerow flowers, grasses, funguses and spores. She consults no textbook or journal. Just tells him when to turn left, and right, and where to park, and holds his hand as she leads him down overgrown tracks and tangled glades, seeking out scents, flavours; some quality in the air. Today it's birch. The leaves will serve as a painkiller and the sap, taken as a cordial, is a diuretic. An unguent distilled from the twigs and leaves eases rheumatism and joint pains. Her father had requested the potion when last they spoke. The weeks hiding out had taken their toll on him and his brothers. He was feeling his age. Roisin had been thrilled to do something of use, and has fallen back in love with the herbal medicine she learned from older family members as a girl. Already she has transformed the house on Exmouth Street into something more akin to a witch's pantry. DC Buller moved out three days after Roisin moved in. He'd been a bit awkward; a little embarrassed, but he'd given McAvoy the closest he'd ever had to a manly punch on the shoulder and called him a 'sly dog' who was 'punching way out of his class'. McAvoy had glowed crimson. Roisin had laughed like a drain.

'Valentine . . .' says Roisin, unexpectedly.

'Sorry?'

'My brother. He's asked if he can be best man.'

McAvoy laughs, bemused at the absurdity of the suggestion. 'He's ten!'

'Eleven . . .'

'I barely know him.'

'You barely know any of us.'

'And it's just a small wedding, isn't it?'

'Did you have anybody in mind?'

McAvoy chews his cheek. He hadn't even given it any thought.

He doesn't want sympathy over the fact he has no real friends, but he's aware his side of the church is going to look a little empty. His mother told him she would be unavailable even before he suggested a date. His dad and brother, both sounding more than a little sceptical, had told them they'd do their best to be there but could make no promises. His old sergeant from Cumbria Police is more of a mentor than a friend and at work he's seen as the odd, shy giant who came back from a family emergency with stitches in his face.

'He likes you . . .'

'Well, that's nice to know, but . . .'

'Thank you. He'll be thrilled.'

Aector chews his lip. Holds her close. Shivers in his wet clothes and feels her grip tighten on his arm.

'You're thinking about it again,' says Roisin, concern in her voice. 'Beating yourself up. Whipping yourself.'

McAvoy says nothing. She unnerves him with the way she seems to read his thoughts; to take the temperature of his moods just by tasting the air.

'It's done with, Aector. Put to bed.'

'Perhaps for you,' he says, even as he wishes he could keep his mouth shut. 'I'm a police officer. There are detectives still looking into what happened. The half-brothers are listed as missing people. Red knew I was going looking for them. There's a DC who looks at me strangely every time I go to the canteen. I can't stand the thought of her murder being written off as unsolved – not when we know that the man who did it is in the ground somewhere.'

She turns. Looks up and into him, her eyes blurring. She places her damp, dirty palm on his cheek.

'Nobody else could understand, Aector. It was a feud. It wouldn't mean much to country folk but to Pavee, it's everything. And it got so far out of hand that somebody died. Somebody who didn't deserve to. But that person is dead, Aector. And the people who tried to hurt me are dead too. There's nobody for the Guards to arrest. It's all done.'

'And I just live with that, do I?'

She shrugs, not unkindly. 'Life's full of pain, my love. Frustrations. Imperfections. Terrible things happened, but somewhere in the world, terrible things are happening every moment. People try and make it neat. Arrests, jail terms, all that bollocks. Nobody asks the Guards to take this stuff on. We live outside, Aector. We're Pavee . . .'

'I'm not,' says Aector, his voice catching. 'I'm joining CID, Roisin. There's a detective superintendent, Doug Roper, I know I can learn a lot from him. I don't know how to have a conversation without blushing so how the hell do I stop myself blurting out that I can tidy up one of his outstanding cases for him?'

Roisin laughs. 'You can't, Aector. You don't know where anybody is. There's no forensics. And do you really want anybody looking too deeply? Going and making that statement, that was terrifying, but I did it for you. And if I know coppers, it won't stay unsolved for long. They'll pin it on somebody.'

He shoots her a reproving look. 'Roisin, that's not how things are done.'

She squeezes his arm. Leans back against him. Stares at the water. When she shivers, he holds her tight.

'I just want to be a good man,' he whispers, his voice lost to the breeze. 'How do I know I'm doing things right . . .'

She takes his hand and places it on her chest. He feels her heart, beating against his palm; a bird in a cage. In moments, they are breathing in tandem: his own heart keeping pace with hers. She laces her fingers through his. Moves his hand down her damp body. Presses it to her stomach.

'We'll keep you right,' she says, smiling, as she feels him tense.

It takes him a moment. His voice is a croak. 'We . . .?'

He feels her nod. Feels her fingers kneading at the backs of his hands. Feels the yearning; the desperate hope for his delight.

'Really?'

She nods. 'I'm sorry. I thought we'd have time, just you and me. I didn't do it on purpose. I didn't even know if I could, after . . .'

He turns her to face him. Presses his forehead to hers. 'You're happy?' he asks, quietly.

'So happy. Scared, but happy.'

He grins, surprising himself with how easily the grin comes to his face. He feels a lightness in his chest, as if he were suddenly filled with a different, gentler blood. Then he gasps, panic gripping him. 'The dress,' he says. 'Will it still . . .?'

He feels her laughing. Hears her call him a fecking eejit.

And here, now, the dead are forgotten over the roar of the living.

THIRTY-TWO

Roisin McAvoy: white-faced, the skin peeling from her lips. Her dark hair falls over her features like pond weed. She's standing in reception, all but vibrating with nervousness; with outright fear.

'Jesus, Roisin,' says Pharaoh, under her breath, as she appears at the top of the stairs. She feels her temper bleed out. Feels nothing but pity.

'Trish, I wasn't sure if . . . well, whether I should, I don't . . .'

Pharaoh passes through the security gate and takes Roisin's elbow. Puts her face close to hers. She doesn't smell right. Smells of stale cigarettes and unwashed clothes. Smells of sweat. There's an iridescent shimmer to her cheeks; the salt of spilled, untended tears.

'What's happened?' asks Pharaoh, her mouth so close to Roisin's that her lips brush her ear. 'Is he OK? Hector? He left the crime scene, ran – I can't get hold of him . . .'

Roisin opens her mouth. Closes it again, biting a sigh in half. Looks up from under heavy, tear-rimed lashes. Stares into her with glassy eyes. 'I don't know,' she hisses, angry and desperate. 'I think I'm being punished. We're all being punished. For what I did, for what I said . . .'

'It's OK,' says Pharaoh. Soothingly. She glances over her shoulder. Two people are sitting in the uncomfortable chairs in front of the reception area, trying to pretend they're not watching. 'Meeting room two, Frank?' she yells, to the desk sergeant. She gets a grunt in reply and the security gate swings back open. She puts her arms through Roisin's. Pulls her close. She's shivering. There's so little meat on her bones that Pharaoh feels as though she is comforting a child. She has spent so long feeling jealous of this woman; resentful of her perfect love, her perfect life; the nearness of the man they both adore. But here, now, she feels no sense of superiority. She feels like a mother coddling a child.

'You're going to arrest me, I know you are,' whispers Roisin, half to herself. 'I didn't know. I swear. He doesn't want me to be here, he said not to bring you into it – said you'd only try to save him and end up incriminating yourself. But I have to. I have to try . . .'

Pharaoh shushes her, making small cooing noises as if rubbing the back of a weeping infant. Leads her through a double door and down a corridor, swiping her card against the keypad outside a small, darkened room. She flicks on the lights. Whoever was here last hasn't tidied up after themselves. There are operational scribblings on the whiteboard and empty cups of coffee scattered around the horseshoe of tables and chairs. She helps Roisin to sit down. Spies a half full jug of water on a desk by the window and pours a splash into a glass that looks relatively clean. Hands it to Roisin, who takes it with shaking hands. It rattles against her teeth as she sips.

'Fin,' she says. 'And Lilah. Lilah was hurt . . .' She folds in on herself as the tears come. Shakes, as the sobs bind her like rope.

Pharaoh crouches in front of her. Tries to put herself in her eyeline – to make a connection; to show her that she is in a safe place. She pushes her hair back from her face. Wipes her tears with the palm of her hand and cups her cheeks. 'Let me,' she says, gently. 'Let me tell you what I know, and we'll go from there, yes?'

Roisin nods, gratefully. Sniffs hard. Gives a silly little smile and instantly swallows it back. Pharaoh stands. Crosses to the door and leans against it, arms folded.

'You've dropped Lilah off with Sophia,' she says. 'Sophia says she's hurt herself – a nasty puncture wound to the hand. Says Lilah isn't talking much, and by Christ that girl's a chatterbox. And Hector isn't where he's supposed to be. Now, I don't pretend to be Miss Marple, but given what I know about what happened to you all those years ago, and the fact that you look fucking dreadful, I'm guessing Fin is the one we have to worry about, yes?'

Silently, Roisin nods. Pharaoh takes a breath. Thinks about the big, quiet, red-headed lad she has known and loved since he was five years old. Forces herself to keep her emotions in check. Breathes steadily, keeping calm.

'The man who killed your auntie,' says Pharaoh, slowly. 'Eva-Jayne Puck. I'm thinking your family may have taken their revenge on him . . .'

'I didn't know,' mutters Roisin.

'I'm thinking that he's suffered at their hands,' continues Pharaoh.

'My daddy,' she sniffs. 'He only just told me, I swear. He thought he was dead. We all did. Aector wanted things done properly but by the time he was well enough to ask questions, everything had been taken care of and there was no way anybody was going to cooperate with an investigation or tell him where the bodies were.' She looks past Pharaoh, as if staring into a memory. 'And by then, we were in love.'

Pharaoh sighs, rolling her eyes. Re-crosses her arms. 'He wasn't dead, was he? Your dad was taking his time with him. Took too much time, didn't he? He got away.'

'It was years ago,' says Roisin, desperately. 'Daddy thought he was under the ground. That he was gone. It was only a few months ago that he came back – like some demon, something undead. He sent Daddy an Oracle card. Death. Daddy came home one day to find his brother's hand nailed to the caravan door with the card on the palm. He's got enemies, has Daddy. Thought it was the Heldens. But the same fecking thing had happened there. It were a tongue. Can you believe that?' Roisin swallows, and the action seems to pain her. 'His son's tongue, nailed to the doorframe – Death card right in the centre. And he started coming for us. For both families. Daddy didn't know for certain who was doing it until one of our boys got away. Described him – the way his face was all hollowed in down one side – missing half his scalp where Daddy took the blade to him . . .'

'And Daddy did that because he killed your aunt?' asks Pharaoh, softly.

'He got my aunt, but he came for me,' says Roisin. She chews at her lips. Sips the water. 'And now he's here. Here, and he's got Fin, and he hurt Lilah, and I know he's going to keep killing and killing until there's only me left, and then he'll really take his time. I'm the one who did it, you see. I'm the one who told Daddy that it was him who killed Eva-Jayne.'

Pharaoh squeezes her own forearms, a chill creeping into her flesh. 'And that's not true?'

'I don't know,' says Roisin, quietly. 'I was in Scunthorpe hiding away from bad men. And then I see a stranger butchering my auntie, and I run, and I just get away, and I go to what I think is a safe place, and they drug me, and the next thing I'm waking up and there's this bastard fighting Aector – it was like watching Satan beat on my own guardian angel, and I rammed the van into him. Made a mess of him. I didn't even think about any of it. I just knew he was the bad man who'd done those terrible things, and that God had sent me my own protector, and he was bleeding. And after that I was too in love to think about any of it. He was dead, I was sure of it. Then Daddy had to tell me the truth – about what happened, about what he'd done – about what was coming for us. I've been so scared, Trish. Scared and guilty and desperate . . .'

Pharaoh screws up her face, trying to keep her feelings from showing in her expression. Inside, her guts are churning. There's prickly heat upon her skin and ice water in her bones. She has to keep forcing herself to do this right – to get the information she needs, and to keep Roisin talking.

'There have been other murders, Roisin,' says Pharaoh, gently. 'Other clairvoyants. Palmists. Fortune tellers. This morning, that's where we were. We were looking at the body of a woman who'd been butchered on her own kitchen carpet. A crystal, hammered right through her heart. And my best sergeant fled the scene because of something he learned, or saw. And now your boy is missing, and . . .' She stops. Locks her teeth. Glares at Roisin with eyes that flash with absolute fury. 'And you took your daughter to Sophia's house. You put my daughter in danger . . .'

'No,' says Roisin, shaking her head. 'No, he could have taken her. Could have grabbed her when he took Fin. No, that's not what he wants. He wants me, Trish. He wants my daddy to know all the pain and suffering that a person can endure. '

'You can't know what he wants,' snaps Pharaoh, flicking her hair behind her ear. 'Has he been in touch? Made demands? Is that where Hector is now – waiting by the phone . . .?'

'I've seen it,' says Roisin, flatly. 'In my dreams. In those moments when I'm not asleep or awake, I hear him. Hear him telling Aector to choose. He can save his son, or his wife, but not both. He can have his son back, but only if he gives me over. And I know Aector won't be able to do it. So I need you to do it. I need you to find this man, and tell him that I agree. Give me to him, and let Fin go free. Do what Aector can't.'

Pharaoh stands immobile. Stares at her as if reading a map of an unfamiliar world. 'No,' she says, teeth clamped together. 'No, you get those thoughts out of your head. We're going to go to Aector. I'm going to make some calls. We're going to do this properly, and if your daddy ends up on a slab or spending the rest of his life in prison, that's too fucking bad. Whatever the fall-out, all that matters is that boy. You need to tell me everything. We can talk on the way. I'm supposed to be seeing one of the bosses, but . . .'

'No, Trish, no – I've seen it. This is how it has to be. It's OK. After I'm gone, you can have him. I know it's what you want . . .'

'Shut your fucking mouth, Roisin,' says Pharaoh, without emotion. 'Shut it now. You did the right thing coming here. Aector was correct in what he said. Of course I'm going to try and protect him. I protect him every bloody day – just like he protects everybody he comes into contact with. And sometimes, the world gives him these situations where he doesn't know what to do or how to be or who to protect first. Well, I make those choices for him. And right now, whatever it takes, he needs to protect his son. Yes?'

Roisin wipes her eyes. Swallows. Takes a breath. She nods. 'Please. Please keep him safe . . .'

Pharaoh shakes her head. Reaches into her bra and pulls out her mobile. Ends the ongoing call with a discreet touch of her thumb.

'You know what he's going to do, don't you?' asks Roisin, her eyes locked on Pharaoh's. 'Why he sent me away. Why he's on his own, right now, refusing to answer my calls, refusing to speak to you. You know he's looking for him, don't you? And he'll find him. That's what he does. But he can't beat this man. He's the devil, Trish. The very devil . . .'

Pharaoh bends down. Takes Roisin's hands in hers. Gives her a little smile. 'Yeah? And he's Aector Fucking McAvoy. I know who my money's on.'

'But . . .'

Pharaoh takes a cigarette from her pocket. Takes another for Roisin. Puts both in her mouth and lights them. Puts one between Roisin's lips. They sit in a cloud of smoke, eyeing each other like cats.

'Now,' says Pharaoh, at last. 'Let's go save our daughters from each other, yes? And on the way, you can tell me all you remember about the day Eva-Jayne died.'

Roisin nods. Her eyes shine through the smoke like crystals in firelight.

One hundred and sixty miles away, in a quiet little office at the end of a long corridor, Helen Tremberg looks at the notes she has scribbled down. Checks that the recording is clear. Replays a few snippets of the conversation she has spent the last half hour listening to. Saves the file to her laptop. Takes a handful of Minstrels from the open bag on her desk, and drains her bottle of Fanta. Finally, she opens up the database. Cross-checks the information that she has just been party to, against times, dates, and unsolved crimes.

Ten minutes later, a warning sign appears in the centre of the screen. She has accessed a confidential file, linked to an ongoing multi-agency operation. The point of contact listed for all further enquiries, is a senior Gardai officer, and an extension number for a secure line at the Home Office.

'Oh Aector,' whispers Tremberg, shaking her head. She thinks of Fin. Of the boy she met, seven years before, in Hull's Holy Trinity Square. He's been a brave boy. Sweet, and clever and too good to be true. She glances at the photo of her own daughter, Penelope, in a silver frame on her desk. Thinks of Roisin, and all she has endured. Thinks of Aector McAvoy, and the day he saved her life. Chews on her cheek. Picks up the phone.

'Sir,' she says, in her most ingratiating voice. 'Sir, you know that favour you owe me . . .'

THIRTY-THREE

Twelve years ago

'So just the men now, so. Ladies . . . no, if you could just leave that be . . . excuse me, aye, son, no . . . . . . just the men . . . put that back . . . no, no of course I don't want to fight you, you're ten . . .'

McAvoy feels more than a little sympathy for the photographer. Trying to get the wedding party to follow instructions is proving near Biblical in its level of suffering. It's only a small wedding, but half the guests are children and the others are Pavee men and women with hard-wired aversion to doing as asked. The drink has been flowing merrily, and there's a decent buffet going cold on the table. None were keen to leave their velour seats or take their fists off the golden tablecloths. It has taken almost an hour to get everybody to assemble in the little wooded glade at the back of the hotel. The photographer – a pot-bellied man with scabby red hair over a flaky scalp and an air of the recently alcoholic – is losing his mind.

'Look, you . . . I don't understand, these are your photographs, you're paying for them – why do you keep flicking V signs every time I ask you to smile – you're wasting your own money . . . no, please, put them back . . .'

McAvoy finds himself grinning as he watches his best man run off into the woods carrying two lenses from the photographer's open bag, followed by a gaggle of young girls in puffy skirts and glittery makeup. On the path, treading rose petals and confetti into the damp gravel, a semi-circle of Traveller men and women are roaring with laughter, raising half full glasses and occasionally bursting into song. It had been a beautiful service, apparently. Valentine, with fresh tramlines shaved into the neat fuzz on his skull and looking exceptional in a pure white three-piece suit, had brought the place down when he pretended to pinch the wedding rings. McAvoy had been grateful for the laughter, as it had covered his stumble when reciting the vows. He'd been so nervous he could barely speak. He just kept his eyes on Roisin's and tried to behave like somebody who might be worthy of her love. She glowed. He'd heard the expression before, but had never seen it so perfectly exhibited. She wore ivory, bare-backed, slim-waisted; a black Madonna necklace on a gold chain at her neck and a dainty floral headdress in her dark hair. She was barefoot, her feet leaving neat prints on the cold flagstones of the church as she walked up the aisle on her daddy's arm. McAvoy had dressed as the Teagues had suggested. The suit, tailored without his knowledge, had been waiting on the peg in his hotel room: a soft grey tweed with a sky blue lining and a waistcoat patterned in gold-and-blue silk. He'd worn a neckerchief, pure white, and pinned at the throat. The congregation has told him he looked like a model. The mirror in the hotel room told him he looked absolutely ridiculous. Still, Roisin had delighted in his appearance, and Papa Teague, beaming with pride, told him that he looked more like a Pavee than a policeman: a curious compliment that McAvoy has yet to process.

'You've made her the happiest lass alive,' comes a voice, at his ear.

He turns. Papa Teague. Gold sovereigns on his fingers, fat cigar in his mouth; black porkpie hat brushed clean. He's grinning, happy in a cloud of poteen, Guinness and tobacco. He nods across the clearing, to where Roisin, still barefoot, is having a kickabout with two male cousins, the hems of her skirt already soaked through.

'She's made me happy too,' says McAvoy, earnestly. 'More than that. I don't even know what to call it . . .'

'Call it smitten, boy. Call it love. And don't be fretting, we don't need to have the chat.'

'The chat?'

'You know, the one where I tells you that if you mess around on her or hurt her or make her feel second-rate, I'll skin you and feed you your own face. No need for such unpleasantness.'

McAvoy holds the smaller man's gaze. He's getting better at looking people in the eye. People at work have noticed the change in him. There's something in his gaze: a sense of resolution. Papa Teague sees it too. Smiles, and looks away.

'Not much of a turnout from your side,' he says, conversationally.

'Dad's got problems on the croft. My mother, well . . .'

'Don't feel obliged to explain yourself, boy. You're family now.'

They stand in silence for a moment, letting the words sink in.

'That wee boy of yours is going to be something special,' says Teague, blowing out a cloud of smoke.

'As long as he's healthy and happy,' says McAvoy.

'Aim as high as you like, lad,' says Teague, leaning closer. 'You're married to a sorceress, lad. Touched by the spirits, so she is. Got the sight. Always had a mind like a rocket. I don't know if she can read the cards and the leaves but she knows right from wrong and can tell what you need before you even tell her there's a problem. Whatever spell she cast to get you, it's worked, eh?'

McAvoy laughs, politely. Watches as Roisin scores a goal then turns a celebratory handstand in the grass. He'd like to tell her to be careful; that the baby is more precious to him than he could have ever dreamed, but she has a habit of laughing at him and telling him to not be so fecking soft, and he'd rather avoid that in front of her family.

'Spell?'

'All those letters she wrote you, for all those years. Weren't the half of it. She'd be down the glen first dew of each new moon, washing her face in flowers, whispering to the spirits to bring her what she wanted – the man she wanted, her true love. Bringing you, lad. And it worked, didn't it? Turned up at the right moment. Christ, if you didn't, I'd never have forgiven myself.'

McAvoy looks away, unsure if he wants to think about it all right now. 'Just luck, I suppose . . .'

'Luck can be all sorts of things to all sorts of people, lad. Me, I knew what my little girl wanted. And nice as it is to have faith in things working out as you want them, sometimes the spirits need a nudge. Her mother thought I was a mad man, sending her to stay with Eva-Jayne. Said there were many people better suited to looking after her. But not all of them were so close to where a big fecker of a policeman was working. Did me good, to know she was near you.'

McAvoy steps back, heat rising up from his gut, sweat breaking out at his temples. 'You sent her to be near me? Why? How could you have known it would work out as it did? She could have been killed!'

'I didn't know they'd send Cromwell,' says Teague with a shrug, chewing his cigar. 'That were all a bit much. But I did have my hopes you'd gravitate together. All her spells, and wishes, and you – this big bumbling giant with a punch like a fucking wrecking ball and no idea what you're for . . .'

'No,' says McAvoy, gritting his teeth. 'No, you don't treat people like that. Life isn't like that. The danger she put herself in . . . what happened to Eva-Jayne . . .'

'He's paying for that,' says Papa Teague, sniffing and looking away. 'Paying every day . . .'

McAvoy is about to reply when the sound of running feet makes him turn. Roisin leaps into his arms, both legs around his waist, sweat running down her cheeks. She kisses him. Grins. Kisses him again.

'My best men getting on OK? Jesus, but Valentine's leading the poor fella a merry dance. Up a tree, so he is, dancing on a branch with the poor man's bag. Shall we go save him, husband? Oh I like that. Mr and Mrs McAvoy. Jesus but I'm dizzy.'

McAvoy finds himself being pulled away. Turns back to Papa Teague and sees him walking away.

'You OK?' asks Roisin, looking up at him. 'By Christ you look handsome. I heard Mammy saying she'd ride the arse off ye . . .'

'Your dad,' says McAvoy, pinching the bridge of his nose. 'Just something he said. I must have misheard.'

'It's the accent. And the poteen. And the fact he's got a cigar in his teeth. Come on, let's get your best man out of that fecking tree . . .'

McAvoy lets her lead him. Lets his thoughts turn to his wife, and his son, and the new house they're looking at up on the Kingswood estate. Pushes the nagging voice into a recess in his mind. Almost succeeds in convincing himself that it had been a slip of the tongue.

Doesn't listen to the whispering doubts until they start to scream.

PART THREE

PART THREE

THIRTY-FOUR

11.58 a.m.
The Humber Estuary

'There's no chance he's there. None.'

McAvoy leans towards Kincaid. Squints through the spray. Angles his head, trying to hear the other man over the chainsaw whine of the motor. 'Sorry?'

'No way he's there. It'll be a set-up. A trap. We've been looking for years and he doesn't make mistakes. Do you know the people he's put down? The jobs he's done. He's not . . .'

The rest of the sentence is swallowed up by the slap of the inflatable smacking down onto the iron-grey water. The wind is rushing in from the open ocean, pushing the small, bright-orange craft back towards the shore. Barrington is having to push the little craft hard, grinding his teeth as he pushes down on the throttle. He glares past his passengers, white amphibian eyes fixed on the horizon, his face dripping salt-spray and sweat. He keeps glancing at his passengers, as if to check whether this is really happening. He doesn't look afraid – just baffled at what he has stumbled into. He has no doubt there will be hell to pay for somebody when all this is done, but he's pretty sure it won't be him.

McAvoy allows himself to move with the boat, his body swaying as if his feet and the deck were an elbow joint. He's always been a good sailor. The estuary is choppy today and the grey air is hazy with rain and spray, but he's known far worse conditions than this. He moves as if dancing to slow music. He's soaked to the skin, his clothes sticking to his flesh like molten plastic. He'd refused the all-weather suit. Shook his head, wordlessly, as Barrington handed him the lifejacket. He's not being deliberately reckless. He doesn't know how much time he will have; how quickly he will have to move, when they reach the fort. He wants to be unencumbered. Wants to have his hands free for whatever is to come.

'They'll hang you for this, you mad bastard,' yells Kincaid in his ear. 'He'll say you made him do it. Made him ferry you out here. And if it comes to it, I'll say the same. You had me at gunpoint. Made me come, when I was all for calling in back-up and telling the bosses . . .'

McAvoy turns away from him. Fixes his eyes on the little black square on the horizon. It's been getting steadily bigger. He swivels back to look at the distant shoreline. It's just a smudge now: a line of lights, like the last embers in a dying hearth.

'McAvoy,' shouts Kincaid, again. 'I said, they'll hang you . . .'

'I heard you,' he growls, his voice snatched away on the wind. The boat lurches as a hard wind hits them side-on. Overhead, gulls whirl against the ugly, badly Artexed skies. The clouds are great cakes of sun-bleached cowshit: all whorls and vortexes.

Stay, Fin. I'm coming. Whatever it takes, you fight. You fight to live, and I swear, I'll get to you . . .

A burst of static, sizzling like hot oil.

'RNLI station at Cleethorpes,' shouts Barrington, behind them. 'On the radio. Reports of a small craft near the base of the fort. They know about our break-in and wanted to check the description. What do I say?'

McAvoy wipes the salt water from his face. Turns his back on the rain and gives Barrington his attention. 'You say thanks and you tell them you're on a training exercise. You'll redirect towards the fort. If they offer to lend back-up, you politely decline.'

Barrington licks his lips. Nods. Lifts the receiver and does as instructed. McAvoy turns to the horizon. The fort emerges from the grey. He narrows his eyes. Makes out the shape of a building he has seen so many times from the shore.

'Like something from a film!' shouts Kincaid, nervousness in his voice. 'Christ, how did they build it? What's it even for?'

McAvoy ignores him. He can't seem to find the right words. He knows all about the forts. They were built a century earlier: great, forbidding armour-plated castles constructed to defend the Humber from German U-boats. They've stood empty for decades, their steel skins turning to rust, their concrete struts barnacled and slimed by the waters that lap at its great grey belly.

'You still think you can get through all this without anybody you care about doing time? You're a fantasist, mate. I'm on your side, but there should be a whole tactical team with us! He's insane, McAvoy. Insane and very good at killing people. What have you got? You're not even armed!'

McAvoy doesn't respond. Hears a clatter from behind him and spins around to see Barrington holding out a hard plastic toolbox, the lid flipped open. 'Take your pick,' he yells, as the wind screams around them.

'Are you people fucking mental?' yells Kincaid, despairingly. The boat slaps down again, and he lurches right, retching and heaving over the side.

McAvoy wishes he'd left Kincaid back at the boathouse but he couldn't be sure he would do what McAvoy asked. Couldn't be sure he would keep his mouth shut for long enough for Aector to try and recover his son his own way.

'Just do me in,' growls Kincaid, wiping his mouth. 'Kill me now.'

McAvoy reaches past him. Takes a hammer, and a length of cord from the box. Grabs two long white tubes and stuffs them into the waist of his trousers. Nods his thanks to Barrington.

'Are they fucking flares?' yells Kincaid. 'What good are they? Look, McAvoy, this isn't right, mate – you're just going to get killed, and me killed, and your boy killed, and that's if he's still alive to begin with . . .'

McAvoy takes him by the lapels and hauls him close. Looks deep into his eyes. Places one big hand on his wet face and shoves him down to the deck. Shakes his head. 'No,' he says. 'No, my boy's alive.'

Behind him, Barrington kills the engine.

'Tide will take us from here,' he says. 'Your man – he'll have been tired if he paddled out against that tide, especially if he had, erm . . . cargo.'

McAvoy nods. He's already made the calculations. He knows they can't be far behind their quarry. Prays to God that whatever is in store for Fin, it will not have begun in earnest.

The fort looms ahead: all rusty metal and slimy concrete, rising from the water like the lair of a Bond villain. It's circular, rusting steel plates and reinforced concrete, rivets seaming every panel, bleeding rust like weeping bullet holes.

'There's no ladder down,' says Barrington, quietly. 'Water

should be high enough, but you're going to have a bitch of a time getting up . . .'

McAvoy nods. Looks down to Kincaid still sprawled on the deck. 'You go back with him,' he says, softly. 'Go to the nearest lifeboat station. By the time you get there, this will either be done or it won't be. I was never going to make you come with me. Thank you for telling me what you have. I hope that whatever comes next, you'll remember that I did my best.'

Barrington looks up, confused. Flinches, as the craft drifts under the base of the fort. Looks back to McAvoy. 'No, seriously, you can't . . .'

McAvoy reaches up. Grabs the rusting metal that encircles the first concrete strut. Feels the sharp steel puncture his palm, opening the wound in his skin. Heaves himself upwards.

Begins to climb.

THIRTY-FIVE

The darkness is assembling itself into patterns now. Shapes. The ink-dark patch of nothingness in the top left corner of his vision is becoming a rectangle. Ahead, the pitch dark is glinting, as if some distant light were striking metal. Below, somewhere near his face, the night-time black is becoming great wormy coils of damp rope.

Fin McAvoy feels a weariness in every part of him. Has never been more aware of himself. He is hot with pain: glowing needles in every patch of fleshy softness; brutally cold pliers twisting at the places where his bones don't quite meet. He knows terror, suddenly. Knows true fear as if the monsters in his nightmares have followed him into wakefulness.

He breathes out, softly. Sucks in a bitter lungful of dust. Stifles his cough and the action causes him to gag. He tucks in his elbows, trying to stop himself coming apart as he wretches, bucking and twisting like a rabbit in a snare. He can't seem to make his hands work. They hang from his torso like rubber prosthetics.

Memories drift in. He'd been with Lilah. There had been a pile of leaves. He'd gone looking for her pocket calculator. And then the earth was alive and cold, leathery hands were grabbing for him, and there had been a stink of wet fur and fresh graves and the sudden burning static of metal upon his flesh. Then a nothingness – an oblivion that stunk of unwashed flesh; of petrol and dirt and sea salt.

He tries to move. Coughs again. Squints into the dark. He feels like he is inside a broken radio. The air is a smashed mirror in an unlit room; black and white and black and white.

It's snowing, he tells himself, and the thought arrives in his own voice. *Snowing.*

Fear comes, rising up from his gut in great acid waves. Lilah. Had something happened to Lilah? He was supposed to be looking after her. She was his responsibility.

He twists, becoming aware of fresh points of pain. He's on a cold, damp floor. His bones feel as though they have been pulled out of their rightful places and rearranged. One side of his face is tingly, the way his gums feel after an injection from the dentist. He can taste blood. The snowflakes, crusting his lips, are chemical, like washing powder.

He wriggles, trying to work out how to move his feet. Glances ahead and behind, the darkness so thick he could take fistfuls of it and squeeze out handfuls of black paint.

He tries to speak. Feels ridiculous, childish, as the first words croak out of his throat.

'Mammy? Dad? Hello . . .'

The sound comes echoing back, a little-boy voice, helpless, shrill.

'Please . . .' he says, and he doesn't know who he's saying it to. 'Please . . . Lilah. Lilah, are you there? It's me. It's your brother . . .'

Thinking upon his sister stills the terror that grips him. Forces himself to take control of himself. His sister may be here. She may be in worse trouble than him. She needs reassurance – needs to know that he will get her out of here, take care of this, as surely as if Mammy or his father were here.

'Lilah, if you're there I need you to say something, OK? Are you hurt? Do you know where we are? I don't think I can move very

well – I think I'm tied up, it's all sort of . . . cloudy . . . I think I
can see a bedframe, an old-fashioned one, metal – and there's ropes
here. The floor's all wet. I can taste something . . . talk to me, Lilah
. . . don't worry, we'll be OK, it's all a mistake . . .'

Fin's lips feel rubbery. He isn't sure if the words are coming
out or if he's just reciting them in his head. He tries to pull
himself up but a sharp pain at his wrists causes him to cry out.
He pushes his face closer to his hands. Feels a point of cold
metal graze his cheek. Clarity hits like a fist. There's a nail
through his wrists, a gleaming metal tip emerging from the back
of his left hand. His hands are fastened together as if in prayer.

Fin gasps, fear pulsing through him. Little mewing noises
escape his lips. He wriggles backwards, his back touching the
cold steel hardness of the wall. Swivels around at the contact
and feels the rope bite into the flesh of his neck. He understands,
suddenly. A picture flashes in his mind – a scene from a film.
His feet are tied together and the rope is around his neck. He's
been dumped on a hard floor in a darkened room, his hands in
front of him, stapled at the wrist. If he tries to kick with his legs,
the noose will close around his throat.

'Lilah . . .' he says, and this time the voice is real. There is
something snake-like about the tone, a soft hiss to his words.
'Lilah, please tell me you're safe . . .'

'Safe?' comes a voice, somewhere in front of him. 'Where's
safe in this world, eh?'

Fin squirms back, the sweat on his body turning to
ice-water.

'Hello . . . who's there . . . Dad?'

'Not yet, boy,' comes the reply. It's emotionless. Joyless.
The words sound as though they have been programmed into
something lifeless; spoken by an automaton.

'What's happening?' begs Fin, trying to keep still. The pain
is everywhere, an agony beyond enduring. He can't feel his hands
but now he knows what has been done to him he is fixating on
the wound at his wrists. He can feel nothing where the nail has
gone through his skin and bones. He feels a wetness on his
forearms but there is just a cold lifelessness at the place where
he should hurt most. 'Is Lilah here?' he whispers, and a wisp of
chemical-tasting ash lands upon his tongue.

'She's not my concern,' comes the voice. 'Took her pain like a proper fighter, so she did. Didn't cry. Must be how it goes in your family, eh? The women are the strong ones. The men snivel like kittens.'

Fin feels his cheeks burn. Chokes on a sob and feels himself lose control of his bladder. His face burns as the sudden rush of urine soaks his school trousers, his front suddenly hot, and quickly cold. There's a little laugh from the darkness.

'Don't worry, boy – there'll be no shame after,' comes the voice. 'They won't know you pissed yourself. The sea will wash it away.'

Fin tries to be brave. Fills himself with images of his mammy. Of his dad. 'What is it you want?' he asks, his throat agony – his larynx bulging against the rope.

'From you?' comes the voice. 'Truly, not very much. I'll settle for your death.'

Fin grinds his teeth, swallowing blood and gritty, bitter air. Focuses on the voice. Manages to locate a little column of darker air, somewhere off to his left, where the sound seems to be coming from. He focuses on it. Watches the darkness delineate into a form. Broad shoulders, stocky legs, the perfectly smooth outline of a domed head. He glares at the shape, trying to make sense of it. There are no blurs to the edges – no suggestion of clothing. He can make out the exact outline of a physical form: a silhouette; a cardboard cut-out, black and silky, like tadpoles.

'Why? Why me . . . ?'

A flash of flame. The sudden suggestion of a long, sunken face, all hollows and dips, as if the features were an assemblage of twisted tree roots and wet earth. A burning ember, now. The rasp of fire eating paper; the sudden pungent stench of cigarettes.

'I made you, boy,' comes the voice, smoke bleeding into the air. 'If it weren't for me you wouldn't exist. Your mammy, your daddy, they made you while I was being buried in the earth. Brought them together, so I did.'

Fin tries to reply but the pain in his throat is becoming unbearable. His legs are cramping up. He can feel dizziness, a bone-crunching weariness, starting to take little bites out of him. He wants to close his eyes. Wants to let go, and drift into a place without pain.

'Your grandfather,' he says, a hint of true feeling creeping into the lifeless voice. 'He thinks I begrudge him his vengeance. He thinks I'm hurting his kin because I'm angry about what he did to me. Truth be told, I understand. I came for his daughter. He was entitled to do whatever he saw fit. Kept me in the dark, underground, more dead than alive, watching the worms fall from the earth like rain, watching my skin devour itself, my bones twist and splinter, feeling myself decompose while I was still alive. He did what any man would do. Did less than your mammy would do if she were here now.'

Fin can't seem to make sense of the words any more. There's a thudding in his ears. He's aware of his heart – can see it pumping, flexing, a fist-sized lump of gristle expanding and diminishing like a bullfrog's throat. He gasps. Tries to shout. Feels spit run down his chin.

'Don't go dying yet, boy,' comes the voice, and Fin is suddenly aware of movement, a ripple of silk as the black figure moves quickly towards him, the cigarette's tip a lance-point bearing down upon his exposed, upturned face.

A flash of a blade, and then the sudden blessed release as he crumples onto the hard ground, his knees and face smacking down on concrete. He sucks in a breath. Throws up. Gags on mucus and blood and the salty snowflakes and curls into a ball, feeling returning to his wrists and hands with such sudden savageness that he lets out a shriek.

'We've a way to go, boy,' says the man, crouching down in front of him. 'Don't you think about dying. I need your mammy and your daddy and your grandfather to see you breathing, so they know I'm a man of my word. You're no good to me dead, boy. Do you know how many years I've thought about this? About your mother? She did it, you see. She told her daddy that it was me. Maybe she was mistaken, maybe she really didn't recognize me, with all the mud and blood and tyre-tracks on my face. Maybe she was too loved up and didn't even give it a thought. But your grandfather took her at her word. Put me through the trials of Job, so he did. Left me to devour myself, like an animal beneath the ground. And that's what will happen to your mammy, boy. I'll make your father an offer. He can have his boy back, but it will cost him his wife. That will be his punishment. Your grandfather, he'll be the last to die. He'll know what's happening to his daughter, because he did it to me. And as for your dad, I want him to know that life isn't what he thought it was. He's not my enemy, boy. He's not Teague blood. But he was there. He could have asked questions. Could have asked about the man who did all those things to Eva-Jayne Puck. Could have told Papa Teague that he was visiting Hell on a man who only killed those he was paid to kill. I'd never have gone for Roisin Teague if the brothers hadn't tried to cash in. The Heldens wouldn't have harmed her. Nobody knew where she was. And I spent years under the ground as punishment for something I didn't do!'

Fin spits. Sobs. 'I don't know what you're talking about! I don't know these names! My dad's a police officer. I don't know what was done to you, but I swear, if you ask him to choose between me and Mammy, he won't do it. He'll just kill you. He's not a violent man, Mammy always says that. But for me? For Mammy? You need to stop this now. Whatever you think you're doing, it won't . . .'

A movement in front of him. The rush of flesh and bones and the sudden, sickening impact of a boot in his gut. He jerks, vomit surging acidly up his throat. Curls into a ball. Bucks, as another boot thuds into his chest. Tries to cover up and feels the sudden release as he yanks his wrists apart. Stares at the tip of the nail that skewers his right wrist. Presses his lips to the open wound in his left hand, his mouth filling with the iron foulness of his own blood.

'Your father!' he hisses. 'Hurt me? I've watched you all, boy. Your father's a big man, but he's weak. I've seen him when you're all asleep – seen him sitting there, tears on his cheeks, holding himself like a fucking child. I've seen him standing at your bedside, looking down on you like he's staring into a coffin. He lives his life in fear, boy. Always got one eye on the grave, so he has. Always preparing for the day when it all ends, when payment is demanded for his happiness. Well, that's what I am, boy. I've come to collect. To show him that he doesn't get to have life and love and contentment. No, he gets to agonize. To grieve. To hate himself every day.'

Fin looks up. The cigarette gives off just enough light for him to see the face of the man who has sworn to make his bloodline suffer and die. Wrapped up in himself, he chews on his cheek. Stifles his cries as he fastens bloody fingers over the head of the nail and begins to slide it free of flesh and bone.

'All these years,' spits the man. 'Putting myself back together, setting my bones, patching my skin, trying to clean the corruption from my blood. All these years of healing, of waiting, of letting Papa Teague forget, to feel safe, to believe himself absolved and redeemed. They weren't expecting me, boy. Thought they were free. But the devil doesn't forgive, boy. The devil comes for payment. And the price is going to be . . . everything . . .'

In one fluid movement, Fin slides the nail free and grasps its bloodied head in his left hand. Lashes out and feels it strike home. The nail plunges into the fleshy leg of his abductor like a fork into succulent meat.

A shriek of pain, the sound of flesh hitting flesh, and then Fin is wrapping his head in his hands as the sounds of violence, of skin on skin and bone upon bone fills the cold, gritty air.

He hears curses and grunts and the clatter of metal hitting the concrete floor. Looks up through the pleached branches of his arms and sees two black shapes, fighting like the shadow of flames. Sees the man who took him, hacking down, hacking down, a wooden club in his right hand, striking again and again at a big, spread-eagled figure on the floor.

The rush of panic, the sudden understanding of what he is seeing.

'Dad!'

And then Aector McAvoy is reaching up and closing his palm around the face of the man who took his boy, and is running him back towards the wall and slamming his skull against the reinforced metal, again, again, and dropping the limp, waxwork body onto the floor.

And then Fin is looking up as his father shines a light in his face, and stares at the bruises and cuts and the ugly wounds and welts, and tears run down his cheeks and into his bloodied beard, and he gathers him up in arms that tremble and holds him so gently that even if he were made of cobwebs and dew, he would not come apart.

'He said he was going to make you choose . . .' whispers Fin. 'He said . . .'

And then Fin is clattering back to the floor as the devil fastens his arm around McAvoy's neck and begins to squeeze, clinging to him as if riding a wild horse, and McAvoy is falling forward, on his knees, eyes bulging, bloodied teeth bared, grasping behind him, smashing him back into the wall, tongue sticking out from the wet blackness of his open mouth, hand scrabbling in the pocket of his coat.

Fin looks up just as his father smashes the white tube into the face of the man on his back. The cylinder squelches, hideously, into the hollow eye-socket. There is a scream, and then the sudden white hot flame, the hiss and squeal of white-hot fireworks and sparks, shadows dancing, flecks of fire skipping on the air with the flakes of gritty snow.

McAvoy, on top of his son, shielding his body with his own.

A soft, wet explosion.

An instant of warm rain and the pitter-patter of fragmented bone.

Then the clatter of the devil's headless body slumping to the floor.

And Fin lets the darkness take him.

THIRTY-SIX

12.44 p.m.
Snuff Mill Lane, Cottingham

Roisin's mobile starts to trill a moment before the speakers in Pharaoh's little convertible vibrate with the sound of an incoming call.

Roisin, childlike and silent in the passenger seat, snatches up the mobile. 'Aector?'

Pharaoh, her knuckles white, an ache from her fingertips to the top of her head, stabs the button on the centre of the steering wheel. 'Hector?'

Silence for a moment. Rain and traffic and the screech of bald windscreen wipers over dirty glass.

Then the tension in the car pops like a glistening blister.

Tears flow in rivers down Roisin's face. She nods. Grins. Begins to shake.

'Thank fuck,' whispers Pharaoh, and puts one hand to her heart. 'Thank fuck.'

Pharaoh pulls up onto the kerb and flicks on the hazard lights.

The cheerful voice of Andy Daniells fills the vehicle.

'Nice to hear your voice too, boss.'

'Oh he . . . and you . . . no, bollocks to Daddy, he did this, he can deal with it . . . is he cross with me – no tell him Lilah loves him, he saved her, she'll know he's a hero . . . I didn't mean it to be like this, Aector, oh Blessed Jesus and all the Saints I'm so glad to hear you . . .'

'Save me, Andy,' says Pharaoh, rolling her eyes. 'It's so sickly sweet in here my diabetes is starting to bite.'

'Heard from the big man,' says Daniells, emphasizing the words to indicate that he's overheard and recognized the other voice in the vehicle. 'Said he's sorry he did a runner like that but it was a family emergency. He'll call you when he has a moment . . .'

Pharaoh looks across at Roisin. Shakes her head, smiling a little. She's grinning from ear to ear, whispering 'love yous' and 'so-so-sorrys', her voice the rustle and hush of bare feet through dry leaves. She lets herself enjoy the moment. She'll have to tidy things up, she has no doubt about that. But she sees something more than simple relief in Roisin's expression. Her boy is alive.

'Well,' says Pharaoh, loud enough for McAvoy to be able to hear her voice through Roisin's phone. 'Family emergency, is it? Whatever could that have been?'

The complex four-way conversation comes to a brief pause. A light rain begins to pitter-patter on the windscreen. An arsehole in an Audi leans on the horn, complaining to anybody who will listen that some silly cow in a clapped-out convertible has blocked his drive.

In the passenger seat, Roisin grimaces. 'Yes,' she whispers, into the phone. 'I had to. I didn't know what you were going to do. It's OK. She knows. She'll help.' She wipes her eyes. Gives

Pharaoh a look that she recognizes. 'She'd do anything for you, Aector.'

Pharaoh laughs, an exasperated little bark. Reaches into her jacket pocket and retrieves her little black cigarettes. Lights one, slowly, and blows out a thick cloud of smoke.

'Guv? Boss? You there? The ACC is looking for you. I've told the sarge. And the press office is fielding endless calls. Is there going to be a briefing? Sophie Kirkland just reported in. Followed up on a doorstep call by a PCSU. Reports that the victim's partner was mouthing off in the Burns Head, reckoned she was seeing somebody else. Didn't seem ready to do murder over it but he wasn't exactly happy neither.'

'Name?' asks Pharaoh.

'According to Sophie, he reckons it's somebody from the letting agency that dealt with her house. Based in Patrington with another office in Withernsea.' He stops, something awkward in the pause. 'Called him Marathon Man when he was giving out about it. Mr Fucking Fit was another charming little pet name . . .'

'Go on, Andy,' says Pharaoh, as Roisin hangs up on her husband and sits back in her seat, the colour slowly returning to her cheeks.

'I saw a runner this morning,' says Daniells, as the rain starts to come down harder. 'When I arrived at the scene there was a jogger outside the cordon. He had a Covid mask and those big sunglasses that athletes wear. He asked a few questions about it all and started trying to sell me and Stefan a holiday home. Didn't seem unusual at the time but I've kind of been mulling it over and, well, all things considered I thought I should maybe see if I could track him down. I've been on the company website and there are only two male employees and he doesn't fit the bill, but then, the photos look pretty dated. I was thinking of ringing the agency and asking some questions but then I thought there was a chance you'd stab me in the face if I didn't run it by you, so, well, I'm running it by you.'

Pharaoh takes a drag on her cigarette. Stares through the rain-speckled glass. The sky is darkening; clouds curling like great twists of damp rope. She closes an eye, trying to move the pieces around inside her head. 'Who owns the company?' she asks. 'If you chat to some office junior then chances are they'll have no bloody Poker face and be straight onto their colleague and telling him to get themselves prepared. It'll be on Facebook in no time.'

There is a rustle of pages, a sudden muffled sound as Daniells moves his phone beneath his lower chin. 'Seth Brimley,' says Daniells. 'Address out Fitling way.'

'Fitling?'

'Pig farm, tea room, near Burton Constable Hall . . .'

'Far from Cottingham?' asks Pharaoh. 'Far from Sunk Island?'

'Erm, about the middle really,' says Daniells. 'I'll send you some details if you want to take it.'

'Sure. Tell the ACC something urgent came up but we'll both be in this afternoon.'

'Sure. Oh, the sarge says he knows what happened to your anarchist, by the way.'

Pharaoh snorts as she laughs. Buzzes the window down and chucks her cigarette butt onto the driveway of the Audi as he goes volubly insane behind her. 'Course he does. I'll talk to you later.'

She ends the call. Sits back. Lowers her sunglasses and gives Roisin her best stare. 'All good, then?'

'He's hurt. Fin too. But they're OK.'

'And I'm going to have to sort out a lot of mess, am I? But I'll do that because it's him, and I'll do anything for him, yes?'

Roisin takes a cigarette from her bra. Pharaoh lights it for her. 'I mean it in a good way,' says Roisin, meeting her eyes. 'He's alive because of you. He's all that he is because of you. When I think of all the times it could have gone differently, honestly, I promise you, Trish, you're always in my prayers. I thank God for you. I might give you shit but that's because I know how easy it is to love him and because sometimes he comes home smelling of you, and the thought of losing him breaks my heart. But when that bastard came for Fin, I didn't think of calling Aector – I thought of calling you.'

Pharaoh looks away first, flicking her glasses back up and wishing she still had a cigarette on the go. She blinks a couple of times. Looks away before Roisin can spot the tear that spills from her tired eyes.

'Ever been to Fitling?' she asks, flicking a V-sign to the driver behind and pulling into traffic.

'Pig farm? Tea room? He took me there for an afternoon tea once. Nice cakes, bad smell.'

'You should work in advertising,' says Pharaoh with a smile, and switches on the radio. The local news is just finishing. Bad weather to come. The lifeboat has been launched from Cleethorpes to attend an incident at Haile Sands Fort in the Humber estuary. She glances at Roisin, who is wincing in advance.

'Is he . . .?'

Roisin nods. 'Taking Fin to be checked out. He's with an Irish copper. There's been an . . . incident . . .'

Pharaoh growls. Takes the cigarette from Roisin's lips and inserts it between her own. 'Course there fucking has.'

Eleven years ago

'McAvoy.'

He jerks upright, banging his head on the door of the people carrier. Closes his eyes for a moment as the pain travels around his skull like a satellite in orbit. Opens them again when he realizes that for the briefest of moments, his son is technically untended. Checks his boy. Two months old now and putting on weight. Salami arms and apricot cheeks and chubby little fingers gripping at the air as if digging through clay. Brown eyes, red hair. Just shy of seven pounds when he was born. Smaller than they'd expected. Roisin reckoned he was keeping himself on the dainty side so as to spare her as much agony as he could.

'Thought that was you – I saw you from the window . . .'

Wilma Bradley is making her way across the icy car park towards him, placing her feet with purpose. The car park at the back of Queens Gardens Police Station is almost empty. Ragged flurries of snow tumble down from a purplish, fish-scaled sky. The earth is iron hard. There will be accidents aplenty today. The staff who live over the Humber Bridge will be reluctant to make the journey in. The A180 and the M62 will both be gridlocked before seven a.m.

McAvoy ducks back into the vehicle. Unclips his son. He's not fully asleep; a slight grizzle and the occasional grimace

betraying the fact that he's not given up the fight. He recently
declared war on his parents, ensuring that they enjoy neither the
opportunity to sleep, or to create a sibling. McAvoy has taken
to driving around the city in endless meandering configurations,
listening to classical music on the radio while the boy intermit-
tently dozes and screeches in the back. It's the only break Roisin
gets. He'd be on the breast every moment were it up to him. So
would the boy.

'Hello there,' says McAvoy, straightening up, holding the boy
to his chest. He retrieves his little stripy hat from the pocket of
his overcoat and slips it on him. Presses his cheek to the boy's.
Gives him his warmth.

'Oh my!' says Bradley, stopping a few feet away. She hasn't
pulled a coat on. Is shivering in dark trousers and a thin fleecy
pullover. She grins, unable to help herself. 'Oh he's gorgeous,
McAvoy. Double of you, isn't he? You can see he's going to be
a bruiser. Does he blush like his dad? Oh . . . what's his name?'

'Fin,' says McAvoy. 'I won't assault your ears with his middle
names.'

'He looks a Fin,' says Bradley, clearly fighting the urge to
tickle his cheek. 'Not sleeping?'

'He gives us thirty seconds or so once a fortnight. Can't ask
for more.'

She considers McAvoy. Looks him up and down as if considering placing a bid. 'You look well. Tired, of course. But well.
The scar's almost gone.'

'Wasn't much there to begin with.'

She laughs at that. Shakes her head. 'I won't keep you, I know
you'll be wanting to keep him warm. It's just, when I saw you
there, I kind of thought . . .'

'Yes.'

She looks a little awkward, as if she's not sure she's done the
right thing. Rubs her hands together. 'The items taken from
Eva-Jayne's flat . . . they're back from the lab. I wondered whether
you could pass them to the family.'

McAvoy takes care not to let his expression change. The beard
is proving a comfort, camouflaging the worst of the embarrassed
flush that grips his cheeks whenever he feels wrong-footed. He
gives himself an extra moment before replying.

Of course she knows, he tells himself. Of course she will have put the pieces together. You married a witness. You went looking for the brothers. You came back from a holiday with a facial wound. You haven't replied to her emails. Here it comes, Aector. Here it comes . . .

'You heard, then,' he says, holding Fin close.

'About your happy event? Yes. Good on you. Seems a nice girl. Fiery temper, of course, but that's in the blood. Seems to have done wonders for you.'

He smiles, unable to help it. 'I've tried not to tell people, but I know word gets around . . .'

'You should have just told me,' she says, looking a little disappointed in him. 'None of my business, of course, but were you seeing each other before it happened?'

He shakes his head. 'No, I just knew the family. Kind of a whirlwind, I suppose.'

'That's what she said.' Bradley nods. 'Wish I had better news for them. I'm not part of it anymore. The file's still officially open but we've nowhere left to take it. You'll have heard about the two brothers? Missing for months now. Maybe recipients of some summary justice but Roper's not giving it any more resources than needs be. Did I hear you're moving onto his team?'

'Possibly,' says McAvoy, conscious of the falling temperature and his son's warm breath at his neck. 'I need to make sense of some things first.'

'Don't we all.' Bradley smiles and shakes her head again. 'They never listened to me anyway. Roper and his hangers-on. Lost interest in Eva-Jayne pretty quickly. Chalking it down to somebody feeling pissed off about hearing their future wasn't much better than their present. I can't say for sure. We've traced her regulars – all had plenty nice things to say about her. A lovely lady. Wouldn't be a bad inscription on a headstone, would it? Is she OK, your wife? Memories like that . . .'

'She never really saw anything, as she said in her statement,' says McAvoy, fidgeting. He fiddles with Fin's little bootie. Unlaces it and laces it up again.

'The chap she bumped into on the stairs – you can tell her he's grand, by the way. Still has the odd nightmare about the girl who jumped down the stairs and put him on his backside but I think he rather enjoys having something else to occupy his time. Bit of a saddo, if that isn't too cruel. Armchair detective. Rings me every couple of days for updates. Wish I could tell him something other than the truth.'

McAvoy presses his lips together until they become a single, bloodless line. 'Wrong place, wrong time, eh? Thanks for asking, though. I'll pass that on.'

'It's the crystal that's doing me in,' says Bradley, talking more to herself than to McAvoy. 'Not one of hers, that's pretty clear. Labradorite. It's a beautiful thing, once you've sponged the gore off. Hammered right into her, like a stake through a fucking vampire. It's a healing stone, your Roisin will know that, I'm sure. To cleanse and realign your chakras – to protect you from bad spirits, bad vibes.'

McAvoy nods, afraid to speak.

'The mouth injuries too. Roper has it that the tongue was cut out but I've seen the photos. Looks to me more like a mutilation – like somebody was cutting it in two.'

'Jesus,' whispers McAvoy, putting his palm over Fin's tiny ear. 'I'll pick up the stuff, drop it off. No worries . . .'

'I'm leaving anyway,' says Bradley, brightly. 'Detective sergeant, West Mercia. Can't come soon enough, if I'm honest. I don't feel particularly appreciated. My boss, Trish, she said I needed to have a fresh start and I trust her judgement. Been through some horrors. Did you hear? Husband's had an aneurysm – isn't likely to walk again. Finances are all over the place too. Sorry, I do blab when I get going. Don't worry – I'm usually the soul of discretion. Take my secrets to the grave, as it were.'

McAvoy meets her stare. Holds it. 'I really hope it all works out for you,' he says, and means it.

She takes a moment. Doesn't smile. 'There are some personal letters she might want back,' she says, at last. 'I'm a softie at heart. When she came in and made the statement and I put two and two together . . .'

'I don't follow.'

'Her notebook. It was taken as evidence. You can give it back to her. Maybe don't tell her if you read it.'

'I don't understand.'

'Lots of letters to "my darling Aector". Written over the years.

She's had a thing for you for a long time. I'm not judging. Nice to see it's all worked out. But you know how people can be.'

McAvoy blushes scarlet. Holds Fin so tightly that he lets out a little cry. McAvoy pats his back. Tries to stop himself coming apart: crumbling into ash and billowing away with the swirling snow.

'That's private,' he says. 'Of course I won't read it.'

'I believe you,' says Bradley, with something like sadness. 'Anyway, there are a couple of bin bags by my desk. I'll mark them for your attention. I'm having some drinks at the Country Park Inn next Friday, if you can get a babysitter. Bring your lady.'

McAvoy doesn't speak. Just wants to get his son in out of the cold. Wants to go and hold his wife. Wants to stop being Aector McAvoy and go live in the safe little bubble where the world can't get to any of them.

'I'll try,' he says. 'Best of luck.'

'And to you,' she says. 'You too, Fin,' she says, smiling again. 'Take care of Daddy.'

She turns away. Walks sure-footed across the car park. As she leaves, a snatch of melody, off-key but recognizable, carrying on the cold air. Classic Nina – the song they danced to at the wedding.

I Put a Spell on You . . .

THIRTY-SEVEN

Nine years ago

Four hundred yards past the sign declaring 'PRIVATE PROPERTY', is another, scrawled in a noticeably less kindly font. This one reads: 'TURN THE FUCK AROUND'.

Papa Teague, at the wheel of the red Toyota Hi-Lux, allows himself a wry smile. Whether it is due to the bluntness of the sign, or simply a response to the nearness of his prize, he would not be able to say. He is not an educated man. He's quick-witted, intuitive, begrudgingly literate, but his schooling was sporadic and his interest in the contents of weighty academic tomes is minimal. As such, Papa Teague has never heard about Pavlov's dogs. He is unaware of the theory that carries the scientist's name: the discovery that dogs could be made to salivate if they associated feeding time with the ringing of a bell. Were somebody to inform Papa Teague, he would be spectacularly unimpressed. He has owned Rottweilers that drool the moment they see him pulling on the leather gloves that he wears when he is taking care of what he always refers to as 'some business in town'. The 'business' covers a multitude of sins, but the Rottweilers know that before the day is out, they will be licking blood from leather. Papa's smile upon nearing the little farmhouse at the end of the track, is no less a work of classical conditioning. Once he passes the sign, he is only minutes away from pleasure. And Papa Teague takes his pleasures very seriously.

The vehicle jerks left and right as it hits the trenches and rises in the dirt track. On either side, the trees reach out their branches; black, claw-like twigs intertwining overhead: a spindly mesh that turns the early-morning sunlight into a camouflage pattern on the rain-speckled metal of the car.

Papa Teague slows as he reaches the squat, white-painted farmhouse at the end of the road. It sits in the centre of some fifty acres of arable farmland, though the fields haven't been turned these past twelve years. Nobody has knocked on this door in years. The nearest neighbour is three miles away, and they know better than to come asking for a cup of sugar. This is a bad place. People were hurt here, years ago. They say there's still blood on the ceiling; brains turning the flock wallpaper to gory woodchip. Papa Teague cannot verify the truth of the statement. Just knows it's a safe place; a sanctuary, where no bugger would be fool enough to come asking questions or causing problems.

He switches off the engine. Enjoys the silence. There's a little shiver in his gut; a suppressed tremble of anticipation. It used to be this way in the day before a fistfight. He could already feel the cold agony of his own healing wounds; the broken bones, the blood trickling down his throat every time he slept lying down. He could look at his hands and call to mind the sensation of their breaking; swelling; bleeding. He would force himself to confront the pain that was to come. By the time the fight began, he would already have endured the worst he could imagine. Had experienced it, and come through the other side. And he could concentrate instead on inflicting pain.

He steps from the vehicle. Admires himself in the darkened glass. Still a forbidding figure, all in all. Hasn't turned into his father yet. Still got broad shoulders and arms that strain at the fabric of his dark-blue shirt. There's a gut, behind his mustard-coloured waistcoat, but not one to be ashamed of. He's man-sized. Man-shaped. All fecking *man*.

He takes off the porkpie hat and chucks it on the driving seat. Rolls back the sleeves of his shirt. Slowly takes off his big gold rings and the identity bracelet at his wrist. Places them all in a little black velvet bag and chucks the lot inside his hat. He reaches across and removes a wooden crate from the footwell. It's heavy, but he doesn't let himself show that it's a struggle. Even here, even alone, he doesn't want to show weakness.

He looks up. Watches the rain. Wonders how long he'll keep doing this. When he will receive the sign from the Almighty that enough is enough.

Says a prayer. Crosses himself with his hands full. Nods, as if making his peace with God. Then he crosses the muddy forecourt at the front of the farmhouse and trudges past a series of outbuildings. They are rarely empty. He has stored all manner of contraband here over the years. He reminds himself to pick up a crate of the stolen cut-throat razors that one of his boys helped himself to at the docks. They're German. Quality steel. Perhaps his son-in-law would like one as a birthday present. He rather likes the thought of that, much as he likes the lad. His hatred of coppers outweighs his love for his daughter's husband.

He turns right at a patchy stretch of hedge and trudges across long, damp grass, soaking himself to the knees. He counts as he walks, his strides uniform, his eyes fixed on a point at the far end of the field, screened by a low stand of trees and a small drainage ditch running down to the stream.

He stops when he reaches one hundred. Looks around him at the tangled wildflowers and grasses. He can just make out the indentations; can see the subtle changes in the colour and texture of the greenery. He looks around, checking that he remains unobserved. Raises his eyes, ever alert for the presence of the Gardai helicopter. Sees only the blurry outlines of two ling-necked white birds, briefly illuminated by a blade of whitish sunlight. He wonders at its meaning. Can think of no negative interpretation of such a joyful scene. Sees only beauty, elegance, purity; the kiss of the dawn. He takes comfort in it. Takes strength.

From the crate, he removes an extendable, military-issue spade. Stretches the handle to its extremities and begins to work. Plunges the dull blade into the matted ground, taking care to keep the sods intact. He works up a sweat as he works, his back twinging as he rises to deposit each fresh chunk of black earth and green grass in a neat pile to his left. Spies the bone-bright roots; things that scuttle and squirm and burrow. Thinks of the poem that he used to know by heart and which now comes only in snatches. Thinks of the place where the shaft of the spade meets his palm; the rasp and suck and scrape of necessary toil.

The spade hits wood. A slow smile creeps over Papa Teague's face. Dropping to his knees, he begins to clear the area by hand, pulling up tufts and weeds; letting the nettles and thistles assault his skin; wildflowers bleeding green upon his sweat-soaked shirt and forearms.

Soon, his hands are touching the curved black wood, his fingers searching out the edges of the hatch. It had pained him to so mistreat such an elegant wagon. It's a proper vardo, crafted in the 1930s and home to generation after generation of distant kinsmen. It has witnessed births and deaths and all that comes in between. It was in a state of disrepair when he took it, in part-payment against an unmanageable debt. He'd planned to have it restored and to present it to his daughter as a gift: a way to keep her Pavee roots even while living within static walls. Instead, it serves as something that is at once jail cell and tomb.

Papa Teague checks the sky again. Inserts his fingers into the tiny space that he sawed into the bowtop roof. Pulls it back, arching his neck away from the opening before the stench can engulf him. Something like steam rises from the ink-black square. A warmth. The mingled scents of decay and filth and spilled, clotted blood. Fat flies hover briefly in the air above the hole, the light dazzling on their iridescent bodies. Papa Teague covers his mouth. Fights the bile. Reminds himself of what this man did. Of what he would have done had fate not intervened.

He takes a torch from the crate. Steels himself. Shines it into the darkness.

The man known as Cromwell cowers in the furthest recesses of the wagon, wrapped up in his own stark-white limbs; arms and legs drawn up, face pressed against bloodied, shit-streaked knees. Papa Teague thinks briefly of Hell. The Hell the priests used to talk about at Mass: of suffering beyond endurance – the flames devouring the eyes, the endless agonies, the wail and despair of the sinners beyond redemption. He feels a surge of compassion. Fights it down.

Perched on the lip of the hole, Papa Teague pulls a pack of cards from the pocket of his waistcoat. It's a fresh pack, the seal unbroken, the cellophane catching the light. Slowly, silently, he opens the pack of Oracle cards. Shuffles them, his movements languid, deliberate. He keeps his eyes on the figure in the dark. Hopes that this time, he will be given permission to dispense mercy instead of justice.

He blesses himself. Splits the deck. Stares at the Oracle card and feels his heart sink. The image is of a furry cat, inscrutable eyes, sketched against a red carpet and yellow wall. It is the sign for 'falseness': a reminder to be alert to those who will lie and cheat and manipulate. A card of lies, corruption, negativity. It is the card selected for him by fate, and the ethereal presence of those who serve as his guide. It is not a card that allows him to be merciful. Cromwell's punishment must continue.

He spits into the hole. Up-ends the crate. Packs of Army rations spill into the darkness like coal. Dry food, desiccated fruits, sugar-packed chocolates and barely-edible biscuits. They land in the pool of stagnant muddy water that swills upon the floor of the wagon; circles on the surface as it steadily drains away through the rotting floor into the black earth beneath.

Papa Teague hopes that by the time he returns, the earth will have swallowed him. That the weight of the dirt and the rain will cause the wagon's roof to sag, and that he will have drowned or suffocated, or his heart have simply given up through poor despair.

He shines the light upon the man who killed his kin, and who would have taken his daughter to pieces and driven a crystal through her heart. Feels the familiar rage rise. Takes comfort in it. Hides behind it.

A moment, before the hatch closes. A heartbeat. The figure in the darkness looks up. Sees. Papa Teague locks eyes with the creature he has imprisoned beneath the earth. Sees the spark in his eyes: the burning, ceaseless hatred. Looks into eyes that carry a promise, an oath, a prayer. Sees his own unmerciful death; the annihilation of all that he loves; the crimson agony of his own death.

He slithers back. Slams the lid shut. Tries to catch his breath. When he lights his cigar, he notices that his hands are shaking. It takes an effort of will to calm himself. To look up into the sky, and search for something with which he can soothe himself. He cannot see the birds. The light has been folded within a great dark fist of cloud.

He doesn't make a sound as he starts to pack the sods back on top of the wagon. Keeps his thoughts only on the task at hand.

As he crosses himself, work complete, there is a moment when he fancies he hears the faintest of sounds: a low, keening song, rising up from the earth beneath his feet. He turns his back. Walks away.

Doesn't stop asking the Lord for forgiveness until he is back in the car.

Cannot shake the feeling that there are voices other than his own, whispering in the echo of his *Amen*.

THIRTY-EIGHT

1.22 p.m.
Haile Sands Fort

'Jesus, Mary and Joseph' says Garda Kincaid, ducking under the metal doorway and shining a light on the mangled corpse. 'I'm taking it that you hit him quite hard.'

McAvoy steps back into the dark space. Covers his nose. It smells of damp and wet metal, gun smoke and blood. 'The flare,' he says, under his breath. 'I didn't know that would happen.'

'No?' asks Kincaid, swivelling around to face him. 'What did you think? That it would just look pretty?'

'My son,' says McAvoy, leaning back against the wall. All the strength has gone out of him. Fin is still waiting for him in the lifeboat, surrounded by the crew from the Cleethorpes station. Lucas Barrington is with them, whispering quietly in their ears, unsure whether he has been involved in a heroic rescue mission, or been the victim of a kidnapping. Fin, wrapped in a blanket and with bindings on his wounds, is staring towards the shore like a fisherman saying goodbye to a lover.

'It's best all round,' says Kincaid, looking down at the body. 'Best for you. Best for me. Best for Papa Teague.'

McAvoy looks up. Rubs the grit from his eyes. 'I don't understand.'

'I've spoken with my guv,' he says, quietly. 'He's not disappointed. This prick had a lot of bargaining chips. He . . . did things . . .'

McAvoy rubs his hand across his face, turning the tumblers in his mind. 'He killed for important people?'

Kincaid shrugs. 'My lips are sealed, mate. Suffice to say, my boss, and your boss, are going to have a chat that's more about silences and knowing glances than words and handshakes.'

'Trish?' asks McAvoy. 'She doesn't know anything . . .'

'Not your fucking line manager, McAvoy. I mean your chief constable. He's going to get a phone call from a number that rarely calls. And he's going to go to bed tonight feeling very happy. A murder cleared up within twenty-four hours – another cold case put to bed, and maybe even a bravery citation for whichever officer he chooses to stick it on.'

'He said he didn't kill Eva-Jayne,' says McAvoy. 'And as for the case at Sunk Island, that doesn't make any sense. The crystal, the Oracle cards . . .'

'Symbolic.' Kincaid shrugs. 'Papa Teague used to ask the fates to decide whether to let him die. Always had a touch of the second sight, so he did. Makes sense as a calling card.'

'And why Dymphna?'

'Christ knows. Maybe just to get you away from the house?'

McAvoy shakes his head. 'I saw her body. Everything that was done to her – it was done with intent.'

Kincaid crouches down beside the body: a crumpled swastika
of twisted limbs. Pats at the pocket of his military-issue trousers.
'You said yourself you found a charm bracelet near the scene.'

'A charm bracelet,' he says, tiredly. 'Yes. Roisin's, I'm sure
of it.'

'So who else?' asks Kincaid. He waves the torch around.
'What's with all the snowflakes?'

'I think it's asbestos,' says McAvoy. 'Don't worry, a little bit
of exposure won't do you any harm.'

'Won't do much fucking good either,' grumbles Kincaid. His
torchlight picks out the curve of a single canoe, pushed up behind
a lopsided cabinet. 'At least you know what happened to the
anarchist. And if he's got this shit in his lungs it will be another
one to pin on this prick.'

'So you think we'll be allowed to name him?'

Kincaid laughs. 'Christ only knows what story they'll cook
up, but yeah, they'll let you put a name to the crimes. Any
suggestion that he's got links to powerful people – that will be
shot down at once.'

'You mean shut down?'

'No,' says Kincaid, flatly. He retrieves a slim black mobile
phone from the dead man's pocket. Grimaces as he rolls the
glove from the lifeless hand and presses the thumb to the screen.
He scrolls through the data.

McAvoy moves away from the wall. Looks down into the patch
of darkness where his son was hogtied and tortured. Makes fists,
his blood surging in his ears as if he were underwater. His brain
feels as though it has been punched again and again. Despite it,
he can feel something squirming inside his skull, as if a single
green shoot were trying to push its way clear of the muck of his
thoughts. He knows he's missing something. None of this feels
right. He needs to stop thinking about Roisin. About what she may
have told Trish. Needs to clear his head of everything else and
just focus on what his mind is trying to tell him.

'Oh, my boss is going to be happy,' mutters Kincaid, as he
pulls out his own mobile and starts snapping pictures of the data
on the screen of the dead man's phone. 'If you were wondering,
he's taken pictures of the dead Heldens and the dead Teagues.
He's proud of his work. If you're going to give yourself sleepless

nights, just remember what this cunt was willing to do. If you hadn't come along he'd have gone through with it. Made you choose.'

'I couldn't have,' says McAvoy.

'Then they'd both be dead,' says Kincaid, simply. He lets out a little hiss. 'That makes sense,' he mutters.

'What does?'

'Internet search. Chondrosarcoma. Treatments, a guide to pain management, possible life expectancy if untreated . . .'

'That's a bone cancer, isn't it? He'll have been in agony.'

'And on borrowed time if he had revenge on his mind. See – even given you a motive.'

McAvoy shakes his head. 'He didn't do the clairvoyants. Didn't do Eva-Jayne.'

'Well, your wife says he did. That's why her daddy put him in the ground for years. Who else?'

McAvoy closes his eyes. Tries to tease out the facts that matter from the whole flicker-pad of memories. Thinks all the way back to the first time he heard about the murder at the flats in Scunthorpe.

'01964,' says Kincaid, behind him. 'That's here, isn't it?'

'Holderness,' says McAvoy. 'Why?'

'Several calls to a local number over the course of two days last week. Some at strange hours. Two a.m., three oh five a.m., five a.m. . . .'

'Read it out,' says McAvoy, sharply, and keys the number into his own phone. As he punches in the area code, the screen fills with contacts and recent calls from any number beginning 01964. First among them is a call received at nine fifty-eight a.m.

'What you got?' asks Kincaid, noting the change in the bigger man's body language. 'Don't be making life difficult when it just got so simple, now.'

McAvoy says nothing. Pictures himself, driving home at break-neck speed – the call coming through as he neared home and learned about the abduction of his son. He'd spoken to Andy Daniells about it at the crime scene. Had he ever been given a name?

'McAvoy? What you got?'

'Just a moment,' he mutters, and wedges his finger in his ear as he listens back to his voicemails.

'Hello, Sergeant McAvoy, I think we were cut off. This is Seth Brimley, I understand you were eager to talk to me regarding one of our rental properties at Sunk Island . . .'

The name ignites like a flare. He recalls the witness statement from years before, given by a businessman hurt by a fine-featured, dark-haired girl as she fled the scene of Eva-Jayne Puck's brutal murder.

'Seriously, McAvoy, what's happening in that big head of yours?' Kincaid sounds worried now, as if his almost-completed jigsaw puzzle is missing some pieces.

'Brimley,' mutters McAvoy, putting the name into a search engine. 'Seth Brimley.'

'Who's that?'

'Estate agent. Letting agent. Land agent. He was there when Eva-Jayne died.'

'No, I told you, the Heldens sent this prick to do Roisin and she got done instead . . .'

No,' says McAvoy, scanning an article on a property website. 'No, the Heldens sent him after. He's always said that. He worked it out, Kincaid – worked out who'd done it. Maybe he was blackmailing him, needed a place . . . oh Jesus.'

'What?'

'Brimley's company handled the sale of this place in 2017,' says McAvoy, quietly.

'What, this fort?'

McAvoy nods. 'And there's an article here . . .'

Kincaid leans over his shoulder. Reads the headline.

Colleagues Line Street to Honour A Glorious Spirit.

'*Holderness Gazette*,' says McAvoy, quietly. '2009. Evangeline Brimley, office manager for a local estate agent, laid to rest after a short battle with a brain tumour . . . no children . . . husband gave tearful eulogy . . .'

Kincaid points to the screen, his voice hushed. '"Colleagues spoke about her 'deep and abiding' interest in spiritualism and say she put her faith in New Age healing practices instead of conventional medicines . . ."'

McAvoy turns to Kincaid, so close their noses almost touch. 'Jesus, it was there all along.'

'You don't know for certain,' says Kincaid, shaking his head.

'You just want to preserve your neat little story,' spits McAvoy.

'It helps you out too, boy,' says Kincaid.

'I don't care about me. My boy's safe. My wife's safe. My daughter's safe. Whatever happens, this man needs to be arrested. God knows how many he might have killed.'

'I'm calling my guv,' says Kincaid, angrily. 'Don't do a fucking thing . . .'

'I'm calling mine,' says McAvoy, punching Pharaoh's number. 'He at least needs to be questioned.'

'No,' says Kincaid, eyes flashing temper. 'No, you're going to mess things up.'

McAvoy turns his back on Kincaid. Curses as the call goes straight to voicemail. Rings Andy Daniells, struggling to hear as Kincaid launches into a furious rant to his own boss.

'. . . silly bollocks here is going to fuck it up . . . thinks he's got an accomplice, or another killer, but won't do the sensible fucking thing . . .'

'Andy?'

'Now then, sarge. You after the boss? I think she and your good lady have gone all Thelma and Louise on us. Bit of good news though, I've got the preliminaries through from the pathologist. Seems the tongue wasn't excised, so much as split. Cut down the middle, like a snake's . . .'

McAvoy swallows. Forces himself to stay calm. 'Andy, just stop. Where's Trish?'

'She's speaking to a potential love interest of the victim's,' says Daniells, more slowly. 'Estate agent, lives out Fitling way. Tried her myself a moment ago but the reception's awful out there. You might want to give your good lady's mobile a go, I think they're making an outing of it, though the ACC will go fucking spare if she hears me say that . . .'

McAvoy feels his legs go out from under him. 'Seth Brimley?' he asks, weakly.

'That's the chap,' says Daniells, brightly. 'You OK, sarge?'

And McAvoy is suddenly pushing past Kincaid and vaulting the headless man, feet pounding up the darkened stairwell, sprinting towards the light.

'All units,' he's shouting, into the mobile. 'All fucking units, now!'

THIRTY-NINE

Eight months ago

An X-shaped building.
Grey, stained almost black by the ceaseless rain.
The sky an endless smear of damp graphite and charcoal.

A pink corridor, paper peeling, ceiling curved. Rubble in open doorways, floorboards peeking out from beneath frayed trenches in the linoleum.

Smashed glass, here. Graffiti sprayed haphazardly on plaster, on wood, on stone.

Papa Teague holds the phone to his ear as he walks softly down the hallway, his other hand white-knuckled around the handle of a slash hook.

'I can't hear you, Danior . . . the fecking echoes in here . . . Jaysus, but I turned left four times, chavva . . .'

He passes an open doorway. Glimpses a white, metal surgical bed, abandoned in the centre of an unlit room. Paper hangs in torn strips from the wall. Changing his position, he spies a wheelchair, abandoned in the furthest corner, as if some invisible occupant had been left there and told to face the wall.

Papa Teague turns right, moving swiftly down a staircase patterned with pigeon shit and smashed tiles. He can hear the echo of his own footsteps. Can feel the damp in his bones. The meeting place wasn't his choice. The old mental hospital has been closed for years but he is old enough to remember the stories about what happened to people once they were dragged within its great forbidding walls.

'Feck it, Danior, any more of this shite and I'm away, boy . . .'

He stops, the echoes of his voice disappearing into the walls like shy spirits. Only one door is open in the hallway. It matches the image that Danior Helden sent him an hour ago. They've been trying to meet for days, but each time they have left their hiding places in a desperate attempt to parlay, the presence of the Gardai or the mere presence of an unfamiliar vehicle has been enough for one or both of them to call things off. The Heldens and Teagues have known war far longer than they have ever known peace, but the relative truce between the clans has now lasted over a decade. There have been wobbles, of course, and there was that bad business with Valentine Teague and Shay Helden over in America, but by and large the peace has held. They still distrust one another, but for now, they are united. A common enemy has ensured they pool resources.

A large, broad-shouldered man with dark hair and a tatty bomber jacket steps into the corridor from the open door. He looks Papa Teague up and down, his eyes coming to rest on the weapon in his hand.

'Won't be enough,' says Helden.

'Why? You got more with you?'

'No, cousin. I'm alone, as I swore I'd be. I mean that won't be enough if you were followed.'

Teague opens his coat. Shows the revolver in the pocket of his waistcoat. 'The knife's got friends.'

'They say you don't hear him coming. By the time you get your gun out you're already watching your blood pool.'

Teague sniffs. Spits. Shows his teeth. 'Butcher's bill?'

'Duke and Lash,' he says, quietly. 'Menowin's boy and his friend.'

'Dead?'

'Duke made it home. We won't see Lash again.'

'He badly hurt?'

'If he was a horse I'd fecking shoot him. One side of him . . . just fecking hangs there. Went at his spine with a screwdriver.'

Papa Teague crosses himself. Looks down to the floor. 'He came for my daughter, Danior.'

'No,' says Danior, shaking his head. 'No he didn't. I was there, cousin. We'd have put any of you boys in the ground but why the fuck would we waste a hired gun on some nobody across the water?'

'Eva-Jayne?' asks Papa, scowling. 'He got himself confused – thought she was the target, or she disturbed him before he got to Roisin . . .'

'How many times?' snaps Helden. 'Time and again, all through the peace, I've fucking told ye! We sent Cromwell over the water because those half breed animals, those Godless half-brothers, were offering her for sale. And by Christ, though we hated you then and we'd have been glad of the bargaining power, he was in the middle of the Irish sea when the fortune teller died. You had your boys tucked away all over. Doncaster, Hartlepool, Falkirk. Don't act like you didn't, but you think we'd have gone for your girl? Your pride and fecking joy? After what she'd already endured? Fuck, cousin – you've been torturing the wrong man.'

'No,' says Teague, shaking his head. 'No, you sent him. He killed Eva-Jayne, he would have done the same to my daughter. He shouldn't have lived, not after what was done to him. He was more broken bones than whole ones when my man found him, found Ro, found her husband more dead than alive. Scared the almighty shite out of him when he sat up. I swear, my Jonjo still can't fecking talk about it without turning white. Zipped him into the body bag, almost up past the nose, and then the fecker sits up. Half his face stoved in and he sits up like his alarm's just gone off. I didn't think he'd survive. Getting him across the water, getting him home, even as your family and mine were breaking bread and toasting the future . . . he should have died. He just wouldn't.'

'And we didn't ask the right questions because it spared us settling his bill,' says Helden, rubbing his jaw, closing his eyes. 'Swallowed every word you said. And all the while you had him. Tortured him. Year after year . . .'

'And you'd have been merciful, would you? If he'd come for your daughter, you'd have put a bullet in him?'

Danior Teague doesn't reply at first. Sucks his cheek. Picks at something trapped between his canines. 'He won't stop, cousin,' he says, quietly. 'Not ever. What he's endured, what you put him through . . . to survive that, to emerge, to heal . . . and then come for all we hold dear . . .'

Papa Teague feels his energy sag. Looks at the slash hook in his hand and feels pitiable. He feels his age, suddenly. Doesn't want to skulk and hide and fight for his life. Wants to play with his grandchildren and tell old stories and settle in to being a grand old has-been. Until a month ago, he hadn't thought about Cromwell in years. The visits to the farm had become less frequent; the supplies less plentiful; the rage less fierce. Eventually, without ever making a decision, he simply stopped going to the farm. The wagon would have caved in years before, he was certain about that. The earth had chewed him up and swallowed him down. He had endured Hell beyond imagining. Justice had been done.

Then the killings began.

The Heldens and Teagues have lost daughters and sons. Distant relatives, family outliers, countryfolk with even a whiff of connection to the two clans – all have become targets for a killer who seems to emerge from the air and who disappears again when the carnage is done. Danior's own son was the first to escape. He fed back a description of the demon that had come for him. And though the years had leeched the colour from his skin and turned his features into those of something long-dead, there had been enough familiarity about his methods, his singularity of purpose, to remind both families of the killer they had both employed against the other in years gone by. Papa Teague had driven out to the farm. Had found the patch of earth where he had buried his foe. Had dug down, into rotten timber and buckled iron wheels, through food wrappers and bloodstained bandages. He'd excavated half the damn field. Didn't find a body. Not a bone. And he'd had no choice but to tell his kin that for six long years he had exacted a father's revenge on the man who came for his child. It doesn't matter that the Heldens still deny complicity. The monster is free, and he is out to end the bloodline of the man who locked him up, along with the family who did nothing to help him.

'You'll tell her,' says Helden, quietly. 'Your daughter? The copper? He'll come for them, sure as shite.'

Papa licks his dry lips. He is losing people he loves; is terrified of every shadow and sudden sound, but the thought of telling Roisin that her attacker still lives is something that he cannot bring himself to do. She has found a happiness he did not imagine she could ever feel. He knows what he will do to that fragile contentment were he to tell her that the man who killed Eva-Jayne is free and seeking vengeance.

'He can't kill us all,' says Danior, thoughtfully. 'Those years, the injuries. He's fast, he's lethal, but somebody will get him. You've heard what he's become. A demon. Maggot-white, that's what the lad says. Fingers like claws. Not a tooth in his head or a hair on his head. Somebody will see him. We'll stop him. But we need to be on the lookout. Everybody needs to be prepared. You have to tell her, cousin.'

Teague doesn't speak. Looks around, slowly. Jerks his head at the door. 'Why here, Danior? All the fecking places . . . why here?'

Danior smiles, though there's no joy in it. Jerks his head at the doorway and gestures for Teague to follow him. Leads him into a single room: a white metal bed, leather restraint straps dangling from the frame like flaps of skin. Green linoleum, scuffed down to nothing, white coats hanging on pegs by the far wall.

Teague takes a sniff of the dead air. Mould, rotten wood, damp feathers. And something deeper. Something earthy. Something that reeks of the grave.

He crosses to the bed. There is an indentation in the mattress. A stain upon the mottled grey covering; a paint-blot; open mouth, staring eyes; a ghoulish twist to the mouth. Teague touches the pillow. Puts his fingers to his mouth. Crosses himself.

'He's been home,' says Teague, softly. It's real, at last. He survived. He's come for blood. He'll want Roisin. Her husband. Her children . . .

'Came back to where we first found him,' says Danior, softly.

Teague looks to the weapon in his hand. Hates it all. Hates the violence, and the back-and-forth, and the endless waves of blood and pain and retaliation. He throws the curved blade. It sticks into the plaster beside the white coats, the handle juddering like a diving board.

He turns away from the bed. 'We need to make ourselves scarce, cousin. Keep him guessing. Keep moving. Keep giving ourselves a fighting chance . . .'

Danior nods. 'Or I could just give him you and see if that satisfies him.'

Teague nods. Sighs. Looks up to see the other man holding an old, black service revolver, the trigger cocked.

'Maybe if I do you, it all ends. I wish it weren't like this, cousin . . .'

Papa Teague fires his weapon through the fabric of his waistcoat. Feels the heat of the bullet, the kick of the recoil. Hears the endless reverberations as the sound of the shot echoes off the walls.

Watches the other man fall to his knees, the back of his head now a streak of lumpy red against the damp walls.

Papa Teague makes the sign of the cross. Takes a pack of cards from his pocket. Cuts them, and drops a random picture card on the swiftly-emptying corpse of his kin.

He doesn't look at it. Doesn't need to.

Ever since Cromwell resurfaced, every card he has picked up has promised Death.

FORTY

1.58 p.m.
Fitling, Holderness

'You were right about the smell,' says Pharaoh, wrinkling her nose.

'Oh that's outside, is it?' asks Roisin, innocently. 'Didn't like to say anything.'

'You're funny,' says Pharaoh, scowling.

'I know.'

Pharaoh glances at her phone. There's no signal, but she had the foresight to download a map of the area before they were swallowed up by the endless flatness of Holderness. Brimley's house is at the end of a long track, half a mile from the nearest neighbour and just on the periphery of the sweet, porcine stench.

'I thought there was good money in being an estate agent,' mutters Pharaoh, as the tyres struggle for purchase on the slick, arrow-straight little lane.

'Maybe there's a castle at the end,' says Roisin, helpfully. She's tutting at her phone, trying to get the damn thing to send a picture to Pharaoh's daughter, Sophia. She was able to have a quick chat with Lilah before she was cut off, but Pharaoh can tell she's regretting the decision to come with her. She wants to be with her children. Wants to hold her husband. Wants to call her father and tell him that she will never forgive him for all that his actions have put them through. Instead she has to settle for staring out of the window, staring at mile upon mile of nothingness.

'You can see why people don't want Travelers on their land,' she grumbles. 'No room.'

'This can't be right,' says Pharaoh, ignoring her.

Up ahead is a small, unkempt little bungalow, plonked by the roadside like a discarded toy. It's pebbledashed at the front but random chunks of plaster and stone are missing from the side walls, showing bare, damp brick beneath. The window frames are peeling, the front door streaked with dirt, as if kicked with a muddy boot. There are dead flowers in the window boxes. Dirty lace curtains. The front lawn is overgrown, speckled with a mulch of windblown leaves. There are dead rosebushes in the raised beds, twisted with the barbed wire of free-growing bramble-bushes. A Toyota Land Cruiser is parked in front of a little blue-roofed garage.

'Nice,' says Roisin, as Pharaoh pulls in to the grass verge and kills the engine.

'Shall I crack a window? Dogs die in hot cars.'

'It's OK, if I feel unwell I'll cut a hole in the roof.'

'Peachy. Back in a bit.'

Pharaoh slams the door hard enough to make Roisin's head ring. She grins to herself as she walks to the front door. She's rather enjoying Roisin's company. They've talked a lot on the journey, both attempting to show the other how well they understand the man who connects them – sharing stories and memories and finding common ground in exasperation. It seems he causes them equal amounts of worry and despair.

The gate hangs open, black paint and rust. Pharaoh pushes it with her boot. She snatches off her sunglasses and tucks them into her jacket as the door swings open and a figure appears in the empty frame. He's pushing sixty. Skinny, but in decent shape: as if his limbs were made of tarred rope wrapped in air-dried ham. He's wearing jeans and a long-sleeved shirt under a baggy cardigan. Short grey hair and an angular jawline, his chin more straight lines than curves.

'Mr Brimley?'

He nods, all smiles. 'You'll be the police, I shouldn't wonder.'

'Detective Superintendent Pharaoh,' she says, wafting her lanyard.

'I wasn't expecting a home visit,' he says, casually. 'I don't get many callers out here. Not a lot of trouble with Jehovah's Witnesses.'

'Lovely area,' says Pharaoh, conversationally. 'Must have taken somebody an age to flatten out all the hills.'

'Topographically underwhelming,' he says, looking past her to the little convertible on the grass verge. 'Just yourself, is there?'

'Near as damnit,' says Pharaoh. 'Do you mind if I come in?'

Brimley looks at her for a moment. Angles his head, as if listening for a distant voice. Then he steps out of the doorway and ushers her inside. 'Living room's through there.'

'You estate agents,' says Pharaoh, wiping her biker boots on the coarse mat. 'The patter never leaves you.'

The living room is small and cluttered, as if the furniture were designed for a bigger house. The huge sofa would look luxurious in a grand, high-ceilinged living room but here it just looks cramped. There's a little coffee table in front of it: providing a plinth for books, magazines, dirty plates, all weighed down with a red bowl full of glass beads. The wallpaper's old-fashioned: erratic swirls of avocado, kiwi and tangerine that make Pharaoh wonder whether licking the paper would sort out her vitamin deficiency.

'It's about Dymphna, yes?' asks Brimley, sitting down in the rocking chair. He shakes his head. 'Bad business.'

'Can I ask how well you knew Ms Lowell?'

He pauses before answering. 'It is murder, then? The police officer wouldn't say when I asked but I've listened to the news most of the day and the words "suspicious death" do lend themselves to a bleak interpretation.'

Pharaoh sits down on the lip of the sofa. Spreads her hands apologetically. 'As you can imagine, for operational reasons

I'm unable to tell you very much. It would be a help if we knew
more about her. I understand your firm rented out the property
to Ms Lowell.'

Brimley scratches at his neck. Makes a little clucking noise
with his tongue. 'I thought there would be blue lights,' he says,
half to himself. He waves in the general direction of the main
road. 'Sound travels here. I can't hear sirens.'

Pharaoh shuffles in her chair. Glances around the room. Her
eyes rest on the green-framed photograph, sitting on the low
wooden cabinet in place of the TV. Sees the pendant around the
bright-eyed, attractive woman's neck.

'That's the wife,' says Brimley, following her gaze. 'Love of
my life, she was. Can't say I've ever really got over it. They
called her "a glorious spirit" in the newspaper. She'd have liked
that.'

Pharaoh licks dry lips. Drinks in the other details of the room.
Picks out muddy footprints on the swirling carpet. Spots the
discarded running trainers by the little armchair, the soles crusted
red and brown.

'You called her Dymphna,' says Pharaoh, chattily. 'I presume
that means you were more than passing acquaintances?'

'Lovely name, isn't it?' says Brimley, dreamily. He rubs at his
chin, his grey beard rasping against his palm. 'She shouldn't
have been using her residential property for business purposes.
Really very much a no-no. But it does almost make you think
there's a purpose to everything, doesn't it? I mean, twenty minutes
away! All the miles I've put in, and there she was, on my own
doorstep. It would have delighted Evangeline. A big lover of
oddities and coincidence and chance. A real Bohemian spirit, my
wife. They got her young, you see. Bridlington seafront. Madame
Rosalita, I think it was. Told her everything she wanted to hear.
Going to travel, going to marry her true love, going to spend
time living abroad. No children. Didn't mention the life-line,
though I suppose now I can see why. Even gave her a message
from her own personal angel, telling her that Grandma was sorry
she didn't make it to her ballet performance and that she was
very proud of her. Of course, you and me know that it's all just
about reading people and guesswork. I mean, even a blind squirrel
sometimes finds a nut, doesn't it? But she believed in them with

all her heart. I indulged it, I realize that now. But it was harmless, wasn't it? Psychic nights, Tarot readings, spiritualist conventions. By God they fleeced her, but as far as I saw it we were just paying for her hobby.'

Pharaoh shifts on the sofa. Breathes out, slowly. 'Mr Brimley, perhaps I could use your telephone for a moment, I'm keen to check in . . .'

Brimley glances at her. Shakes his head. Reaches down the cushion of the armchair and retrieves a large, wood-handled hammer.

'Best you stay there,' says Brimley, his tone still pure reasonableness. He picks at a patch of dried blood on the metal head. 'It wasn't until she got poorly that it became a problem. One of those bastards told her they could cure her. She bought a talisman from Psychic Serena. Told her it had been dug out of the earth intact and enchanted by a Hungarian priestess. Eight thousand, it cost that time. Five more for the incantation she had to say while washing her face in the morning dew. And Psychic fucking Serena had a boyfriend, didn't she? And he saw a cash cow. Told her he'd spoken to the angels on her behalf. He could save her, banish the illness, guarantee her a happy, long life. He said there were black auras surrounding her and he could make them go away. Ten grand was nothing, was it? Not for that . . .'

Pharaoh watches as he rolls the hammer between his palms. Stares through the dirty curtains. She can just make out the rear tyre of her car.

'Didn't work, did it? Apparently she didn't believe hard enough. She'd angered the spirits. Sold her bath salts that would cleanse her third eye. A fucking snip at fifteen K.'

Pharaoh eases herself back in the chair. 'You must have noticed her spending . . .'

He shakes his head. 'Not until after. She was office manager. Paid out the company accounts. Took out credit cards and didn't tell me. Not until the very end, by which time it was too late to get her proper help. She was dying. And that was when her mystical healer told her he could find her a new vessel. For just eighty thousand pounds he could ensure that while her body expired, she would become nothing but positive energy – that she would be forever around me, forever with me, a

perfect painless consciousness that would know nothing but
joy and light . . .'

'Jesus,' mutters Pharaoh.

'Psychic Serena was first. I gave her the chance, of course.
Let her prove herself. Simple test – she had to ask the cards
about me. About what was in my soul. And if she got it right,
I'd know she was the real thing, and I'd let it be. She got it
wrong. Told me I was a kind man who was at a crossroads, and
that I should do the thing that my instinct told me to. So I
did. Did the same to her boyfriend, when I tracked him down.
And then Evangeline died. It wasn't a pretty thing. Not beautiful.
But she convinced herself she was going to be a ball of pure
white light. Told me she would come back. Be there around me.
Said I would feel her presence. Told me to ask the cards. She
would send me signs.'

'How many?' asks Pharaoh, her mouth dry.

'I'm not sure,' he says. 'Sometimes I think I've hurt somebody
and then I realize I can't have because I've been at home the
whole time. Other times I wake up and I'm already hurting
someone.'

'The crystal?' asks Pharaoh, watching, almost hypnotized, as
he hefts the hammer.

'Powerful protection, the labradorite,' says Brimley, nastily. 'I
don't want to cost anybody their immortal soul. I just end this
life, you see. The labradorite . . . well, if they're genuine, that
allows them to become like Evangeline, you see. It keeps the
black auras away. I'm freeing them. And if they're con artists,
if they don't really believe what they are selling . . . well, I will
confess to a certain pleasure at splitting their lying fucking
tongues and hammering one of their silly crystals right through
their beating hearts.'

Pharaoh sits perfectly still. Brimley's lips are moving, as if in
conversation with a voice in his head. He twitches a little. Grabs
at the air.

Pharaoh glances down. On the coffee table is a red glass bowl,
filled with an array of beads. She looks past Brimley.

'The lady in Scunthorpe,' says Pharaoh. 'Somebody disturbed
you. You gave a witness statement.'

Brimley allows himself a flash of a smile. Pulls up his sleeve.

A silver charm bracelet is sticking into the skin of his forearm, the skin a mass of bruises and welts, scabs and flesh jewels of blood. 'I ask them all,' he says. 'Each of the charlatans. I ask them to hold this, and tell me about the girl. She had fire in her eyes, that one. I felt the energy flowing from her. They all lie. All the charlatans. So I slide their lying tongues and skewer their fucking hearts.'

'And now?' asks Pharaoh, nodding at the hammer. 'You're going to do what with that, exactly? Because I tell you what, Mr Brimley, you really do need to have a think about what you're about to try. Because if you come for me with that thing, I'm going to take it off you and put it through your fucking head.'

Brimley runs his tongue around the inside of his lip. 'The Irishman told me I didn't have much time left. Said he knew what I'd done, what I'd been doing. Said he would keep my secret if I let him use the property out at sea. I did what he asked, and got my reward. Told me Dymphna was a fraud. Told me I should go and visit her and put her powers to the test. She got me wrong. Split the cards and the cards told me she had to die. And before she did, she told me that there would be another. That a dark-haired woman with dazzling eyes was going to be the last to die at my hand. And here you are, detective. Here you fucking are . . .'

Pharaoh snatches up the glass bowl and hurls it past Brimley. It smashes through the glass, shards flying like hail.

Brimley lunges forward, the hammer held like an axe. Slashes down, hard.

Pharaoh grabs his wrist. Closes her fingers around his spindly bones. Scrapes the ridged heel of her biker boot down his shin and hears him scream as the skin peels from the bone. He drops the hammer. Pharaoh smashes her right hand into his jaw. Bloody spit flies from his mouth. Pharaoh hits him again, pain shooting up her hand as her knuckles break.

'No,' he spits. 'No, this is wrong – you die, I kill you, you die!'

He throws himself forward, colliding with Pharaoh's middle, taking her down in a tangle of arms and legs. She feels his hands on her face, his fingers in her eyes, his thumb in her mouth.

Bites down. Squirms. Tries to buck and kick, but suddenly

he's got his hand in her hair and he's smacking her head off the
floor, thud, thud, thud, and there's blood in her nose and eyes
and she feels as if she's sinking beneath the floor, and looking
up to see the little man sitting astride her, a strange serene smile
on his face . . .

And then he is sliding off her, onto the floor, the thin end of
the hammer sticking in his crown like a hatchet into a tree stump.

Roisin McAvoy looks down at the man as he fits and squirms
on the floor, his feet spasming, one eye turned inward, his teeth
mashing his tongue. She peers closer, in recognition. Sees a man
she recognizes. Sees the man who killed Eva Jayne.

She pulls the hammer from his head. Hits him again.

Pharaoh hauls herself upright, wiping the blood from her eyes.
Spits. Reaches up and feels Roisin's hand close around hers.

'Trish?' she asks, quietly. 'Trish, did he hurt you . . .?'

Pharaoh massages her throat. Spits the taste of the killer's
blood. Cocks her head and manages a little smile. She can hear
sirens. She rubs the back of her head. Her fingers come away
wet.

'Oh,' she says, as her fingertips trace the ugly wound. And then
the world is a photograph, ripping down the middle, quartering,
disintegrating, turning to fragments and haphazard, monochrome
confetti.

A silhouette, suddenly. Red against black; a shape, a feeling;
a face that forms in the flicker and dance of some distant flame.

'Oh, Hec . . .'

And then there is nothing but the dark.

EPILOGUE

Castle Hill Hospital, Cottingham

'So,' says Pharaoh, popping a grape into her mouth and biting down hard. 'What can we all learn from this experience?'

She's sitting up in bed, regal and as elegant as somebody can be in a Primark nightie, and with a bandage around their half shaved skull.

There comes a muttering from the far end of the snug little room, on the first floor of Cottingham's Castle Hill Hospital.

'Sorry, Andy?' asks Pharaoh, cupping her ear theatrically.

'Communication is key,' he replies, looking bashful.

'Excellent,' says Pharaoh, and chomps down on another grape. 'That, and always be nice to lifeboatmen. No matter how much you want to laugh, you are never to so much as raise a smile at the word "coxswain".'

McAvoy, standing sentry by the door, can't find it in him to speak. He just keeps staring at her; trying to catch her eye, hoping to see some kind of truth written on her ice-blue irises. She seems unchanged by any of it. Woke up from cranial surgery and didn't even have to ask what had happened or where she was. She knows who she is. Knows herself all the way through. There had been something of a rumpus when she discovered the surgeons had shaved her head and that she'd swallowed her false tooth when she collapsed, but she managed to see the funny side. Told the nurses she had always known that getting the cheap denture would come back and bite her in the arse.

Her children were the first to be allowed to see her. In their company, she had no reason to put on an act. Just held them, and wept, and then got back to the business of getting well.

'Stick it on then,' says Pharaoh, addressing her comments to Helen Tremberg, who sits at her bedside and helps herself to the ludicrous pile of snacks piled up beside the bed.

Tremberg, sucking her fingers, fiddles with her mobile phone. Glances up at McAvoy, and gives an encouraging smile. He can't return it. Can't remember which muscle is which.

'. . . going live to a press conference with Humberside Police, where Chief Constable Alvin Craven is making a statement . . .'

'Should be good,' mutters Daniells, craning his neck and staring at the small screen.

McAvoy watches as the chief constable swallows, his Adam's apple pressing against his collar and throat. He's a big man. Shaved head, waxy skin, hairy fingers and forearms. He sips from a glass of water as he reads.

'. . . understand that the officer hurt in the incident at the property in Fitling is now out of danger. They will be put forward for a gallantry award in due course . . .'

'Get you,' says Daniells, impressed.

'Shut up, Andy,' mutters Pharaoh.

'The body found at Haile Sands Fort has now been confirmed as an Irish national wanted by An Garda Síochána in connection with several murders-for-hire. They have been working in connection with the National Crime Agency on a multi-agency investigation into organized crime. As a result of those investigations, Humberside Police is able to close the files on several unsolved murders, including the recent and tragic death of Dymphna Lowell at a property in Sunk Island, Holderness. At this time we are unable to provide further details but I would like to personally commend the officers of the Humberside Police Serious and Organized Unit for exceptional police work, which would have secured the convictions of an extremely dangerous individual. The suicide of the individual concerned is a source of great frustration for anybody with a true belief in the process of justice . . .'

Pharaoh shakes her head. Bites down on a grape. Shoots a look at McAvoy as Tremberg puts the phone away. 'Well played,' she mutters, to the world in general. She yawns, extravagantly. 'I think that may be enough for now.'

Tremberg, quickest on the uptake, pulls herself out of the chair. 'Andy,' she says briskly, 'could you come show me how the vending machine works?'

'Eh?' he asks. 'You put your cons in and . . . oh, right.'

They push one another out of the room, arguing like children. McAvoy stays still, rooted to the spot.

'Come here,' says Pharaoh, and pats the bed.

He half stumbles as he moves towards her. Lowers himself down. Puts his hands on the bedsheet and feels her grab for it: plump and warm, closing around his fingers as if she were drowning.

'She won't tell me,' he whispers. 'I know there's more to it. I know she was there.'

'She wasn't,' says Pharaoh, holding his gaze. 'I hit him. Hit him with a hammer when he tried to kill me.'

'Trish, that's not true! And she's OK, that's the thing I can't deal with. She's laughing and joking at home. The kids too. They hurt, and Lilah's wetting the bed again, but they're OK. I know what she did, Trish.'

Pharaoh squeezes his hand. 'You blew a serial killer's head off with a distress rocket, Hector. How are you?'

'I feel like my insides are eating themselves,' he says, scratching at his chest. 'I feel like there will be some kind of comeback for all this. There has to be! But everybody seems happy. Christ, even Papa Teague is back on the halting site, buddying back up with the Heldens. He's the toast of the site. Sent us presents, if you can believe that. A locket for Roisin, toys for the kids. He even sent me a sovereign ring. He kept a man underground, Trish. Turned him into something repulsive . . .'

'He was repulsive to begin with,' says Pharaoh, and means it.

'But I did so much wrong,' he whispers. 'Fin, Lilah, the people I love . . .'

'Are all OK,' says Pharaoh, softly. She sighs, clearly keen to open the window and treat herself to a cigarette. 'Look, sometimes we get to put the cuffs on the right people and make sure they see the inside of a prison for a few years. Sometimes we don't. There's no real justice because nobody ever really knows what that means. For some it's more about revenge upon the monster who brought them pain.'

'Six already,' says McAvoy, rubbing his face. He looks tired. Isn't sleeping. Keeps waking at three a.m. expecting to find his wife at the window, staring off into space. Instead he finds her asleep beside him, her head on his chest, hands clasped as if in prayer and a look of true serenity on her face. It unnerves him.

'Six?'

'Psychics. Clairvoyants. Palmists. Spread them out. Didn't always display them the same way. Didn't always leave the crystal. Doctor says he'd been on and off his medication – starting from when his wife got sick.'

'It was grief that drove him to start, you think?' asks Pharaoh.

'No,' says McAvoy. 'No, I think he liked killing and found a way to make it seem grandiose. Gave meaning to his impulses. First wife says he was violent when he'd been drinking. Former business partner remembers him smashing up the office when a deal didn't go his way. Ex neighbour believes right down to his bones that it was Brimley who killed his dog . . .'

'It was all there, then,' says Pharaoh. 'From the start. Right back to Eva-Jayne. If it had been done right . . .'

'If I hadn't gone tearing in, you mean,' says McAvoy, looking down at the floor. 'I feel like all this is my fault.'

'You always bloody do,' says Pharaoh, smiling.

They sit in silence for a moment. Pharaoh lets go of his hand. Grabs a grape and rolls it between her fingers. 'I've lost six pounds, apparently.'

'Sorry?'

'While in hospital. I've lost six pounds.'

'Oh,' says McAvoy, giving her a quick glance. 'Was that in hair?'

'You will pay for that,' says Pharaoh with a grin, then stops, realizing she is displaying the gap where her tooth should be.

'Suits you, anyway,' says McAvoy, looking at her for a moment too long.

She gives a nod of thanks. Stares through the dirty glass and out across the fields that hem the edges of Cottingham. 'What did you think?' she asks, quietly. 'What did it feel like, when you thought that we were . . . that maybe . . .'

He shakes his head. Pinches the bridge of his nose. 'I can't,' he says. 'Can't imagine how . . . I mean, if I lost you . . .'

She sniffs. Blinks back tears. 'And Roisin? When you thought she was in danger?'

He can't meet her eyes. Stares at the backs of his hands. 'What about you?' he asks. 'Did you go towards the light? Life flash before your eyes?'

Pharaoh breathes out, slowly. For a moment, she remembers. Remembers the absolute darkness; the warm black oblivion of the void. 'Yes,' she lies. 'There was something more. Something else. Some kind of peace, maybe. Something that felt, I don't know . . . good.'

McAvoy reaches out for her hand. Squeezes it tight. 'It matters, then,' he says, mostly to himself. 'What we do. Right and wrong. Good and bad. It really matters.'

Pharaoh reaches out. Squeezes his arm and pulls him closer. He rests his head against hers. She feels the sweat of his forehead; feels as though she can hear the endless static of his thoughts.

'Of course it matters,' she whispers. 'Of course there's something more. You're on the side of the angels, Hector.'

She feels the tension bleed out of him. Strokes his back. Clears her head, lest he somehow read her thoughts.

'I thought of you,' she says, into his crown, her lips muffled by his damp, red-grey hair. 'All I thought of was you.'

And then she is stroking his back, her cheek against his head, as his breathing finds a rhythm, and he gives in to sleep.

Pharaoh closes her eyes. Leans back.

Thinks of the moment that Roisin McAvoy stuck a hammer through her attacker's skull. Thinks of the ease with which she delivered the killing blow. Thinks of the recording, safely stored on her phone – a confession of murder, and more.

Breathes him in, and makes a promise to herself. It's good to know where the bodies are buried, so to speak.

And as sleep envelops her, she smiles.

ACKNOWLEDGEMENTS

It's been a little while since the last McAvoy outing. Sorry about that. Authors are self-indulgent beasts and I've been off writing all sorts of other thrillers. Some of you may have read them, and for that, I'm grateful. There is little more depressing than pouring your heart, soul and pulverized brain matter into a book only to find that it's been read by two librarians and an insomniac. So, please accept my nod of affection for following me into the places my imagination dictates.

Everybody else . . . thanks for coming back to Aector. He wouldn't ever speak up about it but he does feel a bit lonely and abandoned when he's not risking his life on your behalf and is grateful that you still like him. He's blushing and doesn't know quite how to say it, but he wants you to know that you mean a great deal to him and that he's here if you want to talk. Trish thinks you probably need to pull yourself together.

As for me, I just want to say a quick thanks to the people who ensure I still have something approximating a career. Kate and Rachel at Severn House, you are superb editors and always work extra hard to keep your most delicate author from shattering like a smashed plate. It's not gone unnoticed and I think of you very fondly. Natasha, I appreciate your patience with the world's most disorganized man. I will get that email back to you shortly.

Mam. Dad. Phil, Selena and Maisie. I like you. Sorry if it doesn't always show. And Bernard. You'd have loved this book. Miss you, mate. Wish you were still around.

A fist-bump to my few friends who keep me going when I'm struggling. Sarah Stovell, Babs, Richard V, Mike and Jo Craven, Rachel the Witch, Tony Blake, Steve and Linda Page, Di Gammage . . . you all mean the world to me.

And finally, my beautiful family. Artemisia, you are my madness and my salvation in one explosive package of glorious insanity. Elora, you wrap your wings around my heart and hold it safe. Amber, Honey and Connor, I'm so very proud of you

David Mark

and love how little interest you have in my career. Go and do the dishes. And Nicola. I'm here because you save my life every night and day. You have given my brain the elasticity of a yoga master's extremities and I don't always know what you're talking about, but my heart beats to the rhythm of whatever mad song is playing on a loop in your head. We are made of the same stars and I will love you always. Sorry about that.